STAR CURSED

ZODIAC WOLVES: THE LOST PACK #2

ELIZABETH BRIGGS

STAR CURSED (ZODIAC WOLVES: THE LOST PACK #2)

Copyright © 2021 by Elizabeth Briggs

Cover designed by Natasha Snow

Cover photo by Wander Aguiar

ISBN (paperback) 978-1-948456-27-2

ISBN (ebook) 978-1-948456-15-9

www.elizabethbriggs.net

CHAPTER ONE

WHEN I WAS A CHILD, my father told me I'd been born under cursed stars. As I sat in my new prison, I worried he might be right.

Every time I closed my eyes, I prayed I would open them to somewhere else. I wanted this to all be a dream, for the last few days to have never happened, but I could see the walls of my cell imprinted on the backs of my eyelids. When I opened them again, the bars were still there, reminding me I was really trapped here, inside of yet another cage. Only this time I was being held by my worst enemy.

Jordan had left me alone hours ago, and I'd spent that time studying my surroundings and trying to find a way to escape. So far, I'd come up empty. I'd shifted to wolf form in an attempt to communicate with my pack, but they were too far away. I'd found some plain clothes on my hard cot and donned them, then I'd searched for some weakness in the iron bars holding me or some crack in the cell's defenses I could exploit, but no such luck. Unlike the Ophiuchus prison, this one didn't have any windows and the air was musty, making me think I was underground. At least there weren't any visible cameras or microphones, and no slight electrical hum that would have indicated I was being watched electronically. Two male shifter guards were stationed outside of my cell, and they never even bothered to look at me. If I focused I could hear their heartbeats, slow and measured, obviously not worried about my presence one bit. I was inside of a prison, after all, a caged little wolf, and they didn't consider me a threat.

They had no idea how wrong they were.

Kaden had taught me to fight, and Stella had taught me how to be a wolf. Somewhere along the way, I'd taught myself how to use my Moon Touched gift too. I was getting out of this place and returning to my true pack, one way or another. I just needed to wait for the right moment.

At the thought of Kaden, a pang of sadness and longing went through me, so strong I could hardly breathe around it. It caught me off guard how much I missed him, and it was even worse because I knew he must hate me now. Kaden's face as I'd driven away with Jordan was emblazoned in my mind, clear as day. He believed I'd gone willingly, that I'd been unable to resist the mate bond tying me to Jordan, that I'd chosen the Leo over him. I desperately wished I could explain to Kaden I'd only done it to save the Ophiuchus pack from the Leos and their allies, the Sun Witches. If I hadn't made a deal with Jordan, the entire forest would have been burned to ashes, and my pack with it. It hurt to leave them behind, especially knowing they believed I was a traitor, but at least they were alive.

I rubbed the Ophiuchus symbol on my arm, hoping my sacrifice hadn't been in vain. I'd seen the Sun Witches leave, and Jordan had sworn my pack wouldn't be harmed further. Even though I didn't trust my mate, I could only hope he'd kept that promise. But for how long? And what was Jordan's next move? He'd said he had big plans for me, but he'd left before he'd told me what they were. All I could do was wait for him to return.

As if my very thoughts had summoned him, the mate bond flared to life, so quick and sudden it made me gasp. A terrible longing filled me as I heard the scuff of footsteps outside my door, and my breath caught while I anticipated Jordan's entry. When the door opened, it took everything in my power not to jump up and run toward the new alpha of the Leo pack.

Jordan stood there in the doorway in all his handsome, muscular glory. He was too damn hot for his own good and had the cocky look of someone who knew it. I desperately wanted to slide my fingers into that windswept blond hair and run my lips across his sun-kissed skin, while he wrapped those strong arms around me and—

No! I shook my head to try and clear my thoughts, while Jordan gestured for the two guards to leave us. Once alone, he strode toward me with the confidence of a true alpha, and I clenched my fists and held myself still, though my body trembled with the effort. *Kaden is the one you want, not Jordan. Kaden, Kaden, Kaden...*

As Jordan stopped outside the bars of my cell, I noticed he was holding a plate of food and a bottle of water. Almost instantly, the smell hit me and I began salivating, my stomach growling. I couldn't remember the last time I'd eaten. The only thing worse than my hunger was my thirst.

"I thought you could use some refreshments," Jordan said, sounding magnanimous, as if he hadn't left me alone without food or water for hours and hours.

He stuck the water bottle through the bars first, and I tentatively got to my feet to take it from his hand. I was careful not to touch him since I knew that would only make the pull toward him stronger. He obviously wanted something from me, and I had to keep a level head around him.

"I haven't tampered with it," he said, mistaking the reason for my hesitation.

I raised my eyebrows as I opened the water, and I did hear the snap of the cap showing it was brand new. I chugged the cool liquid down, desperate to ease my thirst, but after a few long sips, I made myself stop so I wouldn't be sick.

Jordan passed the food through to me next. I couldn't help but stare at the bacon and cheese omelet with sausages and toast arranged neatly on the paper plate. I had to physically stop myself from shoving it into my mouth, and instead, I inhaled deeply, using my wolf's senses to check if there was anything out of place. Spices, meat, cheese, egg, and bread. Nothing else.

"I didn't poison the food either if that's what you're

trying to figure out," Jordan said, and he sounded almost amused. "I'm not going to hurt you, Ayla."

"No? You had no problem hurting me before." I went to sit back on my cot with my meal. I might as well take advantage of the food to get my strength back up. Jordan watched me silently as I used the knife and fork—plastic, just like the plate—to cut into the omelet and take a bite. Delicious, although anything would be delicious at this point. I forced myself to take small, slow bites instead of devouring it.

Jordan leaned against the cell bars as he watched me eat. "Have you reconsidered my offer to be my alpha queen?"

I chewed my bite and stared at him, not breaking eye contact even as my emotions warred between hatred and desire. "You killed my brother and stole me from my new pack. I'll never be your mate, let alone your *queen*."

"You're already my mate." The arrogance of his assertion rubbed me the wrong way, even if it was correct. "The stars have decreed it, and now that my father is dead and I'm alpha, things are going to be different."

"You don't sound very sad about that loss," I muttered around a mouthful of toast.

"Killing your family was my father's decision, not mine," he continued. "I don't want any more bloodshed."

I let out a harsh laugh. "Hours ago you threatened to kill children, but now I'm supposed to believe you're a saint?"

Jordan's jaw clenched. "The Sun Witches have promised to help me bring all the other packs under the rule of the Leos. With you at my side, we can unite what's left of the Cancers with the Leos, and then the other packs will fall in line without a fight. We'll rule over the Zodiac Wolves together like the stars have wanted all along."

"The stars can go fuck themselves, for all I care," I said. "And you can too, for that matter."

Jordan cocked his head at me, looking surprised as if he'd expected me to just give in. *No fucking way.* I might still feel the overwhelming pull of the bond to him, but I wasn't going to roll over and be his mate so easily. I'd agreed to go with him to stop the Sun Witches from killing the Ophiuchus pack, nothing more.

"This is our destiny," he said. "I know it. You know it. The sooner you give in to it, the easier it will be."

"Never," I growled.

Jordan moved closer to the door of my cell, and I suddenly became all too aware of the way his muscles moved under the light, and how his white button-up shirt was open at the neck, and the way he smelled, like sunshine and desert air. My heart beat faster as my body urged me to get to my feet and meet him, and I found myself moving forward before I realized it. My fingers wrapped around the iron bars as if they could tear them apart to help me get to him. No matter what I said, or how much I fought, I couldn't deny the base desires of the bond. Even my half-finished meal seemed inconsequential in the face of Jordan's allure.

I closed my eyes, hoping that would be the thing to break me free from the spell, but it didn't work. The longer I tried to fight it, the more urgent the *need* to be with Jordan became. To his credit, he was a very handsome male, obviously strong and healthy, everything a woman might want in a mate. On the outside, anyway. His personality sure left a lot to be desired. I let out a huff of frustration and opened my eyes.

When I did, I saw Jordan staring at me with hunger in his gaze. I'd seen that look before in Kaden's eyes, and I knew exactly what it meant, but with Jordan it was different. Deep under the urge to go to him, I felt a gut-wrenching *wrongness* that made what I'd eaten turn in my stomach.

"I know you want me," Jordan said, with a cold, self-assured grin on his lips. "The mate bond won't be fully sealed until we have sex. That's why you feel like you're crawling out of your skin to get to me. Don't worry, we'll have a big ceremony at the next full moon and we'll truly become mates. You'll officially join the Leo pack then too."

It took all of my self-control to hide that I was one step away from throwing myself at the bars to get to him, even as his words filled me with dread. "That's not going to happen." I held my arm out to show the Ophiuchus mark on it. "I already have a pack, remember? And as for the mating ceremony, I'll be opting out of that too, thank you very much."

"It *will* happen," Jordan said, and it sounded like more of a threat than a promise. "I'll make sure of it."

Jordan shoved himself away from the bars and left the room, and I felt a harsh tug from the mating bond as he went, urging me to follow him. *But I can't because he has me in a goddamn cage,* I thought. Although a part of me was grateful for this prison—I wasn't sure what would happen if Jordan and I were left alone together for more than a few minutes.

The moment there was more space between us, I found I could concentrate again. I took in a deep breath and slowly let it out, then returned to my cot and my meal. No matter what happened, I couldn't mate with Jordan. I wanted *Kaden*, not Jordan, despite what the mating bond told me, or how irresistible I found the Leo alpha whenever he was around.

Vivid memories of the Convergence came back to me as I finished off my food. The shame when Jordan had rejected me as his mate, and then the violence and sheer terror that had followed, along with the horror and grief of losing my pack and my brother—I felt it all as if it had only happened yesterday. Being hunted by the male who was supposed to be my mate had been horrific, almost as terrible as seeing my brother fall. Everyone I'd called family had died that night, all because of the Leo pack.

Anger simmered in my gut, a familiar feeling I decided to embrace. I was going to make them pay for what they'd done. My parents might have treated me like shit, but they were still family. And Wesley? I'd loved him more than anyone else in my life, and he was dead thanks to the Leos and their allies. Sure, Jordan hadn't been the one to deal the killing blow, but he was just as complicit in all of their deaths. He'd pay just as much as the rest of them would.

Of that, I'd make sure.

CHAPTER TWO

HOURS PASSED. I tried to sleep, but my mind was all too aware that I was in enemy territory and there were two guards only a few feet away at all times. Besides, I had no idea how long I'd been out after Jordan had injected me. Days, maybe. Long enough to transport me from the Ophiuchus pack lands in Canada to the Leo territory in Arizona. I touched the injection site, wondering what he'd used to knock me out. My shifter blood should have fought most drugs off, but obviously, he'd found a way to sedate me for hours at a time.

After tossing and turning on my hard cot, my body grew restless and I got up. I was used to spending most of my day fighting and training, not trapped like an animal. I started stretching to pass the time, working through each pose until I was limber and all the lingering aches and pains were gone. Then I began running through the forms Kaden had spent so much time teaching me. It wasn't the same, practicing without him, but it helped keep my mind off of things. Like the mating ceremony Jordan had mentioned.

My body moved smoothly, and it was now second nature for me to dodge, roll, and kick. I had a sudden flashback to the first few days of training when I hadn't been able to stay on my feet at all, and a grim sort of satisfaction went through me as I continued practicing. I'd come so far thanks to Kaden's persistence and his belief in me. I was hardly the same person Jordan had tried to kill at the Convergence.

When I was panting and dripping with sweat I stopped to take a break. It wouldn't do any good to wear myself out too much in case Jordan suddenly came back. I sat down on my cot and went over the facts I knew in my head. The Leo pack lived in Arizona near Phoenix, but I didn't know anything else about their territory. It was currently Leo season, so they'd be stronger than any other pack until we passed into Virgo season. A huge disadvantage for me. Escape seemed impossible, and I had a brief moment of despair as I wondered if I'd ever get out of here. I pictured myself trapped here for years, withering away until I eventually succumbed to the mate bond and let Jordan claim me as his alpha female.

No, I told myself. *You'll figure a way out. You have to.*

Besides, I didn't have years. I had maybe two weeks until the next full moon, that was all. If I could get outside at night, I might be able to use moonlight to escape. Until then, I'd have to bide my time and wait. Giving up wasn't an option. I'd find a way back to Kaden. Somehow.

One of the guards brought me more water, but otherwise, no one spoke to me. I didn't know what time it was, and it drove me a little mad not knowing if it was day or night. I closed my eyes and reached out with my senses. Day, I decided, though I had no way to tell if I was right. I waited, both dreading and hoping Jordan would return, while time trickled by at a glacial pace.

Finally, I heard someone walking down the hall again, and sat up straighter. From the pull in my gut, I knew it was Jordan before I even saw him. I steeled myself against his presence, telling myself there was nothing he could say that would make me fall for any of his bullshit. Since distance seemed to help me keep a clearer head, I backed up against the wall, as far from the door as I could possibly get.

I scowled as Jordan opened the door, but he didn't look put off by my sour face. In fact, all he did was flash a charming smile and make a motion with his hand. Three more shifters walked inside at his command, carrying food, chairs, and a folding table. This was the largest group of shifters I'd seen since I'd woken up. I blinked, wondering what he was up to now. Whatever it was, it couldn't be good.

"I was hoping to have dinner with you tonight," Jordan said.

"And I was hoping to be back with my own pack, but we don't always get what we want," I replied.

Unfortunately, my stomach chose that moment to let out a loud growl. It had been many hours since I'd eaten the last meal Jordan had brought me, and I'd long burned it off with my combat practice. *Traitor,* I thought, looking down at my stomach.

Jordan's smile only widened at the sound, which he'd obviously heard. Fucking wolf senses. "We both know you need to eat. What difference does it make if I do it with you?"

"Fine," I said but tried to convey just how much I didn't want to with that single word.

If Jordan noticed my acidic tone, he didn't acknowledge it. He gave me a cocky smile as the three shifters worked behind him, setting up the table and two chairs, then spreading out the plates and silverware. My stomach gave a quieter grumble at the sight of the food, and once again, the smell made me begin salivating. The only benefit was that my hunger made me forget the mate bond's pull just enough to make it almost bearable.

Jordan nodded to one of the guards, who stepped forward with a set of keys that jangled as he selected the right one. I took note of which key he used, a slightly bigger, brighter one, as if the locks had been replaced recently on this cell. When he let me out, I noted that the other guard stood at attention, and felt his eyes boring holes into my back.

I shot him a glance. "Don't worry, I'm not stupid enough to try and run right now."

"If I thought you were going to run, I wouldn't have let you out," Jordan said, as he held out a chair for me, acting like the perfect gentleman. "But we both know you're not going to do that."

I sat down and looked at my plate, which had a thick steak covered in dark gravy, roasted potatoes, and a side of garlic green beans. I dug in and took a few bites before looking up to see Jordan watching me with far too much satisfaction. He poured a glass of red wine for each of us, almost like this was a date or some shit. Maybe to him, it was.

I took a tentative sip of wine, knowing my shifter metabolism would stop the alcohol from having any effect. "Do you treat all the ladies you're courting like your prisoners, or am I just lucky?"

"I don't want to keep you prisoner," Jordan said, his voice even and calm. Was this the same shifter who had snarled and growled at me, who'd chased and beaten me at the Convergence? I didn't trust this new amiable Jordan one bit, but I couldn't keep my eyes off him either. He looked damn good tonight, with another of those white button-up shirts open just enough to show off a glimpse of his hard chest, and the sleeves rolled up to reveal sexy masculine forearms. A wave of lust made my thighs clench, and I shoved another bite of food in my mouth before I did something I'd regret.

"I plan to release you from this cell the moment you're free from the brainwashing those snakes did to you," Jordan continued.

"I'm not brainwashed," I said. "If anything, I'm finally seeing things clearly. My time with the Ophiuchus pack opened my eyes to everything that's wrong with the Zodiac Wolves."

Jordan arched an eyebrow as he swirled his wine. "Let me guess. They told you that you're special. That only they can help you reach your full potential. They offered you revenge on the people who wronged you. Then they gave you a sob story about how they were cast out unfairly, and how the Sun Witches are evil. Does that sound about right?"

I opened and closed my mouth, trying to think of a good reply. I couldn't find one. Everything he'd said was true, and I looked back down at my plate, disturbed.

Jordan let out a snort. "In a nutshell, they told you everything you wanted to hear, all so they could use you, Ayla. You were the bait, and now that you're no longer useful to them, you've been discarded. We both know none of them are coming for you."

Ouch. The truth of his words burned inside me. "The Sun Witches *are* evil," I finally said. "What they're doing to us isn't natural. Ophiuchus pack members gain their wolves as toddlers, and they find their mates on their own. The Moon Curse doesn't affect them at all."

"They also use dark magic from the Moon Witches. Did you ever consider that might be the reason they've managed to escape the Moon Curse?" He leaned forward, meeting my eyes. "Can you deny that the Ophiuchus pack plans to wage war on the Zodiac Wolves to force us to submit or die?"

"Are the Leos not doing the same thing? I seem to remember my pack screaming and dying all around me not too long ago."

Jordan's jaw clenched. "Like I told you before, that wasn't my doing and I don't want that to happen again. Can you say the same for the Ophiuchus alpha?"

My heart clenched at the thought of Kaden. "He's not the monster you think he is. None of them are."

Jordan's eyes narrowed and his voice turned cold. "Is he the one you fucked during the full moon?"

I froze, a shiver going down my spine. How did he know about that? "What are you talking about?"

Jordan's fingers tightened around his fork and I worried he might stab someone with it. Possibly me. "I felt it when you went into heat that night—and I felt you fucking someone else for hours. It was *agony*. I've never felt such betrayal and desperation in my entire life. I nearly tore off my own skin."

My mouth fell open. He'd *felt* that? Oh shit. I'd never even considered what Jordan might have gone through during my heat, or how it would affect him. For a second I felt a small twinge of guilt, knowing what he must have gone through, but then I pushed it aside. I looked him dead in the eye and said, "Good. Now you know what it felt like when you rejected me."

For a split second, a hint of pain crossed his face. "I suppose I deserve that."

His words surprised me and I took a long sip of wine before answering. "Yes, I slept with Kaden that night. He kept me from losing my mind and fucking every male I could find since I couldn't get to you. But it was just sex. That's it. And we never did it again after that night."

Jordan cocked his head at me. "So you don't care for him?"

"No," I lied. Everything else I'd said had been true, but I didn't want him to know just how much I cared for Kaden. That seemed like something that could be used against me, and I didn't want to give Jordan any more power over me. "And he definitely doesn't care about me."

"Good." Jordan leaned back, his shoulders relaxing. "I didn't think so, but I had to be sure. Unlike you, I've been faithful all this time. The only woman I will mate with is you. And from now on, you won't be fucking anyone but me."

A shudder ran through me at the possessive words, making me squirm in my seat with a mix of desire and revulsion. "Not interested, thanks."

"You can't deny the way you feel about me," Jordan said. "It's obvious from the look in your eyes that you're one second from leaping over the table and climbing onto my lap. Trust me, I'm there too. And since we've established no other man is coming for you, why resist the inevitable?"

He made a good point, and it would be so much easier to just give in, especially when I knew Kaden wasn't going to rescue me. But deep underneath the pull of the mate bond, something told me it was wrong. I shook my head. "Maybe it is inevitable, but I'll fight it for as long as I can."

To my surprise, Jordan grinned at that. "And in the end, my victory will only be sweeter for it."

I rolled my eyes and finished off my meal, taking care not to look at him, which helped me resist the desire to go to him. He finished his food too, and then he tapped his fingers on the wine glass as he stared at me. I felt his eyes all over my body, moving across my skin like a caress, and suddenly it became hard to breathe.

Jordan downed his wine in one gulp. "Tell me, how did you escape me at the Convergence?"

My heart rate picked up at this sudden change of topic. "I ran. You were just too slow I guess."

"Don't lie to me. I know something strange happened. One second you were there, and the next you were somewhere else. Was it some kind of magic?"

"I don't know."

Jordan slammed his fist down onto the table, making me jump. "I *saw* you disappear, Ayla. Tell me how you did it."

Ah, there was the Jordan I knew, the one who'd beaten me and hunted me through the forest. For a moment I'd worried maybe he'd grown a conscience and a heart, and now I was actually glad he was back to being a total dick. It made it much easier to tell him to fuck off.

I shoved my plate away, officially done with this date. "I'm not telling you shit."

"You're my mate!" Jordan roared, jumping up to loom over me with his broad shoulders and muscular frame. He wasn't using his Leo power, but he was imposing all the same. "You have to obey me."

That startled a laugh out of me. "*Have to?* I don't have to do anything. You're so used to getting what you want that you've forgotten what the word 'no' sounds like. Let me remind you." I slowly raised my middle finger. "No."

His eyes flashed with fire, and I thought he might strike me, but then his face grew eerily calm again. A chill went through me at the sudden change. "I'll find out soon enough. In a few days, you'll be my true mate and then you won't be able to deny me *anything*." A villainous grin crossed his face. "You won't want to."

He nodded to one of the guards, who grabbed me by the arm before I could even think of trying to resist. The guard shoved me back into the cell, and the door locked as I stumbled inside. Three other shifters rushed in and began cleaning up silently, while Jordan walked out of the room without another word.

As I sat on my cot, sagging back against the wall, I squeezed my eyes shut against the whirlwind of emotions inside me. *How am I going to get out of this mess?*

CHAPTER THREE

EVENTUALLY, I slept. I'd grudgingly accepted that no one was going to come in and murder me during my sleep, and I finally relaxed enough to let exhaustion overtake me. My dreams were restless, featuring me running through the forest with a lion chasing after me, while I called for help but no one came. I didn't need to be a dream expert to know what *that* meant.

The sound of the door opening roused me from sleep, and I was instantly alert and ready to defend myself if needed. I sat straight up, about to tell Jordan where he could shove it, but to my surprise, it was a woman who'd come to visit me. She looked to be in her mid-forties, with long curls the color of sunshine and a face that would turn heads and make eyes linger. She was tall and very fit, with a commanding presence and an air of importance, making me think of a Viking warrior queen.

She stopped outside my cage and the guards both bowed

their heads to her. For a few moments, she simply stared at me with sharp brown eyes in a way that made me feel overly self-conscious, and the slight curl to her lip said she found me wanting. I realized I was wearing days-old clothes and I hadn't seen a brush for even longer. I didn't even want to think about how I must smell. But I met her gaze without flinching anyway, because I refused to be cowed by the people in this pack.

She lifted her chin. "I wanted to see the girl responsible for my husband's death. I have to say, I expected more."

I swallowed as I tried to figure out whose husband I might have killed. Then it hit me. The self-assured air, the way she resembled a feminine, older version of Jordan—this was his mother, the Leo alpha female. "I didn't kill him."

She sniffed at that, her eyes raking over me with disdain. "Obviously. I doubt you could kill any of us, let alone the alpha. Yet the blame still falls on you."

I lifted one shoulder in a shrug. "I had nothing to do with the alpha's death, though I would have gladly killed the asshole if I'd had the chance, and I certainly don't mourn his loss. Consider it justice for what he did to my father."

A flash of anger crossed the female's face, and she gripped onto the bars with surprising strength. The metal screamed under her hands, and I had a brief second of panic as I wondered if she could actually pull the bars free of their roots in the concrete.

"You will *never* mate with my son," she growled.

"Trust me," I said with a hollow laugh. "That is one thing we can agree on."

Her eyes narrowed, but then she spun on her heel and walked out with a toss of her blond hair, continuing the Leos' tradition for dramatic exits. I wondered what she took most offense with—me being a Cancer originally, or my half-breed heritage, or that I'd been involved in her mate's death. Either way, it was nice to know there was some contention among the Leos about me becoming one of them. With any luck, I'd be able to use that to my advantage.

ANOTHER DAY PASSED.

I woke up feeling *gross*, for lack of a better term. I'd been in this situation before, locked up without a shower for days on end, and I'd forgotten just how awful it was. I ran a hand through my tangled hair and shuddered at the feel of the greasy locks between my fingers.

"Are you planning to let me have a shower anytime soon?" I asked my ever-present guards. From what I could understand in the time observing them, they went in shifts of eight hours, changing three times a day. It was a good way to pace the time, and they were my only clock in here. At least the Ophiuchus prison had a window.

The guards didn't answer, and I smiled humorlessly at the two figures. I didn't know if Jordan had instructed them not to talk to me, or if it was of their own volition, but I had yet to hear a peep from any of the guards.

I passed the time going through my exercises, trying to keep my body as fit as possible so I could be ready to escape or fight at a moment's notice. Also because it was the only thing to do in a small cell like this with no other entertainment or company. They could have given me a book or two at least. Was Jordan trying to wear me down through sheer boredom?

I stopped when I heard the sound of people walking toward me, and I tried to look like I'd been sitting on my cot this whole time. The moment the figures entered the room, however, I threw that tactic out the window and went on high alert mode. Three Sun Witches stood before me, dressed in their warm-colored robes, all of them beautiful and terrifying. I blinked a few times, wondering if I was so bored that I'd just straight up hallucinated Sun Witches, but then one of them motioned for the guard to open the door with the jangly keychain again. He opened it, and all three of the Sun Witches stepped inside my cell—and were securely locked inside with me.

This can't be good, I thought, as I sat up straighter.

The middle Sun Witch was familiar, with eyes so pale they looked colorless, and platinum blond hair falling to her shoulders. Her robe was burnt orange and threaded with gold images of the sun along the neckline and around her wrists. I vaguely remembered her giving me a blanket at the Convergence. The other two witches, wearing robes the color of Dijon mustard, seemed to defer to her as their leader, even though she was younger than them.

"My name is Roxandra," she said. "I am Evanora's daughter."

That explained a lot. Evanora was the High Priestess of

the Sun Witches. Was she here too? I sure hoped not. "I'd say it's nice to meet you, but the circumstances are less than ideal."

Roxandra looked around the cell, perusing it slowly as she talked. "We're here to learn about your powers."

"Powers? What powers?" I clasped my hands in my lap, hoping they wouldn't shake. Lying to Jordan was one thing, but even though I now knew that the Sun Witches weren't the perfect paragons I'd grown up believing them to be, they were still powerful beyond measure, and I didn't know if I could fool them.

"You have Moon Witch powers." She turned those strange eyes on me, and they dared me to lie. "Tell us about them."

"I don't know what you mean." It was surprisingly easy to choke the lie out.

Roxandra stepped forward and bright light filled her eyes. "Don't lie to me."

I spread my hands wide, trying to look innocent and calm, even as my heart raced. "If Jordan told you I have magic, he's wrong. He just can't believe a girl like me could get away from him in the woods, but I've spent my life escaping bad situations. It's what I do."

And I'll escape this one too, I mentally added.

Roxandra's glowing eyes narrowed. "Who is your mother?"

"I have no idea." It was nice not having to lie about that, at least.

"The Cancer alpha must have told you something about her."

"He told me she was human, and that she abandoned me when I was a baby. That's it. Trust me, I wish I knew more about her."

Roxandra pursed her lips and glanced between the other two witches at her side. Then she turned those sunlit eyes back on me. "If you had just cooperated with us, I could have made this a lot easier for you."

I clenched my jaw, wondering what exactly was going on, but before I could open my mouth to ask, the three of them began chanting. All of their eyes glowed, making the room light up like we were outside at noon on a cloudless day. I shielded my face from the sudden brightness, a sharp contrast to my dark cell, and that's when I felt the spell settle over me like a straight jacket, pressing and squeezing, as if it was trying to eek something out of me. I opened my mouth to scream as silvery light shot out of me, right from my chest. *What the—*

It felt like an explosion, and when my vision cleared, all three Sun Witches were on the ground. Roxandra looked shaken as she stood up, and she shouted a word in another language I didn't recognize. The other two Sun Witches scrambled to their feet and advanced on me. I held my hands up, too confused and disoriented to fight back as they grabbed hold of my arms. Before I could respond, they pulled me off the cot and pushed me to the floor.

"What was that?" Jordan's voice called out.

I'd been so shocked by the explosion of power that I

hadn't even heard Jordan approaching, but when I looked up, he stood outside of my cell door, eyes on Roxandra.

"Our suspicions were correct," Roxandra said, as she smoothed two slim hands over her robes and pulled herself back together before standing tall once again. "She's part Moon Witch. Strong, too. Whoever her mother was, she was powerful."

My mouth fell open. Kaden had said my mother was probably a Moon Witch, but there had been no proof of it, and with my father dead, there was no one to ask either. Now there was no doubt in my mind Kaden had been right. Of course, that changed nothing. I still didn't know who she was, or where she was now, or why she'd abandoned me. All this knowledge did was leave me with more questions about my past.

"What caused her powers to awaken?" Jordan asked.

"They must have awakened when she gained her wolf," Roxandra said.

That made sense. My wolf had been locked away for the first twenty-two years of my life, and I'd never exhibited this sort of magic before. I'd been called to the moon, but I'd just thought that was how it was for every Cancer shifter. It was only on the night of the Convergence when I'd first tapped into my power.

Roxandra looked over at me, a slight frown on her face, and in her eyes, I saw fear. She was *afraid* of me, or afraid of my powers at least. "She needs to be controlled, or killed before her powers become stronger."

Killed? I glanced wildly at Jordan. Would he listen to the Sun Witches on this?

"Killing her is not an option," Jordan growled. "She's my mate."

"She's more dangerous than you know," Roxandra hissed.

"She's. My. Mate." His voice was so ferocious that even Roxandra stepped back from it. "I've got it under control."

"As you say," Roxandra said, though she didn't sound too happy about it.

"After the full moon ceremony, she'll be completely bound to me," Jordan said. "Then we'll be able to use her magic to our advantage. She could be a valuable asset."

"Very well. I strongly urge you to keep her locked up until then." She cast me one last look, lip curling in distaste, and nodded to the other two witches. They couldn't seem to let go of me fast enough, nearly tossing me away from both of them, like they thought I might hurt them. *Right.* Me going against three fully trained Sun Witches? I hardly understood my own powers, let alone how to use them against others.

The three Sun Witches left without casting a backward glance. Jordan lingered, watching me as I sat on the floor as I tried to get a hold of myself to return to my cot again. The spell they'd used had taken all my energy with that burst of unexpected magic, and now I could barely move.

Jordan took my arm and lifted me up, helping me to my cot. Desire swirled in me at his touch, and I so wanted to lean against him and let him take care of me. *Give in,* the mate bond whispered. *Why fight it?*

"I won't let them hurt you," Jordan said as he set me down on the cot. Then he lightly touched my hair, smoothing it down almost tenderly. The mate bond purred inside me, wanting more.

"No, you just want to use me." I jerked away with the last of my strength and he dropped his hand with a scowl.

"Everyone is a pawn in this game," he said in a cold voice. "Even me. But together, we could be king and queen instead."

He left without saying anything else, and I breathed a sigh of relief when he was gone. It was too hard to think when he was around. The mate bond clouded my mind, making me doubt my instincts and twisting my emotions into knots.

I sagged back against the wall. I couldn't deny it any longer. I was part Moon Witch, which meant that my mother hadn't been human, and Kaden's theory had been correct. That didn't give me any answers though, and Dad wasn't alive for me to ask him any questions. He probably wouldn't have answered them anyway. Had he even known my mother was a Moon Witch? I had no way of knowing.

It didn't matter that I'd just woken up about an hour ago, I felt the intense urge to nap. That bolt of energy that had hit the Sun Witches had taken most of my strength with it. I collapsed onto my cot, not even bothering to pull the thin blanket up over myself. I just curled in on myself and closed my eyes.

I wished, with an intensity that caught me off guard, that I could talk to Kaden and Stella. They both had Moon

Witch blood, and they might be able to help me understand what was happening. Could they create silvery light like that? I wasn't sure. I knew they could both go invisible, and Kaden had somehow made magical wards to protect the pack lands, but that was it. I was woefully ignorant when it came to anything about the Moon Witches or their magic, and I desperately needed to know more.

I rubbed my Ophiuchus mark absentmindedly, almost as if I could feel it tingling in sympathy. I was determined to find my way back to my pack. They had the answers I needed, and I wanted out of this place with the Leos and the Sun Witches. These weren't my people, they weren't my home, and Jordan definitely wasn't the man I wanted to spend my life with, no matter how the mate bond made me feel.

CHAPTER FOUR

I BLINKED awake and felt an overwhelming sense of disappointment. I'd been having the most wonderful dream about running through the forest with my pack by my side, and waking up to confinement within these four walls was getting worse and worse every day that passed. *This* didn't feel real, but it was what I kept waking up to, rather than my bed in Kaden's house.

It had been a few days since my encounter with the Sun Witches, and the boredom was starting to drive me a little insane. All I could do was sleep, eat, train, and scheme, only to repeat the process again and again. No one came to visit me, and I was starting to think they were going to leave me in this prison until the full moon ceremony. The possibility of escape dwindled with every day that passed, while my despair and desperation only increased. I wouldn't even consider how smelly my armpits were at this point.

The sound of someone walking down the hall caught me

off guard and I sat upright in bed, feeling the mate bond tug at my gut. I slid the blanket off my legs and put my feet on the floor, trying to shake away the last remnants of sleep so I could face Jordan with a clear head.

Jordan and his annoyingly perfect face appeared in front of my cell. "Good morning, Ayla."

I crossed my arms. "Oh, so you remember I exist now. What do you want?"

Jordan nodded to the guard with the keys, who unlocked the door without question. I expected Jordan to step inside, but instead, he held his hand out as if gesturing for me to follow him. "Let's go for a walk."

Although I desperately wanted to get out of this cage, even for a minute, this smelled like a trap. "Have the Sun Witches convinced you I'm a threat now? Planning to take me out back and kill me?"

"I don't know how many times I have to tell you this, but that's not on the agenda anymore," Jordan said.

"Look," I said, but I stood up all the same. "The first time we met you hunted me through the forest like prey and broke multiple bones in my body, and now I'm just supposed to take you at face value that you're not interested in harming me? Especially when the Sun Witches seem more than ready to kill me?"

Jordan cocked his head. "Did you actually see me kill anyone at the Convergence?"

I paused to search my memories and found he was right, but I still scowled at him. "Just because I didn't see it happen, doesn't mean there isn't any blood on your hands. Besides, you *wanted* to kill me."

"I was acting on my father's alpha command. He made me reject you, and he made me try to kill you. Now that he's gone, things can be different between us."

"He...what?" I fell back on my cot, so shocked my knees gave out. I searched Jordan's eyes, looking for any hint he was lying. Could it be true? That would explain how Jordan went against the mate bond's pull and was able to reject and hurt me. Dixon was a powerful alpha, and his command would have overruled anything else. I knew firsthand how impossible it was to resist an alpha command, thanks to my own father. The only time I'd been able to resist was when Kaden had tried to use one on me—but that must have been a fluke.

"I know I was an asshole to you when we met. But I never wanted to hurt you." He stepped back, giving me space to exit the cell. "Come on. Let's talk outside. I bet you could use some fresh air."

I couldn't deny that. I reluctantly followed him, still waiting for the axe to fall. As I left the cell, I kept an eye on both of the guards, but neither of them made a move. No alarms went off either.

Jordan led me out of the room I'd been trapped inside for days, and I realized mine wasn't the only prison cell. There were maybe a dozen or so identical rooms lined up in a row under soul-sucking lighting and no windows. All the other cells seemed empty, which made sense. I hadn't heard anyone else during my stay here.

Jordan took me up a dark stairway and then we passed more guards, some sitting at desks and doing paperwork, others chatting over a water cooler. Up here there were a few windows, at least, and sunlight streamed through them. Every person in the building seemed to stop and gawk at me as we walked by, but no one said a word.

Jordan pushed open a door and led me through it. After spending so many days in a dark cell that was climate-controlled to be slightly chilly, stepping outside was a shock. The hot, dry air of the desert hit me and the sun beat down with a particular intensity, intent on driving nails of pain into my skull. I squinted and tried to resist the urge to cover my eyes.

When they finally adjusted, I glanced around. We were at the edge of the Leo pack village, and beyond it, there was only harsh desert, with hills, and tumbleweed, and an honest-to-god cactus sticking out of the ground. I was definitely not in Canada anymore. The Leo village butted right up against the desert, with rows of nearly identical two-story houses that all looked pretty new, each painted in one of three shades of sand with clay tile roofs.

Before I could take it in, Jordan started walking away, toward a patch of green up ahead. I hesitated, looking back at the prison building, but the guards stayed put. Jordan was going to take me out into the village by himself, with no backup? Was he that confident?

I hurried to follow Jordan. "Aren't you worried I'll try to attack you, or run?"

"Not really." He gave a casual shrug, his face lit up with

a cocky smile. When he glanced over at me, his hair blowing in the wind and the sun kissing his tanned skin, I got the distinct impression that he belonged here in this dry, hot place. "I'm trying to treat you like my mate. If you do try to run, you won't get far. And if you attack me..." His smile turned wicked. "I'd take great pleasure in pinning you to the ground. I think we both know what would happen after that."

His words flared the lust inside me I'd been trying so hard to ignore. I couldn't help but picture us tousling out here in the desert heat, trying to battle one another until we finally gave in to the urges we both felt. No, attacking him was not an option. Not when I couldn't trust my own body to obey. My only choice then was to run. Maybe not now, but later.

"I want you to come to me of your own free will at the full moon," Jordan continued. "That's why I want to talk."

"Then let's talk," I said, taking a step toward him and letting the desire settle over me like a warm blanket. A new plan formed in my mind. If Jordan wanted me to come to him, to be his perfect mate, I could do that. If I made him believe that I trusted him and accepted him, or better yet, that I wanted him, he might lower his guard enough to give me a chance to escape. If he let me out of my cell once, he would probably do it again as long as I behaved. It would be tricky though. It would require subtlety I wasn't entirely sure I was capable of, and worst of all, it would require me to put away my sharp tongue and pretend to swoon over him.

I looked up at him from under my lashes, taking him in.

Damn, he was gorgeous. My body ached for him, my pussy pulsed with need. Okay, so the swooning part would be easy thanks to the mate bond. Maybe *too* easy. I had to reign this girl in before she got me in trouble.

"Come," he said. "I want to show you my favorite part of town."

He lightly touched my elbow and led me toward the gazebo on the edge of town surrounded by a lush garden. It was the complete opposite of the harsh land around it, and I wondered how it could survive this heat. He opened a small gate and we stepped inside, and it instantly felt cooler. I took a long, deep breath, smelling dozens of different plants and flowers in the air. They were thriving, despite some of them being clearly made for cooler climates.

Jordan strolled along the path toward a gazebo up ahead. "This garden was a gift from the Sun Witches. The temperature will always stay comfortable, no matter the weather."

Wow, I thought. *The Sun Witches really have been favoring the Leos.* Had Dad known about this? Did the other packs? With the Sun Witches helping the Leos and giving them their blessings, they really could take over the other packs. That also explained why the Sun Witches didn't lift a finger to help the Cancer pack when the Leos slaughtered us, despite all their talk of how there was no fighting at the Convergence. Fucking hypocrites.

A bolt of worry went through me when I remembered Kaden saying he wanted to take down the Leo pack and all the others as well. What could he possibly do against the might of the Sun Witches combined with the huge numbers of the Leo pack? And if the Leo pack did manage to conquer the rest of the other Zodiac Wolves... I swallowed hard at the thought. I was beginning to realize that even if I did escape this place, I might never be safe from them.

We stepped inside the gazebo and Jordan directed me toward the bench and then sat right beside me on it. The mating bond urged me closer, begging for me to touch Jordan, but the part of me that cared for Kaden howled its disapproval. A war was quietly waging inside me, pulling me apart at the seams, tugging me in two different directions until I wanted to scream. All I wanted was to run back to my cell and hide, but I knew this might be my best chance to win Jordan over.

"What did you want to talk to me about?" I asked, tucking a piece of greasy hair behind my ear. I had to look positively revolting after being in a prison cell for so long, and I doubted I smelled any better, yet Jordan didn't seem to notice. Or if he did, he didn't care.

He looked up at the sky, his face contemplative. "My father used to rule the Leo pack with fear. He would physically abuse pack members to keep them in line, and none of us were exempt. Not even me, his firstborn son."

I sat up a little straighter, no longer having to feign my interest. Dad had ruled with fear and brute force too, and I'd known that better than anyone. "My father was the same."

Jordan glanced over at me, his lips drawn tight in a grim line. "Maybe it's good they're both gone."

My eyebrows jumped up at his words. "Why is that?"

"Because it allows us to do things differently. My father

wanted to wipe out or take control of all the other packs, effectively making everyone a member of the Leo pack with him as its king. I don't want that. I never have. I plan to let the packs keep their individuality, as long as they defer to me as their true alpha. With our pack leading the Zodiac Wolves, we can charge forward into a brighter future for all of us."

With the Sun Witches controlling all of us, I mentally added. It was hard not to say it out loud, but instead, I nodded slowly, as though I was agreeing with everything he said. "It might be tough to convince the other packs to accept you as their leader. Even with the Sun Witches behind you."

"That's why I need your help." He reached over and took my hand, making my blood race. "If the other Zodiac Wolves see that we're together, putting our packs' past rivalries behind us, they'll realize this is for the best. There's been fighting and scheming between the Zodiac Wolves for too long—it's time we were united in peace."

His words sounded too good to be true, and I had to remind myself this was all just a ploy to convince me to join him. He wanted to use me, just like everyone else. Especially now that he knew I had Moon Witch magic. "Do you really think that will work?"

"With you by my side, we'll be unstoppable." He turned toward me, his knee brushing against mine, sending a wave of burning need through me. "We're meant to be, Ayla. The stars decreed it. Can't you feel it?"

"Yes," I whispered. The lie came easily, and I wondered if it was a lie at all. With Jordan this close it was hard for me to think of anything but how much I wanted him. The mating bond drew us closer, impossible to resist, and I yearned to lean forward, to be the one to bridge the distance between us. But Jordan moved first.

His mouth crashed down on mine, and I let out a soft gasp at the sudden burst of lust inside me. Then his hands were on my chin, in my hair, pulling me closer as he kissed me. I kissed him back with the same intensity, unable to stop myself, touching his chest, his shoulders, his jaw. The knot that had been in my stomach since we'd first become mates relaxed, all the tension leaving my body as I finally gave in to the inevitable. Jordan was mine, and I was his.

No, something deep inside of me screamed. Thoughts of Kaden's lips on mine crowded into my head, overtaking the physical sensation of kissing my mate for the first time. But there was something else too, and as the kiss went on longer, the feeling grew stronger. Something was wrong, out of place, like I'd walked into my home and found it completely rearranged. The wrongness of it all grew stronger with each second Jordan kissed me, filling me with confusion...and horror.

I shoved Jordan away with a gasp, finally propelled into motion. Jordan's eyes were clouded with lust as he looked at me in confusion, and I scrambled to get my thoughts together. *Damn quick tongue, where are you now?*

"I—I need time," I said, stuttering over the words. From the way that Jordan's fingers tightened around my shoulders, I worried he wouldn't listen, the words *I'd take great plea-sure in pinning you to the ground* swimming around in my head. If he kissed me again, I wasn't sure I could resist him—I'd barely managed to end it this time. Everything was so jumbled up in my head, a whirlwind of lust, need, disgust, hatred, and longing. All I knew was that I wanted Jordan away from me.

"Time?" he asked, though thankfully he let me go.

I looked at him with pleading eyes, letting down my guard for once, showing him my vulnerability. "Please try to understand how hard this is for me. You rejected me at the Convergence and my pack was killed. Then I woke up with the Ophiuchus pack without any time to adjust or grieve, and just when I felt like I was settling in there, you brought me here, locked me up, and told me everything they said was a lie. And now I've just learned that I'm part witch too?" I let out a strained laugh. "It's a lot to process."

Jordan's brow furrowed, but he nodded slowly. "I understand."

It was absolutely the last thing I expected from him. Everything I knew of him said that he was a selfish asshole who didn't care about the feelings of others, but for some reason, he was listening to me. Technically, nothing I'd said was a lie, but now I had to really sell it. "I want to be your mate, I do. But I'd appreciate it if you gave me a little time to get used to everything first."

"Of course." A grin appeared on his handsome face, nearly blinding me with his good looks. "I have an idea of something that will help you."

"An idea?" I asked, suddenly uneasy.

"More like a gift, actually," Jordan said, which didn't

make me feel any better. This new Jordan was way too level-headed and kind, and I didn't trust him one bit. I wished he'd go back to the guy who'd tried to kill me—that guy I understood, at least.

"What is it?" I asked, trying to keep the suspicion out of my voice.

Still grinning, Jordan stood up and held his hand out for me to take. "You'll see."

CHAPTER FIVE

WE LEFT the garden and headed into the village, which looked like a typical suburb full of big SUVs, perfectly mowed lawns, and basketball hoops in driveways. There was nothing that showed the place was full of shifters, no hint that there was anything out of the ordinary until you caught a glimpse of a wolf loping past or a woman in a burnt orange robe glaring at you. I shuddered and hurried after Jordan.

We stopped in front of a two-story sand-colored house that looked like all the others, except this one was surrounded by guards. All of my alarm bells started ringing and I cast Jordan a wary glance. Where was he taking me now?

He just gave me an enigmatic smile and opened the front door. "Come on. Your surprise is inside."

As he motioned me inside, my nose caught the scent of someone familiar. I stopped dead in my tracks, not believing my own senses, but then rushed forward. I had to see for sure. I blinked as my gaze adjusted once again from the glaring sun to the cool interior of the house, and a familiar figure with long, dark hair turned around.

"Mira?" I asked, my heart leaping into my throat.

"Ayla!" She launched herself at me, and I found myself running forward to meet her halfway. I hadn't seen her since the Convergence when Mira had left with the Pisces pack. She'd been practically dragged away by her new mate after the Pisces alpha had refused to help me for fear of retribution from the Leo pack. It seemed like a lifetime had passed since we'd seen each other.

I wrapped Mira up in a tight hug, nearly sobbing with relief at seeing her unharmed and in front of me, especially after what I'd been through the last few days. I'd been surrounded by the enemy for so long, unable to trust anyone, and it was exhausting. Even in the Ophiuchus pack, I'd felt some of that, though they hadn't been as hostile. They'd all been together for years, or since birth, and I'd been an interloper. Even after joining the pack, I would have had to build years of trust with the pack members before being truly accepted. But with Mira, it wasn't like that. She'd been my one true friend for my entire life, and I'd known her for so long that I couldn't remember a time when I hadn't trusted her.

"I was so worried," Mira said, the moment we pulled away from each other. Her nose wrinkled at the sight—or maybe the scent—of me, but her eyes were full of warmth. "I had no idea if you were dead or alive, or what had happened to you after we left the Convergence. I'm so happy you're okay."

"I'm sorry. I wanted to send you a message to let you know I was alive, but I couldn't." While with the Ophiuchus pack I'd been told I couldn't have a phone or any contact with the outside world until I became a pack member. They wouldn't have let me risk the location of the pack just to send word to my friend. Then once I finally became a pack member, everything with the Leos had happened so quickly, I hadn't had a chance to get her a message.

Jordan moved to my side, flashing me a charming smile. "I thought you could use a friendly face here. And as a show of good faith, I'm going to let you both stay together in this house, instead of sending you back to the prison."

"Really?" I was so excited to see Mira and to know I wasn't going back to my prison cell that I almost hugged him. I'd never expected something like this, especially after the Sun Witches had told him to keep me locked up. Perhaps their grip on Jordan wasn't as strong as I'd thought.

He nodded. "Consider this a trial. You'll have to stay inside the house for now, but as long as you don't try anything, you'll be given more privileges."

He sounded gracious, but his words made me realize there was an underlying threat beneath them. Despite my happiness at seeing Mira, her being here gave Jordan something to hurt me with. If I stepped out of line he could threaten her life, knowing I'd do whatever he wanted to keep her alive. His so-called gift was really just another way of controlling me.

I forced a smile and muttered, "Thank you."

"I'll give you two some time to catch up," he said, as he reached up to touch my cheek. I tensed, not knowing what to expect, but then he kissed me on the forehead. A ripple of need went through me at his touch, making me sigh, and he smiled at me like he knew how I felt. Then he left, closing the door behind him. I almost expected to hear the click of a lock, but nothing came. We weren't locked inside, but we couldn't leave either. No matter how generous Jordan was being, I couldn't allow myself to forget that this house was still a prison surrounded by guards—though it sure beat being in a dark cell with nothing but a cot.

I looked back over at Mira and pushed those worries away. I had so much to tell her, things that she would never believe. But there was something else I needed to do first. "I can't wait to sit down and tell you everything, but I desperately need a shower."

"Good idea. You reek." She laughed. "Go on, I need to unpack anyway."

She shooed me away, and I smiled at her before I went upstairs. It was a nice four-bedroom house, clean and modern and very beige, but it looked like no one lived here. There weren't any personal touches, nothing to indicate that this had been someone else's home before Mira and I had been brought to it. It reminded me of one of the houses the Cancer pack had kept for important visitors, like other pack alphas and their families. It didn't surprise me that the Leo pack had something similar.

I picked an empty bedroom, realizing I had absolutely

nothing to mark the place as mine. No clothes, no keepsakes, nothing. Once again, I was in a place without any worldly possessions. This was getting repetitive to the point of ridiculousness. The thought made me remember the last time this had happened, and I was filled with sadness. I'd only lived in Kaden and Stella's house for a while, but I had a sudden, very strong pang of homesickness. Their home was full of life, and they'd allowed me to become a part of it like I was family. This place was soulless in comparison.

At least there was a shower kit in the attached bathroom. I quickly stripped my days' old clothes off and hopped into the shower. It was amazing to wash the dirt, grime, and sweat off my body, and I lingered in the shower past the point of necessity, grateful to have the hot water pounding down on my skin.

A knock sounded on the door, and I instantly went on high alert.

"I just realized you probably don't have any clothes," Mira said, voice muffled by the door.

I relaxed. "No, I don't."

The door creaked open. "I'll leave them on the counter."

"Thank you so much," I responded, eternally grateful for Mira and her consideration. She was always thinking of others, and I was so glad to have her with me here when everyone else around me was an enemy. I just wished it didn't put her in danger too.

I finished my shower, my mood dampened somewhat by the remembrance of where I was. For a while, under the hot water, I'd been able to let my mind go blank, but now it was back to reality.

I dried off with one of the provided towels and dressed in Mira's clothes. Mira and I were roughly the same size, and we'd shared clothes before many times. When Dad couldn't be bothered to get me new clothes for school, Mira had always given me some of her own. Today she'd left me a gray t-shirt and jeans that weren't the most comfortable, but I would make do until I could figure out where to get my own clothes. Still, they fit a bit differently than I remembered, and I realized that I'd changed since the last time I'd seen her. I'd put on muscle, shed the last bit of baby fat clinging to my body. I glanced at myself in the mirror, and the female that looked back had a stubborn set to her jaw and a hardness in her eyes that I couldn't remember associating with myself before.

Feeling much better, I went back out. I followed the sound of Mira, finding her in a bedroom down the hall, surrounded by many pieces of opened luggage. It looked like she'd packed as if she expected to be here for a long time.

"You look like you're moving in," I said. "What about your mate? Is he here too?"

"Aiden is back with the rest of the Pisces pack." There was a thread of tension in her voice, and she glanced around like she worried someone might be listening. When she spoke again, it was almost a whisper. "They're holding him hostage to make sure I don't do anything, like convince you to run away with me."

My heart sank, though I shouldn't have been surprised.

I'd known Jordan's gift was too good to be true, and this seemed more on par with the Leo pack I remembered. "I'm sorry. It's my fault you're in this mess."

Mira shook her head. "No, it's not. The Pisces pack has totally caved to the Leos' demands. Our alpha is terrified to go against Jordan in case we end up like the Cancer pack."

It was exactly as I'd feared. The Pisces pack had once been Cancer's greatest allies, and they'd turned, just like that. Not that I expected anything better after their alpha had been too scared to help us at the Convergence, and they'd abandoned me when I'd needed them the most. "What about the other packs?"

She pulled some shirts out of her luggage and put them in a drawer. "The other packs are just as scared. They're either straight-up allying with the Leos or trying to stay out of the way. Some are waiting to see where the chips fall, especially with the old Leo alpha dead."

I shook my head. *Cowards.* "There's no staying out of it. Jordan plans to take over all of them with the help of the Sun Witches, and though he pretends he's better than his dad, I have a feeling it won't look much different in the end when every pack is under the Leos' rule. Will *any* of the packs stand up to them, from what you know?"

Mira picked up some light, breezy dresses next. "I don't know. When I was back with the Pisces, we had a couple of packs reach out to see what we were doing, but once they figured out that we weren't actively opposing the Leos, they withdrew. I don't know which ones they were, everyone kept it pretty hush-hush. Especially with me."

"Have you heard anything about the remaining Cancers?" I asked. Not all of them had gone to the Convergence, but what happened to those who stayed behind? Had Dixon sent some of his Leos to wipe them out too?

"I heard they went into hiding, but no one knows where. Or if they did, they didn't tell me." She stared down at the dress in her hand, her fingers idly rubbing the sheer fabric. "As the lone Cancer survivor, everyone was on eggshells around me at all times. They were all polite, of course, and very sympathetic about the death of my parents and the loss of my pack, but they tended to avoid me too."

"That sounds very lonely." I could empathize—I knew what it was like to be tossed into the middle of an unfamiliar pack without warning.

"It was, but at least I had my mate." Her voice grew wistful. "Aiden was the only thing that made it tolerable."

"What is he like?"

Mira's eyes got a far-away look, and a dreamy smile crossed her face. "Aiden? He's...great. Funny, smart, kind, and he loves the water as much as I do. I couldn't ask for anything more."

At least one of us can be with who we want, I thought, and tried not to let the bitterness extend to Mira herself. It wasn't her fault that her mate had come easily to her and that they were a perfect pair—that was how it should be, after all. I was truly happy for her, even if that happiness was tinged with sadness for myself. I was stuck with a mate I didn't want, and I wanted a man who didn't want me. I would have laughed if it didn't hurt quite so much.

"You must miss him a lot," I managed to say. Even if I was a tiny bit jealous of Mira, I still hated that the Leos were using Aiden against her.

"I do." She finally shoved the dresses in the closet. "But enough about me—tell me what happened to you after the Convergence. Have you been here with the Leos all this time?"

"No, that only happened recently." I sat on the edge of the bed. We really did have a lot to catch up on. "After Aiden dragged you away and the Pisces pack left me for dead, I was taken by the Ophiuchus pack. They rescued me from certain death, and even though they didn't trust me at first, they trained me."

Mira blinked at me, the look on her face one of disbelief. "The Ophiuchus pack—you mean those people who showed up at the Convergence out of the blue? I didn't even know they were real before that night."

"They're definitely real. They've been in hiding all this time, but they've been planning to go up against the Zodiac Wolves for years. The Ophiuchus pack might be the only ones with the guts and the power to stand up to the Leos."

"Wow." Mira sat next to me, her eyes wide. "Tell me everything. What were they like?"

"They were..." I drew in a breath as another wave of homesickness filled me. "They were not what I expected at all. Determined, resilient, mysterious, passionate...but accepting too. They've taken in many of the Zodiac Wolves' outcasts over the years, and they allowed me to become part of their pack too, once I proved myself."

I lifted the sleeve of my shirt a bit higher so Mira could see the pack mark there. She reached out and touched it like she couldn't believe it was real.

"And their alpha?" Mira asked, raising her eyebrows. "I saw him at the Convergence. He seemed intense...and hot."

"Kaden," I said, unable to keep the emotion out of my voice as I said his name. "He wants revenge on the Leos for killing his parents, and he trained me to fight. He..." My throat tightened. "He's the best alpha I've ever known."

She sat back, studying me. "You say his name like a benediction. What happened, did you fall in love with him?"

Damn, was it that obvious? "No, it's...complicated. I have feelings for him, but we can't be together because we aren't mates."

"Yeah, but Jordan rejected you at the Convergence," she pointed out. "Although now it seems like he's changed his mind."

I snorted. "Trust me, I'm just as confused about his change of heart as you are."

"How did you end up here?"

I looked down, staring at my hands as I relived the awful memory. "The Ophiuchus pack was attacked by the Leos and the Sun Witches. Kaden managed to defeat the Leo alpha, but the pack was still in danger. I agreed to come with Jordan to save them. He's been holding me prisoner ever since."

"And now he's brought me here to show you what a good guy he is," Mira said, rolling her eyes.

"Exactly. I don't want to be with him, but every day it gets harder to resist the mate bond."

Mira leaned forward, meeting my eyes. "I know this sounds crazy, but hear me out. Are you sure you should resist it? Even when everything was terrible, the mate bond was the only thing that made sense to me."

"I can't be with Jordan. I hate him." I frowned as I said the words. Did I still hate him? I couldn't trust my own feelings anymore. "And even if I didn't, something about our mate bond is *wrong*. I can't explain it, but you have to believe me." I sat up straighter and held my hands out to Mira, who took them, even though she looked a bit confused. "I just need to escape and get back to the Ophiuchus pack. Then I can figure this out."

Mira squeezed my hands. "I'll help you however I can."

"No." As nice as it would be to have Mira backing me, I couldn't risk it. "That will put you and Aiden in danger. I can't ask you to do that."

She let out a huff. "No matter what happens with Aiden, you're my sister. We've known each other since birth and I've always been there for you. I'm not going to stop now, just because it's getting a bit scary."

A swell of gratitude went through me. Of course she wouldn't let me do this alone. She never had before. "There might be a way. I recently learned I have Moon Witch magic from my mom. It's the only thing that saved me at the Convergence. I can teleport in the moonlight, and I used it to get away from Jordan. Maybe I can use it to help us escape."

Mira nodded, not doubting me at all. "I know you'll figure something out. I'm right there with you, the moment you decide you want to go."

I squeezed her hands tight again and sent a silent prayer up to the moon goddess Selene, or anyone who would listen. *Please, let us escape from this place. Before it's too late.*

CHAPTER SIX

I SPENT the next hour searching the house for any cameras or microphones—I wanted to make sure Jordan couldn't listen in on our conversations or watch me in the shower like some creepy perv. I found nothing, which made me feel a little better, although every time I looked out the window I saw one of the ever-present guards on patrol, reminding me I was still in a prison, even if this one was a lot nicer.

That afternoon, a woman arrived with all sorts of clothes in my size, plus shoes, underwear, bras, nightgowns, and even a few hats. When I asked where they came from, she simply smiled and said they were a gift from Jordan. About fifteen minutes after that, another female shifter showed up and filled our fridge and pantry with every food I could possibly think of, ranging from frozen pizzas to watermelon to wine. She told us if we needed anything else to let one of the guards know, and she'd get it for us as soon as she could.

Mira was delighted—she loved to bake and immediately began making a list of things she wanted.

That night we ate one of the frozen pizzas since we were both too tired to cook, and settled in with some popcorn to watch a movie. The big TV in the living room had Netflix, Disney+, and every other streaming service I knew of, all thanks to Jordan. I had to admit, the guy was winning some major points, especially after I'd had none of this with the Ophiuchus pack. Kaden had banned me from anything involving the internet during my time there like he'd expected me to send out our coordinates through Hulu or some shit.

I found a Marvel movie that had come out right after the Convergence and put it on. Mira and I watched and chomped popcorn, and it felt almost...normal. For a few minutes, I forgot where I was, and about everything else, and just enjoyed being with my friend and getting lost in someone else's story.

"Pause it," Mira said when we were about halfway through. "I need more wine."

I chuckled and hit pause, then got up myself. "Good idea. I like the idea of drinking all of Jordan's wine and making him buy more. I need to pee anyway." I started to head toward the bathroom, but Mira let out a little noise of surprise. I turned around and saw her face. "What is it?"

"Oh, Ayla. Your pants." She gestured toward me, and I looked down at my pale jeans and spotted blood between my thighs.

"Oh shit." Panic filled me as I stared down there. "Why am I bleeding?"

Mira's face turned sympathetic. "You got your period. That's all."

"I...how?" I thought periods were something only humans got. I'd lived my entire life without one, as had Mira, as far as I'd known.

"Did you go into heat at the last full moon?"

My cheeks turned red at the memory. "I did, yeah."

"Now that you're mated, you'll get your period after your heat, if you don't get pregnant during it." She cocked her head, her eyes filled with pity. "Didn't your stepmom tell you about this?"

"No, we didn't exactly have that kind of relationship," I muttered, my head swirling with this new knowledge—something I should have known all along, it seemed. I'd never thought I could actually get pregnant from all the sex I had with Kaden, but now that I knew for certain I wasn't, I felt the loss deep in my chest.

Mira stood and walked toward me, sensing my turmoil. "Are you okay? I get the feeling you're upset about more than just a little blood."

"I had sex with Kaden during the full moon. A *lot* of sex. And I guess a part of me hoped I was pregnant, and that I carried a bit of him with me still." I shook my head, blinking back tears. "It's stupid, I know. He's not my mate."

She wrapped her arms around me. "Oh, Ayla. I'm sorry. But you know that even if he was your mate, it's still rare for shifters to get pregnant when we go into heat."

I sniffed, leaning against her. Most shifters only had one child, or if they were really lucky, they'd be blessed with two. The one exception was the Gemini pack, of course, since they always had twins. "Really, it's better this way. I'm way too young to be a mother, and being pregnant here among the Leos would be a nightmare. Can you imagine?"

Mira rubbed my back. "It'll happen someday when you're ready for it. Come on, let's get you cleaned up. I have some pads you can use."

I gripped her arm, a new, horrible thought occurring to me. "Mira, I don't want to have Jordan's baby."

"You won't," she said. "We'll be long gone before the Leo heat comes on in the fall."

I swallowed and hoped she was right—but summer was already flying by, and my window for escape was growing shorter by the minute.

THE NEXT FEW days passed in relative bliss compared to the ones before. I didn't wake up in a cell, no Sun Witches came to squeeze magic out of me, and the best part of all was that I had Mira in my life again. It didn't even matter that we weren't allowed to leave the house, because we spent the days catching up and trading stories of how our time apart had gone.

I told Mira about the Ophiuchus pack, about Kaden and Stella, about the wolf cubs, and about how gay mate bonds were possible. I told her stories of how I'd been trained to fight, about practicing my moon powers, and learning about the stars on Kaden's rooftop.

Mira in turn shared stories about the Pisces pack. How they were similar to the Cancer pack, living up on the coast of Alaska in a fishing village, and how Aiden seemed dead set on providing everything he could for her. I still ached when she talked about how perfect of a match they were, but I managed to smile and actually feel happiness from her. She deserved it, after all. She'd always been so kind to me, so accepting and willing to back me up. *Of course* she deserved to have a perfect mate.

But didn't I?

As I spent time in the house, I began to feel more like a real person again instead of a prisoner and found a sort of clarity I'd been missing ever since waking up in the Leo pack's cells. It was August now, which meant Leo season was still in full swing, and the full moon was approaching too.

I began to form a plan, but I didn't have much to go on. We still weren't allowed outside, but I stared out of every window on the second story and tried to memorize the layout of the town. Beyond that, I didn't know where exactly we were, just that we were somewhere near Phoenix. But how near? Close enough for me to run to, or did I need to steal a vehicle? I cursed myself for not learning more about the other packs from my father, though he'd never been very forthcoming with info either.

Mira seemed dead set on helping me escape, which I

was grateful for, but now I had two of us to worry about. I'd never used my Moon Touched gift on someone else, and I wasn't sure if it was possible, but I had to try. It was the only way we'd make it. We were surrounded by the enemy, and they never let me forget it. Everyone I'd seen gave me suspicious, hostile looks. Not exactly the kind of welcome wagon I'd have hoped for, but I was used to it. I'd spent most of my life growing up in a pack that had treated me a lot like this.

Being here in the Leo pack made me ache for the Ophiuchus pack even more. Even when I hadn't been trusted and Kaden had made sure that I had two guards at all times, I was still treated with basic respect. No one glared at me or whispered about me behind their hands to their friends as I passed, vicious words they knew I could pick up with my wolf hearing. They were my home, my family, and I hoped that soon I could return to them with Mira in tow.

Every night, Jordan had dinner with me in the small backyard of the house under the stars and the waxing moon. I tried to soak up the moon's energy, but it only seemed to taunt me as it grew larger and rounded every night. The worst part was that every night spent with him put me more in danger of losing myself. The mating bond grew harder and harder to resist, and some nights I wondered if I was making a mistake by continuing to fight it. And after Jordan left, I'd return to my room and collapse in bed, twitching with desire, unable to fully satisfy myself, knowing he was probably doing the same thing.

I was frankly astonished by the fact that Jordan hadn't

tried to kiss me again. I could see his lingering gazes on my lips, my neck, the curve of my breasts. I felt the possessive heat in his eyes as he watched me, but he hadn't done anything more than brush his lips over my cheek, not since that time in the garden. Thank the gods.

"You're distracted tonight, Ayla," Jordan said, and I yanked my gaze away from staring at my plate. I hardly had an appetite. It was the night before the full moon, and I was getting antsy. If I was going to escape, it would have to be tonight. I should have eaten everything on my plate to keep my strength up, but my stomach revolted against every single bite.

"Tired," I said, giving him a placid smile. "Mira and I stayed up way too late watching that Korean show on Netflix you recommended. We couldn't stop."

"I knew you'd like it." Jordan smiled back at me and took a sip of wine. "Is your food okay? You've barely touched it."

I looked down at the gourmet salmon dish in front of me, trying to come up with a good excuse. I'd been given such good food here, even when he'd had me locked in prison, better than anything I'd ever had at my house in the Cancer pack. I hated it, and I hated Jordan even more for thinking that he could woo me over with nice food, new clothes, and pretty words. I hated even more how the part of me that answered to the mating bond *liked* his gifts and wanted to stay.

Good mate, it whispered to me. *Will take care of you.*

Right, until the moment he decides he doesn't need me anymore, I thought sardonically.

"I guess I'm just not that hungry tonight. Actually, would you mind if I went inside? I want to make sure I get lots of sleep before tomorrow." I stood before I heard an answer.

"Of course." Jordan stood as well, setting his glass down. He stepped forward, two long strides to get to me, and reached out to touch my cheek. Goosebumps followed in his wake as his hand trailed down my neck, light enough to tickle. I couldn't help the delirious shiver that went through me at his touch, nor could I stop myself from leaning into it.

Jordan seemed encouraged, and slid his hand down my arm, to take my hand I thought. But instead, his fingers traced down to my hip, which he held possessively. When he gave a slight squeeze, I gasped, trying to hold myself still so I wouldn't push him away—or pull him forward. I wasn't sure which would be worse at this point.

"It's okay to be nervous," Jordan whispered, and his breath ghosted along my skin. "But everything will be better after tomorrow night. You'll see."

"Right," I choked out, instead of *let go of me*. I shivered again and closed my eyes, willing myself to feel anything but this mix of pleasure and wrongness.

Apparently, that was the answer Jordan wanted because he let me go, and when I turned to look at him again, he had a satisfied smirk on his face. "Go rest up, Ayla. You have a big night ahead of you tomorrow. We both do."

It sounded like a promise, but it felt like a threat. I managed a shaky smile, thrown completely off by how much I wanted him, and how hard it was to resist staying with him. For days, he'd kept his distance from me, being a perfect gentleman and giving me my space, but now my body hummed with the need to close the gap between us. I couldn't stand another moment of it.

Tonight I would run—or die trying.

CHAPTER SEVEN

I TURNED AWAY a little too quickly and then slowed my steps so it wouldn't look like I was running away from Jordan. No doubt he could hear the way my heart pounded and smell the desire between my thighs. At this point, I think he was enjoying the anticipation, knowing tomorrow we'd be mated once and for all.

I opened the back door, not sparing a glance for the multitude of guards surrounding the house, and when it was firmly shut behind me, I sagged against it. I banged my head against the door, as hard as I dared, and Mira appeared in the doorway of the kitchen.

"Dinner with Jordan again?" she asked.

"I hate him," I said, although that wasn't completely true. I *wanted* him, and I hated myself even more for wanting him to touch me more, to kiss me, to claim me as his own. I shuddered, still feeling the ghost of his fingers on my hips grabbing me in a way that only one person had before. "We have to get out tonight. It's our last chance."

"I'm ready," Mira said, her eyes flashing with determination.

I looked outside at the moon lighting up the sky over the backyard. The only good thing about it being the night before the full moon was that my powers should be stronger. Since I still didn't fully know how to use them, that would be important.

"We'll wait two hours and then go, so they'll think we're asleep," I said. "You have your bag packed?"

"Mostly. I'll go finish up now."

She headed out of the kitchen, and I pushed away from the door and followed her up the stairs. Luckily, Mira had brought two backpacks with her from the Pisces pack, which meant I could shove the little toiletries kit from the bathroom in, as well as some food and clothes. Just enough for a few days. I hoped we wouldn't need more than that.

My heart continued pounding as I picked up the backpack I'd already started packing this morning, knowing tonight would be the time I'd use it. Now I closed the blinds in my room and finished up, then changed my clothes. I'd worn a black sheath dress for my dinner with Jordan, but I put on jeans and a t-shirt for my escape. Then I turned off my light and waited, sitting in the dark, going over my proposed escape route in my head a hundred times, wishing I had more info to make a better plan, wishing Kaden would just come save me, wishing I'd never gotten myself in this situation in the first place. I squeezed my eyes shut and pulled myself away from my dark thoughts. This was the lot I'd drawn in life, and the only person who could save me was myself.

When it was time, I grabbed my bag and knocked on Mira's door. Her bedroom had a balcony that I thought we could use to get onto the roof, since escaping on ground level wasn't an option with all the guards on patrol. They still might see us climb up, of course, but I prayed luck would be on our side tonight.

"Are you sure about this?" I whispered. "This is your last chance to stay."

She gripped her bag tighter. "No way. I'm not staying without you. This isn't my pack, and these aren't my people. You're my people, Ayla."

"What about Aiden?" I asked.

She hesitated, but then squared her shoulders. "He would want me to do this. And I doubt the Pisces alpha would let him be hurt—Aiden is his nephew."

I hugged Mira briefly, overwhelmed by her loyalty to me. Mira had been a constant in my life, and I was so glad she was going to come with me tonight. "Thank you," I whispered. "Once we're back with the Ophiuchus pack, we'll get Aiden out of there, and they'll protect both of you. Now let's go. The sooner we can get out, the more time we'll have before someone comes looking for us."

If this was successful, no one would think to start looking for us until tomorrow, when they noticed the house was empty. For now, they'd think we were sleeping, with the house quiet and dark. Or so I hoped.

Mira nodded and opened the sliding door to the balcony. She peered outside and hissed out a breath. "Crap. They're in wolf form."

That was unusual. They were normally in human form as they patrolled, but maybe they were being especially vigilant tonight with the ceremony tomorrow. Shit. We still had to try though. It was our only chance.

Mira slid out onto the balcony first, watching carefully. I waited inside, antsy and thrumming with energy. Finally, there seemed to be a break in the wolves milling around the first floor, pacing circles around the entirety of the house. Mira crouched down and leaped, grabbing onto the roof above her, using her shifter strength to propel her higher. I watched her struggle to lift herself up, and went out to give her a boost. She tumbled onto the roof, making a lot more noise than I'd hoped, and immediately ducked down out of sight.

I pressed myself back into the shadows as one of the wolves twitched his ears toward us. After a moment, he shook his head, almost as he would have if he'd been in human form, and went back to circling. When it was clear again, it was my turn, and I gathered my strength and jumped. Mira scooted back to give me room to hoist myself up. I almost overshot, expecting it to be as much of a struggle as it had been for Mira, but I'd forgotten that I had a lot more training than she had. She gaped at me as I catapulted onto the roof with one great heave and then tucked into a silent roll.

"Where did you learn to do that?" she whispered, so quiet I could barely hear her.

"Kaden taught me," I whispered back.

Mira shook her head, a little smile on her face. I'd told her about training with Kaden, and she'd watched me warm up and go through a few basic routines a few times. I'd kept up my routine every day, just like Kaden had told me to. Even though he wasn't here to teach me more, it still felt *right*. Like a promise. *I'm coming back to you.*

I turned and stood up once we'd gotten to the center of the roof, where Jordan's guards wouldn't be able to see us, even if they looked up. I tilted my face toward the moonlight and closed my eyes, letting the soft silvery light soak into me. A sudden rush of power went through me, infusing every cell of my body with magic.

I opened my eyes quickly, reaching over to grasp Mira's hand. I didn't even know if this would work, since I'd never tried to teleport anyone with me before, and it had been days—weeks?—since I'd used my magic...but I had to try. I gathered the power inside me and *moved*.

When I blinked, we were on the next house over. I could hardly tell the difference, except for the position of the trees and the sky. This roof was exactly like the roof of the house we were in, and there was a row of more houses just like it, forming a path for me. Like stepping stones.

Mira's hand gripped me so hard my fingers hurt. She'd slapped her other hand over her mouth, and her eyes were huge in her face. She looked like she might throw up, but at least it had worked.

"Thanks for not screaming," I whispered.

Mira slowly lowered her hand and grinned at me. "That was...wow."

"Ready to go again?" I asked. She nodded, and I let out another burst of power, and then we were on the next house's roof. Over and over, I hopped through the moonlight, dancing across unsuspecting shifters' roofs as we made our escape like some sort of midnight fairies.

Finally, we were two houses away from the edge of town, and no one had caught us yet. I paused as I glanced over at the last house. There wasn't anything beyond it, just the endless stretch of desert, somehow even harsher in the moonlight than it was in the sunlight. This was where my plan got a bit murky. Mira believed that Phoenix was southwest of us, but wasn't certain of that, and we weren't sure how long it would take us to get to another town where we might be able to get help.

I saw a car parked on the street below us. That would be the fastest way for us to get out of here, with less of a scent trail to follow. "Do you know how to hotwire a car?"

Mira frowned at me. "Why would I know how to hotwire a car?"

"Fair point." I gazed out at the rugged landscape before us. "Wolf form it is then."

"This is a terrible idea." She was looking out at the desert as well, apprehension clear on her face.

I squeezed her hand tight. "We'll get through this. We have to."

She gave me a shaky smile. "Okay."

I made the final jump to the other roof, and we both started undressing in silence, shoving our clothes into our bags in tandem. I closed my eyes and shifted. It seemed like it had been years since I'd done this, even though it had been a few weeks. I settled into my wolf's body with ease and nudged Mira's dark brown wolf with my nose. Since we weren't part of the same pack we wouldn't be able to communicate telepathically, but we knew each other so well it hopefully wouldn't matter.

We both picked up our bags with our fangs, and then prepared to leap off the roof. For a moment, it felt like I was flying, sailing through the air, and I wondered if I'd even hit the ground at all. Then it came up to greet me, and I rolled to avoid the worst of the impact. Mira landed a few feet behind me with a lot less grace. I glanced back at her, watching her get up and shake herself. She was okay.

Then I spotted something that sent a chill through me. A woman stood in front of the last house, the one we'd just jumped off, and I recognized her immediately.

Jordan's mom.

Shit.

She stood with her arms crossed as she glared at us. Jordan had told me her name was Debra, and that she'd been the daughter of the alpha before Dixon. He'd implied she was fierce and dangerous, and like a true lioness, she was very protective of her sons.

I drew my lips back in a snarl, ready to fight, though I wasn't sure we stood a chance against her. Debra had years of training on me, whereas Mira hadn't gotten much beyond the basics in our pack.

"You're running," Debra said. It wasn't a question. Obviously, there would be no other explanation for our presence on the edge of the Leo village in the middle of the night. "Maybe you're not as stupid or as weak as I thought."

Mira and I froze, glancing warily at each other, tails swishing back and forth. Why wasn't Debra rushing to sound the alarm? Or tackling us to the ground?

She gestured toward the desert. "Go on then. I won't stop you."

I let out a low, wary growl. Was this a trap? Mira cocked her head at me, her ears twitching. She didn't know either. Then I remembered Debra's words back when I was in prison—for whatever reason, she didn't want me to mate with Jordan any more than I did.

I dipped my head briefly to Jordan's mother in thanks, and then nudged Mira with my nose, signaling to her that we should keep going. We leaped over a short wall, landing squarely in the desert, and then we ran.

We dashed across the harsh terrain, unsure if we were going in the right direction, and Mira kept up with me perfectly, matching me stride for stride. Then I heard a howl from the town behind us, and my hair stood on end. More howls joined in, cutting through the cool night air, and then I heard the distinct growl of engines starting up. I looked over at Mira, trying to urge her to run faster while increasing my own pace until my muscles screamed. There couldn't be any slowing or stopping, not now. We *had* to make it.

But even in our wolf forms, we couldn't outrun cars, and it wasn't long before I felt the pull in my gut that meant Jordan was getting closer. *Fuck.* Stronger and stronger it pulled until I almost lost my footing, and the sound of cars in the distance grew louder. Panic filled me, and then suddenly the headlights were on us, illuminating us like spotlights. I tried to bolt to the side, to go into a defensive running maneuver that Stella had taught me. I didn't make it. The SUVs slid in alongside us, spinning around with expert precision to box us in. *Dammit,* I thought, and tried to look for an escape route. There wasn't one.

We were trapped, once again.

CHAPTER EIGHT

MY LEGS SHUDDERED under me as I halted completely, and I was panting hard enough that I was sure Jordan could hear it. Mira wasn't better off beside me, her lips pulled back as she lowered herself into a defensive crouch. But the waxing moon was overhead, and I still had its magic filling me. I pressed against Mira's side and teleported us away from the cars, into another spot of desert. Then I did it again, putting distance between us.

Before I could blink away a third time, the air around me seemed to light up, and fire hit my side. I let out a loud howl of pure agony as I was knocked down, and then a beam of pure sunlight flew toward Mira next, though she narrowly dodged it. From my spot on the ground, I traced the bolt back to Roxandra, who sat in front of one of the SUVs.

As I struggled to my feet, the cars surrounded us again. One of the doors opened and I snapped my head toward the sound. Jordan stepped out and held up a hand, and at his silent command, other shifters emerged from their vehicles and surrounded us. The three Sun Witches moved to stand beside Jordan, and Roxandra's hand lit up as she shot another bolt of light at Mira, this time hitting her square in the chest.

She yelped, falling on her side, and didn't move again. If I'd been in human form, I would have gasped, but what came out of my throat was a whine. I looked over at her, trying to figure out if she was even still alive, but the shifters were closing in fast. I closed my eyes and weighed my options. I only had a few seconds to make a decision, and if I made the wrong one, it could end with both of us dead.

There was no way I'd leave Mira, even if I could teleport, and I didn't see a way that I could carry an unconscious shifter and fight my way out of here. And if the Sun Witches hit me with whatever they'd hit Mira with? I'd be toast. I flinched at the thought of having their magic on me again. I never wanted to come into contact with that again.

"I'm disappointed in you, Ayla," Jordan said with a sigh, as he moved to stand in front of me. "I thought you were finally willing to accept me as your mate."

Never, I thought, as I glared at him from my wolf eyes.

"I told you to keep her locked up," Roxandra said.

"If I had, you wouldn't have seen her power tonight," Jordan said. "I told you she would use it if given a chance."

"True." Roxandra turned a cruel smile on me. "We were wondering what exactly you could do. Now we know."

"There was never any chance of you escaping," Jordan told me, looking down at me with a haughty expression. "The second you used your power, the Sun Witches felt it. We let you keep going for a while so they could study you. After that, it was easy to track you down."

My heart sank at his words. We'd never even had a chance, and now I was going to be trapped with the Leo pack forever. Despair made me want to throw my head back and howl at the moon, but instead, I snarled at my mate. All the desire I'd once felt for him was gone, replaced only with pure hatred.

He bent down and stroked my head, and I snapped at his fingers. "Tomorrow is our mating ceremony. Don't even think about running again. If you try, we'll kill Mira and her mate." From the deadly smile on his face, he was completely serious. "Hell, maybe I'll kill the entire Pisces pack too, just because I can. So do them all a favor, and don't even try."

I balked at his words, and all the fight left me. Surely he wouldn't kill an entire pack because of me? I didn't want to chance it. I didn't trust his mental stability in the slightest. There was no way to escape, and even if I could find a patch of moonlight that wasn't currently being flooded with the light from the cars, I couldn't leave Mira.

I dropped my head in submission and shifted back to my human form, standing naked before them. "I won't run." I held my hands out in front of me in a *don't shoot* gesture. "I promise."

Jordan sneered and didn't even give me time to cover

myself before he grabbed hold of my wrist and dragged me back to one of the cars. I gritted my teeth on the protest forming in my mind and let him throw me in with little ceremony. Another shifter picked up Mira, still in wolf form, and carried her to a different car. I tried to see if she was all right, but didn't get a chance before Jordan was shoving my head into the car.

"Get her out of my sight," he growled, before slamming the door. To my surprise, he wasn't the one who got in the car with me.

The Sun Witches were.

Roxandra sat in front beside the burly male driver, while the other two Sun Witches pinned me between them in the back. The male threw the car into gear, and before I knew it, we were heading back. For a second I debated trying to open the door and flinging myself out, but it was a thought born of desperation, not logic. The three Sun Witches could easily subdue me if I tried anything.

One of them handed me my bag, and a sense of foreboding washed over me as I dressed as quickly as I could in the cramped space. A tense silence filled the car as we drove across the rugged terrain. Neither woman said a single thing until the car stopped.

When I peered out, my breath caught in my throat. We hadn't stopped in front of the house Mira and I had been living in, but outside the prison. I squeezed my eyes shut, knowing what was ahead of me.

The others got out of the car, and for a split second, it

was just me in the back. I had the wild thought of climbing into the driver's seat and mowing over as many of the Leo shifters and Sun Witches as I could. It was nothing more than an idle fantasy though. I couldn't do anything while Mira was being held captive.

One of the males I'd seen guarding the outside of the house reached inside the car. I backed away from him, remembering Jordan's heavy hand on my wrist. He yanked my bag from my hands and threw it down onto the ground before hauling me bodily out of the car.

"You're putting me back in there?" I asked, struggling against him.

"It's only for one night," Roxandra said from where she watched from the side. "After tomorrow, you'll be living in Jordan's house."

And sleeping in his bed, I mentally added, my stomach twisting at the thought.

Another shifter opened the door to the prison building, and the big male hauled me through. I struggled the whole way, digging my feet in, but the male was strong enough that he could just pick me up and drag me along again before I could really get any traction. All three Sun Witches followed us, making sure I didn't try anything. Before I knew it, I was being shoved into a cell again. It clanged shut with a finality that had me closing my eyes and holding back tears. I'd gotten a brief taste of the freedom I'd craved for so long, and just like that, it had been taken away from me.

I shoved the thoughts away before they could overtake

me. I couldn't afford to show any weakness right now. I'd
have to stay strong and think things through logically if I was
going to survive this. Especially as the Sun Witches filled
the room, and the guards took their places in front of my cell
door.

"Where's Mira?" I asked the Sun Witches. At some
point, they'd pulled their hoods up, and I could barely see
their faces under the strange lighting in the prison. There
was no answer, and I growled in frustration, pacing the
length of my cell. I was still thrumming with adrenaline, and
trapped in this tiny cell there wasn't anywhere to let it out.

The sound of footsteps made me pause in my tracks, and
the mate bond hummed inside me. Jordan's face appeared,
just as furious as it had been when he'd been dragging me to
the car. He nodded to the shifter holding the keys, and I
pressed myself against the wall furthest from him as he
entered, wondering what the hell he wanted now.

"This is it," he said. "I'm giving you one last chance to
willingly be my mate."

"And if I refuse?"

He clenched his jaw. "You won't. I know you feel the
same way I do."

I let out a humorless laugh. "I feel *nothing* for you."

"You're lying." He looked like he believed it completely.

Save me from the arrogance of alpha males, I thought. Of
course he couldn't accept that I didn't want him, even after
everything that he'd done to me and my family. To the Ophiuchus pack.

"Or maybe the Ophiuchus snakes truly have poisoned your mind. Especially the alpha." Jordan watched me closely and found something in my face that vindicated what he said. "Don't deny it. You feel *something* for him. But it doesn't matter, because I'll be the only one you can think about once we are truly mated."

Before I could even think to flinch away, Jordan was there, crowding me up against the wall of the cell. I opened my mouth to tell him to *fuck off*, but before I could, he was shoving his mouth onto mine. He gripped my shoulders possessively, so tight it almost hurt. I gasped into his mouth at the sudden flare of desire, and his tongue found its way in. For a few seconds I gave in to the kiss, tugging at his shirt to pull him closer, and then the wrongness hit me again.

No, my gut told me. *This isn't right!*

Fighting off the mate bond was hard, but I'd had plenty of practice during my time here. With a burst of strength, I shoved Jordan away from me, making him fly across the cell. He looked surprised, as if he didn't think me capable of it.

"I reject you as my mate!" I yelled, repeating the words he'd said at the Convergence. *Now you know what it's like*, a part of me thought. *Doesn't it hurt?*

Jordan's eyes flashed with anger, and we both snarled at each other like we might tear each other's throats out. We couldn't kill each other, but that didn't mean we wouldn't try. But before either of us could do anything, a bright light shot out of Roxandra's hands and hit me in the chest, knocking me back against the wall. White-hot pain lanced through me and I screamed, and when it ended, I sagged to the floor.

When I got up, one of the other Sun Witches rested her hand on Jordan's shoulder. He bent his head and she spoke into his ear, and even with my wolf hearing, I couldn't make out the words. He nodded and turned back to me with the kind of anger I'd only ever seen in my father flickering through his eyes. I flinched instinctively, but I wasn't fast enough and there wasn't enough room to properly move away. All I saw was Jordan's fist, flying toward my face.

I was surprised at the power behind it. It sent me sprawling to the floor again, a bright bloom of pain throbbing all along the left side of my face. I lifted my hand to touch my cheek and winced at the secondary jolt of pain it sent through me.

"Hit me all you want," I said, glaring up at him with hatred burning inside me. "I'll never be your mate. You'll have to force me tomorrow, and even when I'm your mate, I'll fight you every step of the way."

"Fine," Jordan snapped. "If that's the way it has to be, then so be it. I tried to make this easy on you, but you've left me no other choice."

I hardly recognized my mate. I'd almost grown lax, so used to the Jordan who'd spoiled me with food, given me gifts, and stopped touching me because I needed time. But this Jordan had been lurking under the surface all this time, just waiting for a chance to be released again.

As he turned away, I said the thing I knew would hurt

him more than anything else. "You're no better than your father."

"I am nothing like him!" He spun back around and delivered a swift kick to my side.

I sucked in a sharp breath of air, or tried to, and I was still gasping by the time he was outside of the door.

"Have at her, boys," Jordan said, with such a cruel note in his voice that I looked up at him one more time to see if I could spot anything human beneath the monster lurking in his skin. "Just make sure she's alive at the end of it. I *do* need her mated to me tomorrow."

He grinned at me through the bars as he closed the doors, leaving the two guards on the inside with me. They advanced upon me, while the Sun Witches stood outside and watched the show.

I gritted my teeth and thought about trying to fight back, but what was the use? I was trapped in enemy territory, surrounded by shifters and witches, and they were holding Mira hostage. Basically, I was fucked.

Instead of fighting, I just slumped back and lifted my arms to try to protect my head as the guards came closer, sharp looks of glee on their faces as they began pummeling me with fists and feet. The Sun Witches hit me with a spell too, though it didn't hurt this time. I wasn't sure it did anything until I realized my body wasn't trying to heal itself. Somehow they'd turned off my shifter healing. *Fuck.* Jordan really did have them wrapped around his finger, ready to act on his every whim.

The feel of Jordan's proximity through the mating bond

persisted for a few moments, still trying to draw me closer to him, even though he was the one responsible for this. *I hate you,* I thought, and then the feeling pulling at my gut faded, and I knew Jordan had left.

It didn't take too much longer for the pain to become too much. As they continued beating me, I slipped gratefully into unconsciousness.

A part of me hoped I would never wake up at all.

CHAPTER NINE

I WOKE when one of the guards who had fun connecting his feet to my ribs slapped me across the face. I sat upright—or tried to. Every inch of my body hurt like I'd been run over by a freight train. I groaned and tried my best to curl up, to make myself a smaller target. How long would this beating go on? But instead of hitting me, the guard shoved some sheer fabric into my hands.

I looked down at it. "What the fuck is this?"

The guard slammed the cell door shut and locked it, then looked at me through the bars, his dull eyes glittering with malice. "Your dress for the ritual, *princess*. Alpha said to strip down. Completely. Then put that on."

His eyes lingered on my body, and I hugged my hands around myself. I'd gotten used to being naked, but nothing could desensitize me to being leered at like that.

"Hurry up," he added, turning around as if I'd suddenly

lost all interest to him. It was jarring, but at least he wasn't looking at me anymore. "I'm supposed to bring you out in a few minutes."

Shit. Not only had I passed out for hours, but I'd only been awoken a few minutes before the ritual. I didn't appreciate the thought of being dragged out of the cell while I was still half-groggy and all kinds of sore from what they'd done to me.

I stripped down, every movement agony, and if I'd been any more lucid, I would have thrown a fit about the dress. As I put it on, I noticed it was extremely revealing, low cut in the front, and almost completely backless. When I moved, my legs slid out from the fabric, all the way up to the spot where my thigh met my hip. The fabric itself was almost see-through, so sheer that if someone looked at me in the right lighting, they'd see everything. The bruises showed through, dark splotches against my light skin. On the front of the dress, plastered on my stomach, was the Leo pack symbol, big and gaudy. *I've basically been marked,* I thought. I looked at the Ophiuchus pack mark on my arm, wondering if this was one of the last times I'd see it.

This is it, I thought, as I realized what this dress meant. I'd thought about mating with Jordan before, of course. The mating bond wouldn't let me not think about it, but the thought of having sex with him hadn't carried the same weight as it did now. Tonight I knew there would be no escaping it.

The guard opened the door, and two shifters entered. I

didn't flinch, but held my head at a contrary angle, daring them to beat me again. Both guards just grabbed me by the upper arms and practically lifted me off my feet so they could drag me out of the cell.

They walked me all the way outside to the garden where the gazebo sat. *Hundreds* of Leo shifters were there, as well as at least a dozen Sun Witches. The garden was over-flowing with shifters, packed so tightly I could hardly see the ground, and there was a long stone altar positioned in the middle of the gazebo. Jordan stood at one end of it, wearing only a pair of black slacks, his muscular chest gleaming under the moonlight. I felt a roil of desire and disgust go through me, equally as strong on both counts.

I looked up at the night sky one last time before they dragged me under the gazebo, fixing my eyes on the full moon. *At least I'm not packless,* I thought, trying to find something, *anything,* good about this situation. *I'd be well into the mating frenzy if that was the case.*

The thought didn't bring as much comfort as I'd hoped. Instead, it made me think of Kaden, about how I should be with him tonight instead of my asshole mate. But fate had never been kind to me, and it wasn't about to start now.

As the Sun Witches parted, I realized the stone altar was human-sized, and the way Jordan stood over it meant he planned to mate with me *right there* in front of everyone. I almost threw up at the thought, but below my disgust, the ever-present burn of desire made itself known too. I tried to shove it down, so horrified by my base animal reaction I could hardly stand it, but it wouldn't go away. I hated how helpless both my mind and body were against the fucking mate bond.

It didn't help that Jordan was standing there, his perfect body on display. I found myself tracing the planes of his muscles before jerking my eyes back up to his face. He smirked, as if he knew what I was thinking about, and motioned for the guards to bring me up to the altar.

The Sun Witches moved closest to the altar as well, a sea of warm-hued colors in the pale moonlight. I struggled as I was brought forward, but I was still hurting, and as I looked wildly around, I saw a half-conscious Mira slumped between two other guards. She was back in human form, but that didn't seem to be helping her any. She looked pale and listless, hardly able to keep her eyes open. Whatever the Sun Witches had done to her had stuck, and I wondered if they'd used the same spell on her that they had on me to keep her wounds from healing. If I fought back, Jordan would have her killed. There would be no escape for me tonight.

The guards forced me to sit on the altar, and I slumped, unable to find the will to fight with all these odds against me. I didn't help them as they shoved me down on it, and when one of them reached for my ankle, I jumped. I tried to tear it out of his grasp, but the shifter held on tight and yanked my leg out to the side.

A wash of shame went through me as I realized they were tying me to the alter, my legs spread apart like a fucking offering, and there was nothing I could do to stop it.

Jordan loomed over me, the hunger in his eyes turning his face sharp. My arms were tied by the guards next, and then they stepped back, leaving me bared for all the world to see. And in this skimpy dress, they saw *everything*.

"It's time for the Leo pack to gain its new alpha female," Jordan's voice boomed out.

The Sun Witches closed in tighter and began chanting, quietly at first, but growing louder with each verse in some language I didn't know. Once the other shifters heard the chanting they began to whistle and yell, the ones in their wolf forms howling. It was a cacophony, and it twisted something in my gut, making the nerves and desire flare up in equal measures.

"Please," I said, pleading at Jordan with my eyes while tugging on my restraints. "If you feel a single thing for me, don't do this."

Jordan ignored my words, and to my horror, he began undoing his pants. I watched, that awful part inside of me howling along with the rest of the Leo pack, screaming *finally!* I swallowed and tried to push the lust down, but it was harder on the full moon. Even if I wasn't in heat, it made all shifters a little wild, as if we still had a trace of the Moon Curse in our veins we couldn't fully remove.

Roxandra stepped forward and looked down at me, face expressionless. "Her pack mark will change from Ophiuchus to Leo when you mate with her."

"Good," Jordan said. "I don't want any trace of the snakes on her."

"Please," I said again, louder. "Jordan, you're better than this. I know you are."

Jordan's eyes flicked up to my face, and for a second I saw something flash like hesitation. He paused, and I glimpsed the part of him that wasn't a monster. Then Roxandra put her hand on his shoulder and his face grew grim and determined again. He loomed closer, hand in his pants, and I squeezed my eyes shut, unable to watch what was about to happen.

There wasn't going to be any way out of this. I was well and truly fucked—and about to *be* well and truly fucked. Everything I'd done over the past few months had been for nothing, and if Kaden ever saw me again, he'd believe that I'd allowed myself to be mated to the Leo alpha. That I *wanted* it.

A sudden commotion broke through the chanting and howling, and my eyes popped open. Jordan's mom pushed through the crowd, and when she got to the gazebo, she shoved aside a Sun Witch as if she didn't care who she was. I had to give the woman credit, she was fierce as hell.

"Stop!" Debra shouted, and her voice carried over the rest of the noise. "You can't do this!"

Jordan growled at her, obviously annoyed by the interruption. "This is our destiny. The stars have chosen Ayla as my mate. I don't care if she's half witch, or from the Cancer pack. She's *mine*." He looked back at me with such possessiveness that my pussy clenched in excitement, while my chest tightened with fear.

"You don't understand," Debra said, her voice urgent. "You *cannot* mate with her."

"Why not?" Jordan asked.

"She's your sister."

My heart stopped. So did everything else. The whole garden fell silent. Even Jordan froze, his mouth hanging open.

His... WHAT?

"What the hell are you talking about?" Jordan asked.

For once, he and I had the exact same thought. Horror filled my chest as I stared at Debra. Her words didn't make any sense. It shouldn't be possible. Unless... Oh shit. "Are you my mother?"

She gave me a condescending look. "Don't be ridiculous."

Thank the goddess. But if she wasn't my mother, that meant...

"How can she be my sister?" Jordan asked. "Are you saying we have the same father?"

Debra dipped her head and lowered her voice. "Yes. I had an affair with Harrison, the Cancer alpha."

Several gasps went up around the shifters gathered there. Cheating on your mate was not only rare and unusual but considered blasphemous. The fact that she'd done it with the Cancer alpha, their pack's worst enemy, only made it more scandalous.

My head was spinning, trying to take in this new revelation, but I felt like a computer that had frozen and couldn't reboot. Jordan was my *brother*. No. Just...no. It wasn't possible. How?

HOW?

I wasn't the only one who was dumbstruck. Jordan gaped at his mom, and I watched emotions flash over his face in quick succession. Shock and horror. Anger. Pain. He looked like he'd been betrayed in the worst possible way.

And that's when I saw his eyes. Blue, just like mine.

Dixon's had been brown. Debra's were brown too. But not Jordan's.

He wasn't the Leo alpha's son. He was the *Cancer* alpha's son.

Oh god, oh god, oh, god. He *was* my brother.

Horror and disgust washed through me, and I wanted to go and scrub every single inch of my body and wash my mouth out with soap. We'd *kissed*. Multiple times! He'd been seconds away from having sex with me! The thought of what had been interrupted made me dry-heave. If I'd had anything at all to eat in the last few hours, I was sure I would have thrown it up.

While I gagged, Jordan just stood there, pants still unbuttoned, looking like his entire world was crumbling all around him. He glanced over at me and shuddered, then turned to the Sun Witches. "How did this happen?" he yelled. "How could I be mated with my own sister?"

The Sun Witches shared uneasy looks, and Roxandra said, "We're not entirely sure..."

Jordan grabbed his head like he might tear himself in two, and let out a roar that made the ground tremble. Then he stumbled off the altar, buttoning his pants before shoving through the line of Sun Witches. The Leo pack parted around him to let him pass, and Debra raced after him without giving me a second glance. Leaving me here to deal with this hot mess of a situation all on my own.

Fuck my life.

The shifters spoke to each other in frantic, hushed whispers, like no one could believe what they'd just seen, and no one knew what to do next. I certainly didn't know either. The Sun Witches huddled together, and no one was bothering to get me out of these bonds tying me to the altar.

"Hey!" I shouted. "Let me free!"

No one moved a muscle. I sighed and tested the strength of the bonds. Unfortunately, they were stronger than I'd thought they would be. I tried to teleport, since the moon was bright overhead, but felt something like a giant wall when I tried. Damn, the Sun Witches must be blocking my magic somehow.

I opened my mouth to yell again when a deep, shuddering *boom* ran through the town. I felt it vibrate the altar below me, and a rustle went through the gathered crowd. Now what?

Sirens started going off, and a few lone howls sounded from shifters in the distance. "We're under attack!" someone yelled. That seemed to jolt everyone into motion, and they began stumbling and jostling as they tried to rush out of the garden. The Sun Witches disappeared in a flash of light like fucking cowards, and still, no one made any attempt to free me. My heart pounded as I struggled with my bonds, knowing I'd be way too vulnerable while tied to this altar.

I'd managed to get one wrist free through sheer desperation when I heard someone shout, "Snakes!"

I froze, wondering if I'd heard the word correctly. Then someone else yelled it too, and I frantically tugged at the bond on my other wrist as a new emotion ran through me: hope.

CHAPTER TEN

IT WAS TOTAL CHAOS, human and wolf forms all crashing into each other around the garden and throughout the rest of the village. I struggled harder against my bonds, wishing I could throw myself into the fight as well. My pack was *here*. For me. They'd come after all. I could hardly believe it.

A shadow materialized beside me, appearing out of thin air. I opened my mouth to scream, but stopped when I saw who it was. Then I wanted to scream for other reasons.

Kaden.

He stalked up to the altar like something out of a dream, the moonlight streaming down on his dark hair. His broad shoulders and muscular frame filled my vision, and he radiated sheer alpha power with every step. He'd let his facial hair grow longer, and there was a hard set to his jaw as he looked me over, something burning in his icy blue eyes. Desire and longing rushed through me, but they felt entirely different from when the same emotions hit me around Jordan. Those felt forced, but this...this was all natural.

"You're here," I whispered, almost scared to believe what I was seeing with my own eyes. I'd never thought he would come for me, and yet now he was reaching down and yanking apart the bindings on my ankles.

When the last tie was undone, I practically launched myself at him. I wrapped my hands around Kaden's neck and pressed my face to his shoulder, nearly sobbing in relief. He was real, and he was here, and he was *mine*. I needed to breathe in his familiar scent, to recommit it to memory, along with the feel of his hard muscles against me, and his comforting warmth wrapped around me. *Home.*

But Kaden was as still as a statue under me, his arms staying staunchly by his side. He didn't hug me back. He didn't react at all.

When I pulled back, he studied my face, where I probably had a black eye from Jordan's punch. Then he lifted one of my arms up as if examining the bruising there. His face flashed with terrifying anger, his body almost trembling with rage. "Who did this to you?"

I jerked my arm back, trying to hide the bruises. "Jordan. And some of the other Leo pack members. Oh, and the Sun Witches got me a few times too."

A low growl rumbled through Kaden. "Your *mate* did this to you? I'll kill him."

He glanced around with wild eyes, and I imagined if Jordan was here, Kaden would rip his throat out.

I frowned, struck again by the shocking realization that

Jordan was my *brother*. Before, nothing would have pleased me more than Jordan being torn apart by Kaden's claws. But now I was so confused by this new truth, that I wasn't sure what I wanted. I'd already lost one brother, and no matter how much I hated Jordan, he was still family. At the very least I wanted to talk to him before Kaden ripped him to shreds.

Kaden must have noticed the hesitation written across my face, because he scowled and stepped back, shaking his head with disgust. "Even after he did this to you, you still want him."

"No!" I added as much vehemence to the word as I could. "It's not that. I don't want him, but—"

"I don't care," Kaden snapped. His strong arms came around me, lifting me up and throwing me over his shoulder so suddenly all the air rushed out of my lungs before I could get out the words *he's my brother*. "We have to get out of here."

I squirmed in his hold, remembering when he'd carried me like this during my heat. "Let me down, I can walk."

"No. You're injured and you'll be more of a hindrance than a help if I let you walk on your own two feet." He adjusted my position, his hand on my ass, using it as leverage to hold me tighter as he hopped off the gazebo and strode through the garden.

I gritted my teeth, unwilling to tell Kaden that the reason I didn't want him picking me up and pressing my body against him was because I was still wearing the skimpy dress with nothing underneath it. I could feel his muscles moving against my skin, and with the full moon overhead, it was driving me totally wild. Even worse, the scent I'd been dreaming about for weeks was now surrounding me, teasing me, tempting me. I could hardly think straight for how much I wanted him, but I needed to be focusing on everything *else* right now. Like the battle going on around me. Or getting the fuck out of this place once and for all.

He didn't say anything else as he walked out of the garden with me tossed over his shoulder like a war prize. All around us were the sounds of fighting, and when I twisted my head to try to catch a glimpse of what was happening, I spotted a bunch of Ophiuchus wolves ambling toward us. I recognized Jack, Harper, and Dane, and actually laughed at how happy I was to see them. They circled around us, keeping the Leo wolves from getting to Kaden since he wouldn't be able to fight with me in his arms.

I could also see that it would be a losing battle. There were significantly more Leos than Ophiuchus shifters, and more of the enemy running toward us to join the fray. Kaden's need for haste made more sense now, even if it had cut into my explanation for why I didn't want him to kill Jordan. We seemed to be rushing toward the edge of the village, where I spotted some cars waiting for us. Then I caught sight of two Leos dragging Mira away, heading in the direction of the prison building.

"Wait!" I turned in Kaden's arms, trying to get him to meet my eyes. "Kaden, please, I need to get my friend, Mira. She's being held captive, and I can't leave her here. She risked everything to help me."

"We can't stop," Kaden said. "I'm getting you out of here *now*."

I struggled against him harder, but he didn't budge. "I'm not leaving without her!"

His jaw was set, and I knew he wouldn't listen to me. Somehow I'd forgotten just how stubborn he could be, especially when he was focused on something. But I was stubborn too, and no way in hell was I leaving my friend behind.

I focused on the beams of moonlight streaming down, praying the Sun Witch spell blocking my powers had been broken. It worked, and the amount of power running through me was almost shocking when I touched it, thanks to the full moon. I didn't even have to try, and then I was about four feet from Mira.

I fell, hitting the ground hard now that I was no longer being held by Kaden, and pushed myself to my feet. Every ache and pain in my body screamed at me to stay down, but I couldn't let them take Mira to some cell, or execute her because of me.

"Hey, assholes," I shouted as I stumbled forward. I was still weak, but growing stronger by the second thanks to the moon filling me with light.

One of the Leos snarled at me, baring his teeth as he shoved Mira into the arms of the other male. I settled into a fighting stance, suddenly glad for all the times I'd practiced while I was trapped here with the Leo pack. My training all came flooding back to me naturally, and when the Leo male attacked, I was ready. I swung and kicked and ducked, and it wasn't long before I'd landed a blow on the male that had him reeling back.

I snapped my head to the side as I saw movement in my peripheral vision. *Kaden.* He looked furious, but when he growled, it wasn't at me. He took down two other Leos charging toward us like it was nothing, proving he always had my back, even when he was pissed at me.

The knowledge that Kaden was by my side gave me confidence, and I lunged toward the shifter in front of me again. He was a fighter too, but he hadn't been trained by the best, and I took him down easily with a maneuver Kaden had taught me. Then I sank my teeth into his arms. The Ophiuchus poison bite wasn't as effective in human form as in wolf form, but it still knocked him out.

The second one dropped Mira on the ground, and I spared a glance for her as he approached us. She looked weak but pushed herself up to a sitting position. Kaden surged forward and took down the male before I even got a chance, like he didn't want anyone getting close to me. I rolled my eyes, though I was secretly pleased he was still so protective of me.

As Kaden stood over the second male, he flicked his eyes to me, the snarl not leaving his face. "Don't do that again."

"I told you, I'm not leaving Mira." I crouched beside her. The adrenaline from the fight had erased what remained of my fatigue, and the moonlight filled my body with the strength it had been lacking before. "Are you okay?"

She nodded and grabbed my arm, her eyes wide. "I'm okay, but are you?"

No, I was very much not okay, because I'd just learned my mate was my *brother*, and he'd nearly fucked me on an altar in front of everyone, and now there was a battle going on around us, but I would be a hell of a lot better once we were far away from this place, so all I said was, "Yeah."

Kaden loomed over us, and he didn't look happy about the situation. "Fine, she can come too, but we have to leave now."

"*Fine*," I echoed, as I helped Mira to her feet. She leaned against my side, and together we began stumbling after Kaden.

Mira turned to me, a slight smile on her face. "That must be the alpha. I see what you mean about him."

I gave her a look that said *shut up*. If Kaden heard—which was pretty much guaranteed—he didn't react in any way. I was happy Mira was lucid enough to be joking with me, but really, did she have to rib me about Kaden when he was right there?

"Come on," Kaden snapped and picked up his pace. It was a struggle to keep up, but Mira and I were able to follow Kaden to the edge of the village, where a few vans were waiting for us. A swell of happiness went through me at the sight. This was really happening. Kaden had come to save me, and now we were finally going to get out of here. I would be away from Jordan and all the shifters who wanted me dead.

Kaden stopped at one of the vans and turned around, then let out a loud howl. Answering howls came from the town, and before I knew it, the Ophiuchus pack members were running toward their alpha. A few snarling Leos followed, most in wolf form, but some of the Ophiuchus wolves broke off to hold them back.

Another explosion shook the ground beneath my feet, and I jumped as I saw a flash of light back the way we'd come. Several of the Leos turned to see what was happening, but a few stayed, locked in a vicious battle with the Ophiuchus shifters.

"What was that?" Mira asked, her voice frantic.

"A diversion," Kaden said.

Suddenly the mate bond tugged at me, and I knew Jordan was close. I turned back, unable to stop myself from being drawn to him despite everything, and spotted him on the balcony of one of the houses nearby. Our eyes met across the distance, but he didn't move.

He's letting me go, I realized.

The pack started piling into the vans, and Kaden stalked toward me and Mira. He grabbed each of us by the arm and shoved us inside the van we stood in front of, then slammed the door shut. This van was the kind you used to transport things and had no windows looking out, and no seats in the back. Our area was closed off from the rest of the van, so I couldn't even see who was driving. In fact, it looked like more of a prison than anything else. *Dammit,* I thought. *Not again.*

The click of the lock confirmed my suspicions. We *were* prisoners, or maybe just a step up from that. The van shuddered to a start, and I was thrown to the floor as whoever was driving took off at top speed. I stayed down and pressed my head to the floor. I was a captive, *again,* and it stung more than ever because it was my own pack that was locking me up. I could understand why Kaden would be a little hesitant to trust me after seeing me willingly leaving with Jordan, but if he'd given me even a second to talk to him, I would have explained everything.

Why did Kaden come after me if he was just going to treat me like a prisoner?

I glanced over at Mira, who was slumped against the wall, her eyes closed. The run to the van had taken the rest of her strength, and we both needed time to heal. At least we were together, and we were getting away from the Leos and the Sun Witches. We were better off with the Ophiuchus pack, even if they treated us like dangerous criminals. It hurt knowing they didn't trust me, but once I explained everything, they'd let us go. I was still a member of their pack, dammit.

Wasn't I?

CHAPTER ELEVEN

HOURS PASSED. I'd tried to stay awake at first, thinking we'd only go a little way and then Kaden would come and talk, but no such luck. We drove, and drove, and eventually, I fell asleep. My body was tired, hurt, and the adrenaline had finally worn off, leaving me with bone-aching weariness and a body desperately trying to heal itself.

When I woke next, it was to the back of the van being opened. Both Mira and I sat up in expectation, and I held my breath, but it wasn't Kaden who opened the door. In fact, I didn't recognize this member of the Ophiuchus pack. He looked vaguely familiar, probably someone I'd seen around the town, but I'd never talked to him.

"Get out," he said, and there was more hostility in his voice than I'd expected. I climbed out, squinting as I took in the landscape. We were no longer in the desert, but it didn't look like the forest of the Ophiuchus pack lands either. I clearly hadn't been out for that long.

I turned and helped Mira down, and then turned back to the male shifter. He crossed his arms as he looked at both of us and then motioned to the gas station we'd stopped at. "One of the females is going to take you to the bathroom, and you'll be provided with food. Don't even think about running."

I gave him a bewildered look. "Why would I run? I'm back with my pack."

Something in the male's jaw twitched. "Just go."

Another shifter motioned us forward, a female. I'd talked to her before, and remembered she was one of the mothers of the cubs that Stella taught, but I couldn't remember her name. She didn't look at me as we walked through the gas station. Where was Harper? Or Jack? Or Kaden, for that matter?

The place was deserted except for the cashier, who stared at us as we walked by. I wondered what we looked like, two battered young females being led by a tough-looking older female. He didn't say a single thing, despite his looks.

Mira and I took turns in the bathroom, and when I got inside, I was shocked at my reflection in the mirror. I'd almost forgotten that I was still wearing that goddamn see-through dress, although at least my bruises had faded and my black eye was mostly gone. No wonder the gas station attendant stared at us when we walked in.

I turned away, used the bathroom, and splashed cold water on my face. When I came out, the female shifter silently led us back out to the van, where the male who had opened the door was waiting with sandwiches that looked like they'd been purchased from the gas station inside. He shoved them into our hands, and I tore into mine quickly. I hadn't eaten anything in over a day, and I was starving.

I took the time to look around. A few of the other cars and vans were stopped, with over a dozen Ophiuchus pack shifters milling around, talking quietly. I tried desperately to find a familiar friendly face and spotted Harper standing with Dane and Jack. I gave them a little wave, and they shot me a wary look, before getting back in their van. What the hell?

"Back in the van," the male shifter said. "It's time to go."

I climbed inside and he handed me some water bottles. I started to ask him where Kaden was, but before I could, he slammed the door in my face and locked it again. I glanced over at Mira, who shrugged her shoulders. I smiled at her, but it probably wasn't very convincing. "I'm sorry," I whispered. "I'm not sure what's going on."

"I'm sure it'll all get worked out soon," Mira said, patting my arm. "They're just being extra careful since they don't know what the Leos have done to you. Or the Sun Witches, for that matter."

I nodded, hoping she was right. As the van started up, I sighed and leaned back against the wall, and we were off again. I tried to stay awake so that I could get a feel for what time it was, but the lack of things to do soon had me falling asleep again.

When I woke, it was to mountains. We were out in the middle of nowhere, in the forest, but not one that I knew. All the trees were different, and the mountains didn't look like the ones I was used to.

"Where are we?" I asked as I jumped out of the van. My body was almost fully healed, and I felt more like myself again.

"Outside Pueblo, Colorado," the shifter said, surprising me with the specificity. "We're in the middle of the San Isabel National Forest, and you won't be getting anywhere if you decide to run. Nearest town is over fifty miles away and it's bear country here. I hear they're a bit hungry this year since winter ran long." He shoved a tent into my hands. "Happy camping."

"You think I'd be dumb enough to run in the middle of a forest I don't know? Also, *why would I run?*" I glared at him. "Tell me where Kaden is. I need to talk to him."

The shifter's lip curled, and he looked ready to say something back when another car came barreling toward us on the dirt road, kicking up dust. It stopped, and Kaden got out. I perked up, but when he saw me, his moody expression didn't change, and he immediately walked into the trees.

I sighed and turned to Mira. "Let's set up the tent."

It only took us a few minutes, since we'd had some experience with camping back in the Cancer pack lands. The tent was barely big enough for the two of us, but another shifter left us some sleeping bags, and I found myself excited to sleep out under the stars after being held under lock and key for so long.

The sun was setting over the mountains, casting a deep shadow into the valley, when Harper brought back firewood that she'd foraged for around the campsite. I cornered her as she was putting it down.

"What's going on?" I asked her. "Why is everyone treating me like an enemy?"

She looked around, like she wasn't sure if she was allowed to speak to me, and then gestured for me to head behind a thick tree with her. Once out of sight, she grabbed me in a hug. "I'm so glad you're all right."

That was more like the greeting I'd been expecting from my pack. I hugged her tight, relieved *someone* didn't hate me. "I'm okay, thanks to all of you for rescuing me. But why won't anyone talk to me?"

"Kaden thinks you've allied yourself with the Leo pack. We're not even supposed to talk to you."

I rolled my eyes. "Idiot male. I'm still an Ophiuchus."

Her face turned sympathetic. "I know. Once you talk to him, he'll see that too."

"Yeah, if I can find him," I muttered.

Dane poked his head around the tree and gestured for Harper to come out. She gave my arm a quick squeeze and then headed back into camp. I waited a few minutes before following.

Kaden returned after the sun had set and did a quick patrol of the perimeter of the camp, and I hurried to reach him. I wouldn't let him get away from me this time.

"I need to talk to you," I said, blocking his path. "Why am I being treated like an outcast again?"

Kaden's eyes finally met mine, and I felt a spark light

between us. "You're an enemy of the pack now, like all Leos."

I pointed to the Ophiuchus mark on my arm. "I'm not a Leo. Obviously."

"What's that, then?" Kaden's eyes dipped to my torso, where the huge Leo symbol was emblazoned on my dress. They lingered a bit longer than necessary as if he couldn't help but stare at what the sheer fabric revealed of my body.

I put my hands on my hips, my anger flaring. "Do you think I had a choice in putting this on?"

His gaze hardened. "I thought you were one of us, but I was wrong. If I could wipe the Ophiuchus symbol off your skin, I would."

That hurt. I gritted my teeth. "Why did you rescue me, if you feel that way about me?"

"Because even if you have turned to the Leo side, we can still use you as leverage. As *bait*."

"Great, I'm back to being bait," I muttered.

Kaden raised his eyebrows. "You went to Jordan of your own free will, why should you expect anything better?"

"I did what I did to protect the pack," I snapped. "The Sun Witches had Stella and the cubs surrounded, and the only way they'd back down was if I agreed to go with Jordan. He didn't give me a choice. I wasn't going to let anyone get hurt or killed for me."

Kaden stared at me for some time, as if trying to gauge if I was lying or not. Finally, he said, "I know."

I blinked at him. "You *know*?"

"Dane saw a vision in the moonlight with his gift a few

days after you left. He was able to show me what happened. But I wanted to hear it from you too." Kaden cocked his head. "Consider it a test."

I wanted to scream in frustration. "Another fucking test? Haven't I proven myself a hundred times over by now?"

He shrugged. "I had to be sure."

I huffed. "Fine, I've passed your test. But you still don't trust me, do you?"

"No, because I don't know what happened *after* you went with Jordan," Kaden growled. "For all I know, you're one of them now. Their alpha female."

"I would never ally myself with the Leos," I ground out. "I hate them more than anything. Did you forget that when you found me, I'd been beaten and tied to a sacrificial altar?"

His jaw tightened, and I watched the muscles in his neck flex. "I don't know what kinky shit you're into."

"Yeah you do," I said pointedly, and heat flashed in his eyes. "You're the *only* one who does."

"I find that hard to believe. Jordan is your mate. Even if you tried to resist him at first, there's no way you could have done it for the entire time you were with the Leos."

"I *did* resist him. It was hard, but I did it."

"So you didn't do anything with him? Not even a kiss?"

I flinched, remembering the two times Jordan had kissed me, made even worse by the new knowledge that he was my brother. My reaction must have answered the question for Kaden, whose face grew hard as stone. He turned away and started trudging through the woods.

"Wait," I called after him, as I hurried to follow. "Let me explain."

Kaden let out a grunt, but he actually stopped. "Go on then."

"Yes, Jordan kissed me," I somehow managed to say without gagging.

He crossed his arms at that, his scowl deepening.

I grimaced. "Twice."

Kaden shook his head and started to turn away again, but I grabbed his arm.

"But he's not my mate! I mean, he is, but it must be a mistake or something."

"I'm not here to play therapist while you try to figure out what you feel for your precious Leo alpha. This conversation is over." He jerked his arm away and tried to shove past me, and I put my hand out once again, slamming it directly into his middle.

"You don't understand," I said. "Jordan is my *brother*."

His mouth fell open at that, shock clear on his face. "What?"

"Jordan's mom had an affair with the Cancer alpha. That's all I know." I drew in a shuddering breath, feeling weak now that the truth was out.

"That's impossible," Kaden said. "Even if he somehow is your brother, which seems unlikely, there's no way a mating bond could have formed between the two of you."

"I don't know how it happened, but he *is* my brother. I felt the wrongness every time we kissed, I just didn't understand it until now."

Kaden's eyes held mine for a moment before he looked away once more. "Brother or not, the mate bond is still there, binding the two of you together. It'll continue to pull you both toward each other until either he's dead, or the bond is fulfilled."

My stomach lurched again at the thought of Jordan looming over me at the altar. "There has to be some way to dissolve it. I'm not going to *mate* with my brother. Obviously."

"There is a way," Kaden said, his voice growing ice cold. "I'm going to kill him. That will put an end to it."

"I... I don't know if I can let you do that." I swallowed hard. "As much as I hate him, he's the only family I have left."

Kaden's face darkened. "And that's why I still can't trust you."

He walked away, while I remained caught in the gravity of his words, my heart pounding in my chest. Would I ever be able to win back Kaden's trust, let alone his heart?

CHAPTER TWELVE

THE NEXT MORNING, Kaden shoved some clothes into my hands, and I wondered if they were his. When I held them up to my nose to inhale, right before I changed into them, I couldn't make out the scent of anyone at all. New clothes then. I tried to tell myself that I wasn't disappointed.

I took special pleasure in ripping the Leo dress up and putting it on the fire just before the others banked it and cleaned up the campsite. Harper came over and gave me her extra pair of shoes since I'd been running around barefoot this entire time. They were one size too big on me, but better than nothing. Then it was time to get going.

Mira and I packed up the tent, and then Kaden waved us over and told us to get in his car. As he looked at me, I saw a glimmer of distrust in his eyes, like he was waiting for me to turn on him. I wished there was some way to convince him that I could be trusted, but no matter what I said, he still thought I'd run back to Jordan the moment he took his eyes off me.

Even so, it was a nice change to find myself sitting in a car instead of in the back of a van. Apparently, my words last night had gotten through to Kaden on some level, even if he was still cold with me. Kaden drove, while Mira and I sat in the backseat, with Jack in the front. Once we were on the road, Jack put on some music, and I let some of the tension go from my body.

We left Colorado and traveled north along the Rocky Mountains, heading for Canada. As we drove, Kaden stared straight out of the windshield, his mouth set in a tight line. He looked like he was wound so tight that he would pop if anyone spoke to him. I wondered if he regretted letting me travel in the same car as him. Jack was unusually quiet too, and I guessed he was still banned from talking to me and didn't dare go against the alpha's word. After a couple of hours, Kaden switched with Jack and took a nap in the front seat, and we all breathed a collective sigh and relaxed a little.

More hours passed, and we stopped to stretch our legs and grab a quick bite to eat. When we got back in the car, I made sure to sit up front with Kaden. There were still things we needed to talk about.

"You're taking shifts driving, right?" I asked. "Mira and I can take one each, so you two can rest more."

"Absolutely not," Kaden said, as he started the car.

"Why? Because you don't trust me? Because you think I'll turn around and drive us straight back to the Leos?"

Kaden shot an exasperated glance over at me. "Because you and Mira still look like shit after what the Leos did to you. You need more time to recover."

"We're fine," I said, though I was still pretty tired. My shifter healing had taken care of my wounds, but spending weeks in captivity had definitely done a number on me emotionally and physically. Now that I was in relative safety again, I felt like I could sleep for a week. Still, I could manage to drive for a short while.

We traveled in silence for some time, and when I glanced back, Jack and Mira were asleep, dozing after their noontime meal. It seemed like a good time to talk to Kaden since it would give us a little bit of privacy.

"Where's Stella?" I asked quietly, careful not to disturb the two sleeping shifters.

"She didn't approve of my plan to use you as bait, so I made her stay behind with Clayton and the rest of the pack." He sounded more annoyed than anything at that, which made me grin.

"At least someone is on my side." My smile fell when I remembered the last time I saw her, trying to save the wolf pups from the Sun Witches. "Was she okay after the attack? How about Clayton? What about all the pups? And the rest of the pack?"

"They're all fine. The Sun Witches and Leos left the pack lands after you made your deal. We all went into hiding not long after that."

I let out a long breath, my shoulders sagging in relief. Jordan really had kept his word, and he hadn't double-crossed me or gone back later to try and wipe out the pack, all things I'd worried about while being held captive by him. "Thank the gods. I feel awful that the village was attacked. It was my fault."

Kaden shook his head. "No, the fault was mine. I set up the meeting with the Leos. I wanted a war with them, and now I have one. For better or worse."

No matter what he said, I still felt responsible. We'd been trying to meet the Leos on neutral ground, but after they never showed up they'd somehow followed us back to the pack lands. I couldn't help but think that I'd led the Leos to us through my mating bond with Jordan. "I'm sorry you all had to go into hiding. That must have been hard on everyone."

"We survived, and we're safe. That's what's important." He clenched his hands around the steering wheel, knuckles going white. "And it won't happen again. We're going to attack the Leos head-on once we recover and form a plan. We got some good information on how they respond to attacks in their territory the other night. Soon we'll gather a much larger force, and we'll be ready to take them down, once and for all."

"You can't," I said with a sigh. "The Sun Witches are allied with the Leos, and a lot of the packs have already submitted, including former Cancer allies like the Pisces." I glanced back at Mira, who was still asleep. "The Leos took Mira from the Pisces and threatened to kill her mate if she helped me escape. Their alpha did nothing to stop it."

Would Jordan kill Mira's mate now? Technically we

hadn't *escaped*—the Ophiuchus had freed us. I wasn't sure if that would be enough to convince Jordan to have mercy though, but maybe knowing I was his sister would soften his heart just the tiniest bit. After all, he'd seen me leaving with Kaden and hadn't tried to stop me. Jordan could have used his Leo lion roar, or directed more shifters away from the explosion to attack us, or ordered the Sun Witches to burn us up. But he'd done none of those things.

"That's because the Zodiac Wolves are weak," Kaden said, breaking through my thoughts. "At the slightest hint of conflict, they back down, tails between their legs. They haven't had to survive on their own like our pack has."

I rolled my eyes. "Even if you think they're weak, you'll need their help if you want to take down the Leos. It's the only way you'll stand a chance."

His mouth twisted as if the idea physically repulsed him. "I won't work with any of the other packs. They don't recognize the Ophiuchus, and last time I spoke to them at the Convergence, they threatened and mocked me. Besides, the other packs would never ally with us. They think we're monsters."

I shrugged, not surprised by his answer. He was right about how the other packs saw the Ophiuchus—I'd felt the same way, before getting to know them. But going up against the Leos and the Sun Witches without backup would be suicide. Kaden was too damn stubborn to listen to me on this, but I had to try. "They might be willing once they see that the alternative is being ruled by the Leos. Jordan plans to make himself a king, and I'm willing to bet there are a few packs out there who won't be okay with that. The Cancer pack, for one."

"The Cancer pack is gone."

"Maybe, maybe not. A large number of Cancers went to the Convergence, but some stayed home. Mira thinks they went into hiding. The beta probably would have taken over, since both Dad and Wesley fell." I fought a grimace as I remembered the last encounter I'd had with the beta's son when he and his friends had smashed my camera and taunted me. "I hate to admit it, but I think they're our best bet. The Cancer pack hates the Leos, and I'm sure that whoever has taken over isn't letting that grudge go. If we can find them, they might be willing to fight back against the Leos, and if they ally with you—with *us*—other packs will be sure to follow."

The car fell silent as Kaden considered what I said, but his face was so hard I was sure he would shoot my plan down. I tried to think of some other way we might be able to stop the Leos, but this was the only way. Unless we could get the Moon Witches to help, but Stella had said they had no idea where they were, or how to contact them. For all we knew, they might not even exist anymore.

"Fine," Kaden said, the word so pointed and unexpected it made me jump. "We'll look for the remaining Cancer members, but when we find them, their pack will have to serve me. That's the only way I'd be willing to work with a pack that shunned our existence before."

Alphas, I thought and rolled my eyes. What was it about them feeling like they had to have control over everything?

Jordan and Kaden were more alike than either of them would ever admit, both headstrong and a touch arrogant. Sure, Jordan had dipped into the completely *mad* side of that, but Kaden made me want to shake some sense into him too sometimes.

"I can try to talk to the Pisces pack," Mira mumbled. Our voices must have risen enough to rouse her from her sleep. "Assuming they haven't all been wiped out by the Leos by now."

I turned around to check on her. She looked a lot better, her eyes regaining some of their normal warmth in them, along with a touch of determination and fear. She was worried for her mate, no doubt, and the rest of her new pack. "I'm sure Jordan hasn't done that," I said.

Kaden gave me a sharp look at that. He probably thought I was defending my mate, but I'd only said it to try to make Mira feel better.

"I hope you're right," Mira said with a sigh.

"I'll send my warriors to escort you to the Pisces pack," Kaden said. "If the Leos are there, holding your mate hostage, they'll deal with them."

"Really?" Mira asked.

"I swear it."

My heart swelled, and just like that, I remembered why he was the man I respected more than anyone else in the world. He didn't even know Mira, had never met her before the other night, and he had no love for the Pisces or Cancer pack—yet he was willing to send his own people to help her rescue her mate anyway.

"Thank you," she said, sniffing as though she was holding back tears. "I'm sure if you do that, the alpha will agree to join you against the Leos."

"Perhaps," Kaden said, drumming his fingers on the steering wheel. "If not, at least there will be fewer Leos in the world."

WHEN WE STOPPED to make camp for the night in a forest somewhere in southern Montana, Kaden went back to avoiding me. Harper took me and Mira down to a small lake a short hike away, and we reveled in cleaning ourselves for the first time in days. Then Mira and I set up our tent, and she passed out almost immediately. Not me though. I was still restless, and this time Kaden was just gone, probably lurking around while invisible, so I couldn't even corner him and force him to talk to me.

I did, however, find Jack standing guard a short distance away, while the rest of the shifters settled down to sleep. This time, out of sight of Kaden and the rest of the pack, he grabbed me in a tight hug.

"Sorry, I couldn't say anything before, not without Kaden ripping my throat out." He stepped back and gave me one of his charming grins. "It's damn good to have you back. Kaden needs someone who will stand up to him sometimes."

"Stella does that," I pointed out.

"Yeah, but he doesn't always listen to her," Jack said.

I snorted. "He doesn't listen to me either."

"He does. I heard what you guys were talking about in the car. With a few words, you got Kaden to consider doing something he's rejected for *years*. Allying with the other packs? He would have torn out his own heart first, before he met you anyway."

"I just want to stop him from getting himself and the rest of the pack killed, but it's hard when he's so damn stubborn."

"No shit. After you left..." He leaned in close, his voice lowering as he looked around to make sure no one else was around. Whoever said men didn't like to gossip had obviously never met Jack. "It was bad. I've never seen Kaden so upset, not even when Eileen found her mate. We all told Kaden something wasn't right, that there was no way you'd go with Jordan and leave our pack behind, but he wouldn't listen. He thought you chose Jordan over him. Then Dane saw a vision of what happened, and I was like, I knew it! I knew Ayla would never leave us of her own free will." He punched me lightly in the arm and I couldn't help but smile at his exuberance, and his loyalty. Then his grin fell. "But that didn't make Kaden feel any better. If anything, it only made things worse, because now he knew you'd gone against your will."

I nodded slowly, my chest aching. "Because he thought I would still end up as Jordan's mate, and the next alpha female of the Leo pack."

"Exactly." He rubbed the back of his neck. "I hate to say it, but we all did. I'm glad you proved us wrong."

"Me too," I said. I couldn't blame them for thinking I'd given in to the mate bond since there were so many moments when I almost had. I was sure the only things that saved me were my feelings for Kaden and some instinctual knowledge that mating with Jordan was wrong.

But the Ophiuchus pack still came to rescue me, even fearing I'd turned to the dark side. Even if Kaden had said it was because they'd planned to use me as leverage against Jordan, I didn't believe it. No, Kaden just couldn't stand the thought of me with anyone else. Especially a Leo. And he was willing to burn their entire pack down to get me back.

Now I just had to get him to admit it.

CHAPTER THIRTEEN

IN THE MORNING, Kaden had a meeting in the forest with some of the other pack members, including Jack, Harper, and Dane, but I wasn't invited. I kept trying to get close and overheard them talking about the best routes to get to Alaska, but then another shifter would always shoo me away. I huffed and went back to help clean up the campsite, even though I felt I should have been involved in the discussion too. What would I have to do to get Kaden to trust me already?

We drove away not long after the sun rose, and I found myself dozing off since there wasn't much else to do. When the car came to a stop, I looked over at Kaden, who was in the driver's seat. "Where are we?"

"Spokane." He motioned to the Walmart in front of where he'd parked. "Do you need anything?"

Shit, what *didn't* I need? I had literally nothing but the clothes on my back. I raised an eyebrow. "Are you buying?"

"Obviously. Unless you packed a wallet in that Leo dress we found you in."

"I'm pretty sure your eyes combed over every inch of my skin, and you know I didn't."

Mira and Jack both snickered in the back seat until Kaden shot them a sharp look. I got out of the car before he could come back with another response.

Inside the store, Mira grinned at me. "When was the last time we went shopping?"

"Seems like a decade ago," I said. Even when we had gone shopping, Dad never let me have any money to buy things. Mira had usually taken pity on me and gotten me something though.

"I'm sorry you had to leave everything behind when we fled the Leos," I said. Mira also had nothing but the clothes she'd escaped in, although at least she'd been dressed more sensibly and was wearing shoes too.

Mira shrugged. "It's okay. I didn't bring anything to their village that I would miss, in case something like that happened."

We both picked out some tank tops and shorts, since the mid-August heat was scorching outside, but also grabbed some jeans and a long-sleeve shirt, plus a jacket, just to cover all the bases. Both the Pisces and Cancer packs lived on the coast, where it tended to be cooler, especially at night. A bra and a pack of underwear were next—the last time I'd had any on was back with the Leos—along with some walking shoes, plus a little travel bag of toiletries, and we were set.

On the way to the checkout, I spotted a stand of burner

phones, and plopped one in the basket too, then grabbed some snacks, drinks, and even some lip gloss, because fuck it, I deserved it. I'd been through a lot lately. Kaden could buy me some fruity pink lip gloss.

When I joined Kaden in the checkout line, he glanced down at my basket and narrowed his eyes. At first, I thought he was judging my lip gloss, but then he asked, "A phone? Need to call your precious Leo mate?"

I nudged him out of the way so I could put my things on the conveyor belt. "Don't be ridiculous. I want to be able to keep in touch with Mira this time. I wasn't allowed a phone before, but I'm getting one now, and I don't care what you say about it."

Kaden's jaw clenched like he might try to stop me, but then he just threw his own snacks and drinks on the belt after my things. Mira joined us too and added her stuff, thanking Kaden for his generosity as he paid for it all, and then we hit the bathrooms to change and clean up a bit.

"Come," Kaden said when we met him just outside the store. "We're going to speak with the others before we split up."

"Split up?" I asked as I followed his gaze to where some other pack members had gathered at a fast food place next door, waiting for us. Harper gave me a little wave as we approached.

Kaden didn't answer me, so I worked on getting my phone out of its packaging as we waited for the rest of the shifters to gather around us. I'd just gotten it turned on and the language set to 'English' when Kaden cleared his throat, and the shifters fell silent.

"Thank you all for your excellent work during the Leo attack," he said, as his eyes took in his people with pride. "We were successful in our mission, and not only did we rescue our pack member, but we learned how the Leos respond to an attack and what their plans are. But our work is far from over. As I'm sure you've heard by now, I require one more task before you return to the rest of the pack." He gestured toward Mira, who stood awkwardly beside me like she wasn't sure if she should be listening in or not. "Our friend here has suffered at the hands of the Leos, and she needs to be escorted safely back to the Pisces pack. It's possible there will be a group of Leos there threatening the pack and her mate. Deal with them swiftly, make sure the Pisces pack is safe, and then you can return home."

A murmur went through the shifters next, but none of them looked unhappy about their new mission, and I was awed by Kaden's ability to command a pack at such a young age. He had the presence of someone much older, and no one seemed to mind following his orders at all.

Harper wrapped an arm around Mira's shoulders. "We'll make sure our new friend gets home safely, and gladly take out any Leos we find on the way. Don't even worry about it."

"Thank you," Mira said, giving the other woman a small smile, and then turning her warm gaze on Kaden too.

He nodded in return. "Jack will be leading you. He's arranged some plane tickets since this mission requires some haste and driving to Alaska would take too long. We'll meet you with the rest of the pack once we've finished our mission."

"We?" I asked.

He turned his gaze on me. "You and I are going to the Cancer pack lands."

"What?" I blinked at him. "Just the two of us?"

"We don't know if the remaining Cancers are holed up and waiting to shoot anyone who enters the pack lands, or if the Leos have overrun them and now control that area. They could have dozens of fighters there, for all we know. A stealth mission is our best bet. You and I can use our Moon Touched gifts to get in and out undetected. Once we know what the situation is, we can go from there."

I nodded slowly, unable to argue with his plan. Kaden's invisibility combined with my teleportation would make us the ultimate spies and scouts. Assuming we could get along long enough to get the job done. I had a feeling the tension between us would only get worse when it was just the two of us in the car.

Kaden said a few more words to the pack, laying out the logistical details of their trip, and then the others headed back to their cars and vans. They'd be driving to the airport in Spokane, leaving the vehicles behind there, and taking a flight to Anchorage. Harper gave me a quick hug and promised to take good care of Mira. Dane gave me a short nod since he never spoke as far as I could tell, and Jack gave me a wink.

He clamped Kaden on the shoulder. "Good luck, you two. Don't do anything I wouldn't do."

"You would do everything," Kaden muttered.

"Exactly." Jack grinned one last time before giving a wave and heading off with the others.

I turned to Mira, who hung back like she was hesitant to go with them. I wrapped her in a hug. "You're going to be okay. They'll take care of you, and help your pack too if they can." I was certain of it after Kaden had called her a friend of the pack. Since he didn't know Mira all that well, I could only assume he did it because of her connection with me, and I was grateful.

She hugged me tight like she was afraid to let me go. "I'm going to miss you."

"I'm going to miss you, too," I said into her shoulder. I hated that we would be split up again. I wanted all of us to be able to stay together and not have to deal with the Leo pack, but I knew that wasn't possible. We weren't kids in the Cancer pack anymore, playing on the beach near our houses. We'd both moved on, joined other packs, and Mira had a mate to rescue. And me? I had a grumpy alpha to deal with.

"I have a phone now, so we can keep in touch," I said. "Oh, I have an idea! Let's get a selfie before you go."

Mira giggled as I pulled her close, and we smiled wide for the camera like we were on vacation and not running for our lives. It wasn't the same as having a real camera, but at least I could have a picture of us in my phone. After I'd taken a few pictures—just in case one of us was blinking in any of them—I frowned down at the little screen, trying to see if they'd turned out okay. The cheap phone's camera was a piece of crap, but it was all I had.

"Did you ever get a new camera?" Mira asked. "After yours was broken?"

"No," I said, trying to keep the sadness out of my voice. "I haven't had the chance to get a new one." Or had the means to do so, for that matter. It wasn't like Kaden had ever paid me a salary during my time with the Ophiuchus. I doubted I'd have been allowed a camera anyway, just like I hadn't been allowed a phone. The Ophiuchus pack had rightfully been wary of anything that might reveal the location of their village.

Mira tilted her head at me, her dark brows furrowing with concern. "I'm sorry, that's such a shame. I know how much photography means to you."

"I have other things to worry about right now." I caught sight of the others waiting for Mira and knew our time was up. "Here, put your number in my phone."

Mira nodded and took it from me, tapping a few buttons before returning it. I looked down, finding she'd put a heart and a fish emoji behind her name, and I smiled. I really would miss her.

"Let me know what happens with the Pisces pack," I said.

She got a hopeful look in her eyes. "I will. I just pray Aiden is all right."

"I'm sure he's perfectly fine and will be very happy to have you back."

She sucked in a breath and nodded. "I really do appreciate everything the Ophiuchus pack is doing to help me. I can't promise that I'll be able to sway the Pisces alpha to stand up to the Leos, but I'll try."

"That's all we can ask."

"It's time to go," Kaden said, making me jump. He was leaning against the car behind me, close enough that he could have heard our whole conversation, looking as annoyingly hot as ever with his muscled forearms crossed over his chest. Had he been listening in the entire time? Probably.

I said goodbye to Mira again, and then she was off, slipping into one of the other cars with Harper. My chest tightened as they drove away, turning down the road and moving out of sight. I quickly typed out a text. *Let me know when you land safely.*

When I looked back up, Kaden had pushed himself off the side of the car and yanked the passenger door open. "Ready to go, little wolf? Or do you need another ten minutes standing around this parking lot?"

"Forgive me for taking a moment to say goodbye to my oldest friend," I muttered as I slid into the passenger's seat. Somehow I'd managed to forget just how arrogant and irritating Kaden could be. But he'd also called me little wolf, a nickname I'd originally hated, thinking it was an insult before I came to realize it was a term of endearment, even if Kaden would never admit that. Maybe he didn't hate me as much as he wanted me to think.

"Looks like you're stuck with me," I said with a wry grin, as he started the car. This would be the first time we'd spent hours alone since... Well, since the previous full moon. It was hard to not think about what had happened then. "Just the two of us, and this time we have a long journey ahead of us."

"Don't remind me," Kaden said dryly.

"I guess you'll have to let me drive now, whether you trust me or not."

He glanced over at me with a raised eyebrow. "Do you even know how to drive?"

"Of course I do," I snapped, but then a wave of sadness washed over me. I looked away, my voice dropping to almost a whisper. "Wesley taught me."

Kaden was quiet after that, letting me sit with my ever-present grief. He understood it, of course. He'd lost his parents to the Leos too.

"You'll have to direct me to the Cancer pack lands," he eventually said, once we were back on the road. "I know they're north of Vancouver on the coast somewhere, but I've never been there myself."

I got the sense he was trying to distract me, but all it did was remind me that I was about to return to my first home, the one that had produced so many bad memories. There were some good memories too, of course, but many of those had been with Wesley, and driving down those same roads would only rub it in that he was gone. I squeezed my eyes shut, dreading what lay ahead of us. "Just drive."

CHAPTER FOURTEEN

DESPITE HIS EARLIER SKEPTICISM, Kaden stopped after a few hours and traded places with me. I hadn't driven in months, and truthfully hadn't done it much back home either, but it all came back to me once I was in the driver's seat.

It would be about a seven or eight hour drive from Spokane to Vancouver, and the closer we got, the more tightly strung I became. I never thought that once I'd escaped the Cancer pack, I'd want to go back. Everyone in the pack other than Mira and Wesley had made it clear that I'd never belonged there, yet here I was, determined to go back and try to win them over. What was I thinking? When we found them, *if* we found them, would they even listen to what I had to say? I might have been the alpha's daughter, but I'd never been treated with respect. Dad had made sure of that. The beta had been just as bad, and he was likely the one running the pack now. Were we making a huge mistake?

"You're very quiet," Kaden said after night fell. He'd been dozing for the last hour, but now his gaze rested upon me and the intensity of it made it hard to focus on driving.

"You're one to talk," I said to the windshield, pointedly staring at the road. Outside, the car's headlights illuminated twisty mountain roads and tall trees. We'd decided to take a more scenic route to avoid Seattle, partly to stay under the radar in case the Leos were looking for us, and partly because I got the feeling Kaden didn't like big cities. "I just have a lot on my mind, okay?"

"Like what?"

I huffed out a breath. "I'm surprised you care."

"Call it boredom if you want." Kaden stretched his legs out in front of him, and I tried not to notice, even in my periphery. Even though his words sounded casual, as if he didn't care at all, there was something in his voice that made me think he really did care.

I sighed but found myself talking anyway. "I'm dreading going back to the Cancer pack lands and worried about what will happen once we get there. I was never popular among the pack. Okay, that's an understatement. I was the town pariah, the alpha's mistake, nothing more, and no one ever let me forget that I was half human and an outcast." I paused as I remembered what I'd learned during my time with the Leos. "Although I guess that's not even true. I know my mother was a Moon Witch now."

"I suspected as much. How do you know for sure?"

"When I was imprisoned by the Leos, the Sun Witches came to interrogate me. They cast this spell that made *some-*

thing come out of me, some sort of light that convinced them I was a Moon Witch. I guess they'd know, out of anyone."

"I told you that weeks ago." A smirk crossed his handsome face. "It's nice to know I was right."

"Like your ego needs any more boosting. I'm surprised it can fit in the fucking car."

"What was that?" Kaden asked, tilting his head toward me, though I knew he'd heard me perfectly. "Surely you weren't talking shit about your alpha."

"Oh, so you admit I'm still in your pack then? Not a Leo?"

"Perhaps." He fell silent for some time, but then his eyes were upon me again—I felt their smolder even without looking. "Tell me what the Leos did to you."

His sudden change in topic surprised me, along with the darkness in his voice. I hesitated, not sure if I wanted to tell him everything that had happened to me. Hell, I wasn't sure I was ready to say it out loud. I would have preferred to talk to someone like Stella, but I wouldn't be seeing her for who knew how long. Kaden would have to do, even though he gave about as much emotional comfort as a cactus.

"At first, they kept me locked up in a cell, much like you did. I was in there for longer though, and there were no windows, and two guards posted at all times. The only way I could tell time had passed was by noticing when my guards changed shifts." My lips were dry and I licked them before continuing, wondering where I'd put that lip gloss. "Jordan came to see me now and then. He told me he wanted me as his mate, that now that he was the alpha things would be different, and that he wanted me to be the queen to his king. I told him to go fuck himself."

"Good," Kaden said, crossing his arms.

"The Sun Witches came to see me, and they said my magic was strong. They wanted to kill me, but Jordan wouldn't let them. He planned to mate with me during the full moon, and he thought I would be more...compliant after that."

"He obviously doesn't know you very well," Kaden said with a snort.

That gave me a slight smile. "He eventually moved me into a house with Mira, and showered me with food and gifts, but I never forgot it was still a prison. I wasn't allowed to leave, and guards were stationed everywhere, but hey, at least I could shower. Jordan had dinner with me every night, and I pretended to warm up to him so he would let down his guard. Eventually, Mira and I tried to escape, but we were caught and thrown back in prison. I told Jordan I rejected him as my mate, and that's when he gave me the bruises you saw. Well, him and his guards. Oh and the Sun Witches scorched me with some of their magic too. Then it was the full moon, and, well, you saw how that was going...." I trailed off and glanced over at Kaden. "Luckily you showed up before anything happened."

He sat very still, but his hands were clenched and his eyes blazed with anger. "I should have protected you better. You shouldn't have had to trade your life for the safety of the pack."

"That was Jordan's fault, not yours. And I would do it

again in a heartbeat."

"You said he kissed you. Twice." Kaden nearly spat the words. "But nothing else happened?"

"Not really." My fingers tightened around the steering wheel. "It was hard though. The pull of the mating bond was so strong, almost like when I was in heat. But I fought it, and over time, it got easier for me to resist. And now..." My stomach twisted. "I think it'll be even easier to fight, knowing we're related."

Kaden let out a low, terrifying growl. "The next time I see him, he's dead. That will solve that problem."

"Trust me, I hate Jordan more than anyone, but I think, deep down, there might be a tiny sliver of goodness in him. I think he might care for me in his own, twisted way. I'm pretty sure he let us escape that night. Maybe if we—"

"He locked you up, punched you in the face, tried to rape you, and you're *defending* him?" Kaden roared, making me jump. "That is not how people show they care. Maybe you don't realize this, since your own father was an abusive piece of shit, but we don't hurt people in our family. Or our mates."

His words shook me to my core. God, was I that fucked up? Was I defending Jordan out of some messed-up daddy issues? I didn't think so, but I couldn't be sure either. I pulled over into the next turnout, my hands trembling, and took a shaky breath. Finally, I was able to whisper, "I know that."

Kaden got out of the car and slammed the door, then began to pace in the dirt on the side of the road, moving in and out of the beam of the headlights. I stared at my white-knuckled fingers on the steering wheel for a moment before getting out, though I wasn't sure what to say. I'd never seen Kaden like this before.

Kaden turned toward me, his body full of energy and his face twisting with fury. "No one will ever treat you that way again, not as long as you're in my pack, do you understand? Not the Cancers. Not the Leos. If anyone tries, I will rip them to shreds with my bare hands. I swear it."

I realized then that his anger wasn't for me, but for all the things that had been done to me, not just in the last month, but over my entire life. "You're right," I managed to say, though my throat felt scratchy. "Everyone in my family either treated me like shit or abandoned me. My mother left me when I was a baby. My dad and stepmother hurt me. Even Wesley is gone. So yeah, maybe I never expected to be treated any better. Not by Jordan or by anyone else. Until I met you. You made me think maybe I deserved something better."

"Ayla..." He slid his thumb across my cheek, wiping away the lone tear that had escaped my eye. Then he wrapped me in his arms, pressing me against his chest. All the breath went out of me as I was surrounded by his warmth and his strength. My eyes filled with tears as I leaned against him, relaxing for the first time since I'd left the Ophiuchus pack lands with Jordan. I was safe. I was *home*.

He held me like that for some time, and it was exactly what I needed. Then he pulled back and stepped away, turning his face so I couldn't get a good look at him. "I'll drive," he said in a low voice.

Once we were back on the road, Kaden behind the wheel this time, we fell into silence again, but some of the tension between us had vanished. At the very least, I no longer doubted my place in the pack anymore.

We continued through the mountains, the road empty other than a lone truck or car now and then, with the forest on either side of the winding road. Only the moon and our headlights illuminated our path, and I wondered if Kaden planned to drive through the night, or if we would stop and camp somewhere.

"Tell me about your parents," I said. Kaden rarely ever talked about them, but the past was looming over us tonight, and I thought I might get a rare chance to get him to open up more.

Kaden didn't respond at first, and just as I opened my mouth to tell him to *forget it,* he said, "They were great alphas, and even better parents. Honest, fair, and kind, though they had a firm hand when it was needed. I never had to worry about taking any issues or concerns to them, and none of the pack did either."

He sighed and pushed a hand through his dark hair, the other one on the steering wheel. My eyes tracked the movement until I realized that I was staring at him instead of the road. I snapped my gaze back forward. If only I had the excuse of being at the wheel to make sure I wouldn't do it again.

Luckily he didn't seem to notice, and to my surprise, he

kept talking. "My mom was an artist. She was always painting, drawing, or crafting something. Our house was always full of things she had made, usually with me or Stella."

"She sounds wonderful. Do you still have any of her work?" I didn't remember seeing it in his house.

"Somewhere, yeah. I put it all away after she died. It was too hard to look at it."

"And your dad?"

"He was really good at fixing things. Cars, computers, plumbing, you name it and he could figure out the problem and get it working again. He did the same with people's problems too. He told me that was the real secret to being a good alpha—figuring out what the problem was and trying to find a way to fix it." His face turned grim. "That's what he was trying to do with our pack. He knew our pack would die out if we didn't rejoin the rest of the Zodiac Wolves. The intermingling of all the packs makes it possible for the bloodlines to remain strong, and for each pack to thrive in numbers without inbreeding, but being exiled cut us off from that. We've scraped by with deserters and outcasts, but we could be so much more if we were allowed to return. My parents realized that, and they tried to do what was best for the pack." His hands clenched around the steering wheel. "But the Leos made sure that never happened."

I wondered what it would be like to grow up with such love all the time, and how awful it would be to have it snatched away from you like that. No wonder Kaden hated the Leos so much. "How did it feel when you got your revenge? When you killed the Leo alpha?"

Kaden's low growl in his throat was answer enough for me. "It felt like justice. Although I didn't just get revenge for my parents. I did it for you, as payback for him killing your father and your pack."

My heart beat faster at that. But before I could respond, something flashed in front of the car, illuminated by the headlights. A wolf, stepping right into the road directly in front of us, too quickly for either of us to react. Kaden had just enough time to swear before we rammed directly into it. The car *crunched,* and to my horror, the wolf didn't budge at all. Like we'd hit a huge boulder instead of an animal.

Then I had the feeling of being weightless, of Kaden's arm pressing me back by my shoulders, before we were tossed back to the ground, rolling over and over. I heard glass breaking and the high shriek of metal being torn, and someone was screaming. It took me a moment to realize it was me. Everything was chaos and confusion and terror, until the car finally came to a standstill, with Kaden and I suspended upside down.

For a moment, there was silence, filled only by the pounding in my ears. Then sounds began to filter in from outside. Scuffling paws, the sound of noses sniffing nearby, and when I craned my neck over, I saw the shadows of a dozen wolves in the headlights, their bodies elongated and cast at strange angles. A single growl pierced the night, and then it was joined by many others, making the air almost vibrate with the sound.

We were surrounded.

CHAPTER FIFTEEN

"ARE YOU OKAY?" Kaden asked, his voice low.

"I think so," I said, wiggling my toes and fingers. Everything *hurt*, but at least I could still move. "Are you?"

"I'll be able to fight. We need to get out of here fast if we're going to survive."

No shit. I struggled with my seat belt, frantic to get it off. I would drop to the car roof the moment I was free, which would leave me vulnerable to attack, but I couldn't stay like this either. "Let's drop on three," I suggested.

"One," he said, softly enough that only I could hear. "Two... Three."

I pressed down, but nothing happened. Kaden fell to the ceiling with a *thump*. Immediately, the growling outside stopped. I pushed the seat belt button again, but nothing happened. "Fuck! I'm stuck."

Kaden cursed, just as a gray wolf snapped its jaws

through his shattered window. "Try to get out. I'll hold them off as long as I can."

I nodded and continued fidgeting with the seat belt. *Dammit,* I thought. *Of all the times...*

Kaden's door wouldn't open either. He bent the metal out of place, the screech of it loud enough to drown out the remaining growls, and then the moonlight spilled inside. Kaden leaped out, shifting into a huge black wolf halfway, and I heard his growl join the group. His shadow blocked the entrance to the car as he turned back and forth, snarling and snapping at our attackers. I saw them lunge at him, and heard the sounds of fighting.

I yanked at the seat belt one last time, trying to use some of my strength to yank it open. It didn't do a damn thing, and I let out a whimper, the thought of shifters tearing the car apart to get to me playing out in my mind. Or worse, letting Kaden fight them on his own and getting injured...or killed.

I considered shifting but wasn't sure if that would work to get me out, or if I'd just be a trapped wolf. I looked outside again. *The moon.* I closed my eyes and tried to calm my mind, to access that part of me that knew how to use my powers, and then I was blinking at the wrecked car from fifty feet away.

I let out a breath. None of the shifters had seen me yet, all of them surrounding Kaden as he fought them off by himself in a flash of fur and fangs. I ran back over, trying to be as quiet as possible, then shifted into wolf form. I wasn't as quick or as smooth as Kaden, but I was able to launch myself onto one of the gray wolves and sink my teeth into its neck, releasing a heavy dose of my Ophiuchus poison from my fangs.

The wolf shook me off, sending me slamming back against the side of the car. He turned and growled at me, snapping his teeth, still very much alive. He didn't even look slightly woozy. What the fuck?

They're Taurus pack, Kaden told me through our pack bond. *Immune to poison. Like all the earth signs.*

Oh shit. I'd forgotten about that. All the packs had some natural ability related to their element—water signs like Cancers could breathe underwater, fire signs were immune to fire (obviously), and air signs could fall from any height without taking damage. It was one of those things I so rarely thought about because it never applied to me, and it hardly ever came up—until now, of course.

If these were Taurus, that explained how that wolf was able to wreck our car too, just by standing in front of it. When a Taurus used bull stance, their pack power, they became totally immovable and nearly impossible to damage. That made fighting them difficult too, especially when we were so outnumbered. Really, was there anything that would give us an edge against twelve shifters who couldn't be slowed down or moved?

Shit, this was bad. I'd never faced so many shifters before, and I doubted Kaden had done so without more pack members to back him up. But he flashed his fangs and fought back anyway, not hesitating like I was. He was the alpha of the Ophiuchus pack, and that meant he was going to fight this to the bitter end. I moved into a defensive position, snapping at the wolf who I'd just bitten as he tried to come closer again and go for my throat. I would go down with Kaden too if that was what it took.

A swell of determination went through me, replacing the despair, and when I glanced skyward I felt a surge of hope. I had the power of the moon to help me, and Kaden did too. Even the Sun Witches had feared me, though I wasn't sure why, or how to tap into the power I'd shown them. But we could use some of that power now to help us.

When the Taurus tried to bite me on the throat, I disappeared, making him chomp down on nothing but air. I reappeared behind him and clamped down on his back leg with my fangs, shaking it like a dog with a bone. That got his attention. When he turned back to swipe at me with a claw, I teleported again, moving to his other side, leaping on his back. I did it again, and again, traveling through moonlight, wearing the other wolf out until I was able to take him down with my fangs.

Kaden had caught on to what I was doing and he went invisible to confuse the wolves around us, who suddenly couldn't see his attacks. As four wolves surrounded where he had to be, I blinked into the middle of them, nudging up against his shoulder. A second later, we were on the other side of them—and I was invisible too.

Working together, using our gifts from the moon goddess, we took more of the Taurus down. I stopped thinking and let my wolf take over, trusting my instincts to guide me. My body moved with the expert precision Stella and Kaden had helped me train into it, and the moonlight shining down on us gave me strength.

And then I looked up to find the remaining Taurus shifters bolting into the dense trees behind us, and Kaden panting at my side. Half a dozen wolves lay dead at our feet, and I hadn't even remembered dealing most of the killing blows.

Once we were sure the remaining Taurus had fled, we shifted back and stood there naked under the moonlight on the side of the road, which thankfully seemed pretty empty this time of night. The Taurus must have purposefully picked a remote area for their attack.

Kaden leaned against the car, letting the metal frame take most of his weight, pressing a hand to his hip. "See if there's anything salvageable in the car."

Both of us were covered in blood, most of it from the Taurus, I hoped. I looked for something to wipe us down within the upside-down car and found one of the Walmart bags untouched behind my seat. The others had been strewn open, and I didn't bother hunting around. Who knew how long we had before the Taurus pack came back with more shifters? *And if they bring Leos as well...* I shuddered. I didn't think I could go for round two right now.

I crawled back out of the wreckage to see Kaden's head tipped back, an expression of pain pinching his features. When he saw me emerge, I watched him fight the emotion off of his face.

"You're injured." I motioned to his hip, which had a lot more blood trailing down it than when I'd left.

"I'm fine," Kaden said gruffly, pushing himself off the frame of the car.

I shoved him back against the car, meeting his eyes with a challenge, then grabbed his hand and yanked it off the wound. The cut was *huge*. Someone had caught him with a claw and ripped along the flesh, and I hadn't heard him make a single noise of pain when it had happened.

"I'll heal," he said, slapping his hand back over the wound, which dripped blood all down the side of his leg and onto the ground.

"Not fast enough. We need to be able to move without you leaving a trail of blood for the Taurus—and Leo—packs to follow." I stepped up to him, preventing him from limping further away from the car. "Sit down and let me heal you. I'm an Ophiuchus now, after all."

Kaden gritted his teeth hard, muscles flexing in his jaw. "No."

I raised my eyes skyward in exasperation. His stubborn ass was going to get us killed. "Fine, I'll do it with you standing up."

I set the bag down on the ground and opened it. Snacks and bottles of water were nestled in with a few changes of clothes, and I took a bottle out and twisted it open. Kaden watched me but didn't do more than jut his chin out stubbornly. I took it as a go-ahead and upended the bottle over one of the shirts in the pack until it was soaked. Then I brought it to his side as gently as I could, though Kaden still hissed out a breath as the wet cloth hit his wound. I daubed at the skin gently, trying not to pull it apart any further and create any more damage. A car passed by, but the wreckage blocked us from view, and they didn't even bother to slow down. We were in the middle of nowhere, but I wanted to get out of here before any human authorities came to investigate the accident.

I tossed the shirt to the side after I was fairly certain there wasn't any dirt in the wound, and then glanced up at Kaden. His eyes were dark on mine, unreadable, and I held his gaze as I slowly lowered myself onto my knees. Kaden's nostrils flared, and he looked away sharply. Being this close to him, bare as the day he was born, made my senses go wild, along with my wolf. Kaden's smell filled my nose, and it didn't escape my notice that I was naked too, or that the last time we'd been in this state was when I'd gone into heat.

I closed my eyes and focused. Now wasn't the time to get distracted by how hot Kaden was, or how much I wanted him. When I was I was fairly sure I had myself under control I opened my eyes and didn't glance back up at Kaden again. I could feel the heavy weight of his gaze on me anyway, prickling at the top of my head, as I lowered my mouth to his hip.

I started at the bottom of the wound and licked the area right below it. Kaden's muscles rippled under my tongue, reacting to the touch almost instantly, and I heard him suck in a sharp breath. I chased his flinching skin, pressing my tongue flat against it. It was salty, the tang of iron overriding any natural taste I might have gotten had he not been bleeding, but not unpleasant. I wasn't sure how exactly to do this, and the last time it had been done to me, I'd been too distracted to remember the exact motions Kaden had used.

Almost immediately, the wound seemed to close up beneath my tongue, and I continued my work, slowly but surely healing the entire area. When his breathing became more labored, I looked up to find Kaden's head tipped back, exposing the long line of his bare throat, and his hands balled up into fists at his sides. The muscles in his forearms stood in stark relief from how tightly he was holding himself back, but he couldn't stop his cock from hardening and growing. It was so close to my tongue, which now traced lazy circles across Kaden's hip, that I debated taking a detour. I'd never sucked anyone's cock before, but I desperately wanted to try it with him.

When Kaden's wound was healed, I pulled back and gazed up at him, waiting to see if he would stop me. Lust clouded his eyes, and I smelled his need in the air, mixing with the scent of my own. My hands rested on his thighs, feeling the strength in them. When I swallowed, his eyes tracked the movement of my throat, and he drew in a sharp breath. It thrilled me, knowing he wanted me even when I wasn't in heat, and with the last sparks of adrenaline running through my blood, I felt completely wild. I began to lick my way up along his hip, then higher, tracing the hard planes and valleys of his abs, unable to stop now that I'd started. He'd never let me touch him like this before, not even when I was in heat. Just when I was about to circle one of his nipples with my tongue, he grabbed my arms and yanked me to my feet.

"As much as I like you kneeling in front of me, this is not the time for that," he said. "We need to get out of here."

I nodded, knowing he was right, and licked my lips, tasting him on them. "I told you I'd be the one healing you someday," I said, my voice breathless.

"You did a good job, especially for your first time." He inspected his hip. "I never should have doubted you."

I pressed my hand to his chest, staring into his eyes, my blood hot as it raced through my veins. "No, you shouldn't have."

We weren't just talking about the healing now, and we both knew it. Kaden met my gaze with a smolder of his own, his chest rising and falling as if he'd just run a mile. Then he yanked me against him, pressing our naked bodies together, and kissed me, hard. The shock of his lips on mine quickly gave way to pleasure and need, and I let out a little whimper as he opened my mouth wider and slid his tongue across mine. His kiss was rough and demanding, and I melted against his body, my hands sliding along his thick neck, feeling his hard cock wedge between my thighs.

My body answered, remembering his smell, the weight of his body against mine, and the unimaginable pleasure we'd shared between us. One of my legs lifted to wrap around him, getting his cock closer to where I needed him. Kaden's hands tightened around my shoulders and I gasped, thinking he might take me right there against the wreckage of our car, with the bodies of our enemies at our feet. We were still high from our victory and the thrill of battle, the lust for blood and sex urging us on. I wanted nothing more than to feel Kaden's cock inside me, to reassure myself that he was still alive and that he was *mine*.

But then his hands shifted position and he shoved me back. "Ayla, we can't do this."

"You're right, we should at least go into the trees so no one will see us if they drive past." I couldn't think why else he would stop this when we both obviously wanted it so much. My nipples were hard in the cool night air, straining toward Kaden, along with every other inch of me too, and he definitely noticed.

"No." He looked away and raked a hand through his hair. "You're still mated to someone else. It doesn't matter that he's your brother—you're still not *mine*."

His words were like a sharp blow to my stomach. I actually stepped back, so hurt by them, and it took me a second to realize why—because in my head, Kaden was mine, and I was his, even without a mate bond between us. But why would I expect him to feel the same? Especially when I technically belonged to someone else?

Kaden leaned into the car and rooted around inside until he emerged with some clothes. I watched as he threw on pants and a t-shirt in quick succession. Then he turned back to the car to find his shoes, which he dragged out of the wreckage.

"Get dressed," he said when he turned to find me still naked.

I clenched my jaw as I grabbed clothes out of the bag and put them on. I understood why he denied me, but it didn't make his rejection any easier to stomach. While

Kaden salvaged anything else he could and put it all in his backpack, I found my shoes beside a dead wolf, where they'd fallen off while I'd shifted. The rest of the clothes I'd been wearing had been torn to shreds when I shifted, but at least these had survived. I checked the car again, and found my burner phone miraculously intact, along with my lip gloss. Thank the goddess for small favors.

As soon as I finished dressing, Kaden started down the road, heading in the direction we'd been driving, with his bag slung over his shoulder. I followed after him, leaving the car and the dead wolves for the Taurus pack to deal with.

They were allies of the Leo pack. I sighed heavily as I realized Jordan must have changed his mind about letting me go and had sent them after me. Kaden was right—Jordan didn't care about me at all, except as a prize to be won or a tool to be used. Brother or not, I was done defending him. If the only way out of this was to kill him, so be it.

CHAPTER SIXTEEN

WE WALKED in silence for about an hour. For once, I
didn't try to break it. My emotions were too tangled up, and
I was too busy trying to figure them out to even think of
trying to get Kaden to talk. Not a single car passed while we
were alongside the road, and our only company was the
waning moon hovering over us. Finally, I was drawn out of
my thoughts by the glimmer of lights on the horizon.

"Is that a town?" I asked.

Kaden still didn't look over at me, but I saw him frown as
he considered the question. "Looks like it. We'll stop and
rest there."

"Oh, thank god," I said. My whole body ached now that
the last of the adrenaline fading. My wolf healing was taking
care of it, but I was starving and exhausted and tired of traveling. We'd been driving or walking since dawn, not to
mention in a bad car accident and then a battle for our lives,
and all I wanted was to lie down for a while.

"How did the Taurus find us?" I asked, suddenly worried they might be able to follow us here too. "Was it the mate bond?"

"I don't think so," Kaden replied. "They probably tracked down the car somehow. I should have changed it out when we split up from the others."

When we reached the town limits, I nearly sighed in relief. There wasn't much to look at, just a sleepy little pit stop in the mountains off the side of the road. The buildings looked like something out of an old Western movie, but they had a gas station at least. Hopefully, they had somewhere where we could rest for the night—and shower. *And forget that this day ever happened.*

"There's a motel or something this way," Kaden said, looking at his phone. "I think. Reception is terrible out here."

We continued walking until we came across what looked like an old Victorian house, painted in pastel colors. All the outside lights were on, and a wooden sign read, *Cascade Bed and Breakfast.*

"Looks like this is our stop," I said, and we walked up the steps together.

No one was in the lobby when we entered, and I went up to the counter and rang the little bell, feeling like I'd gone back in time. A back door opened, and an older woman with a cheery face and red cheeks bustled out. Despite the late hour and the fact that we still had traces of blood on us, she beamed at us. *Top-notch customer service skills,* I thought wryly.

"Good evening. You need a room?" Before we could

answer, she unhooked a key from the wall behind her. "I only have the one left, but you folks got lucky. It'll be the perfect room for you."

Her eyes twinkled merrily as Kaden reached into his pocket and pulled out his wallet. He flipped his card onto the counter, and the woman ran it. "What a lovely couple you are. You will make such beautiful babies."

I looked down at my feet, a denial ready on my lips, but I didn't speak it out loud. A pang went through me as I thought about how that would never happen.

Kaden frowned and held his hand out for the card and the key. "Thank you."

"Your room is right up the stairs. Enjoy your night, dears." She waved from behind the desk. "And if you need any food, feel free to ring me. We have some leftovers from supper."

"Thank you," I managed past the lump in my throat from her earlier words. "Food would be great."

We hauled ourselves up the creaking wooden stairs to our room, and Kaden unlocked the door with the big brass key. When he pushed the door open, he just stood there, staring into the room.

"What?" I peered inside. At first, I didn't see anything wrong. The room seemed perfectly nice, though very outdated, and the king-sized bed had a cacophony of pink pillows on it, but it looked comfortable enough—

"*Oh,*" I said.

There was only one bed.

Kaden closed his eyes briefly as if steeling himself, before walking inside. "I'll take the floor."

"The hell you will," I said, shutting the door behind us and throwing the lock. "Don't be ridiculous. It's a king-sized bed. There's plenty of room for both of us. We can even put pillows between us if you're worried about me being a cover hog or something." I paused to look at the sheer amount of pillows. Really, why did people feel the need for *so many?* "There's definitely enough of them."

Kaden turned to face me, his eyes blazing. "We both know if we're in that bed together, we're not going to be sleeping."

I swallowed as the tension that had faded between us made a sudden and valiant reappearance. "Would that be so bad?"

I took a step forward, and to my surprise, Kaden didn't move back. His eyes smoldered as they took me in, and I waited with bated breath for whatever he was going to say next.

Then a knock came at the door.

"Who is it?" I asked, but my voice came out breathless. I cleared my throat, embarrassed that my reactions were so telling.

"I brought you up that food," the lady's voice said, just as cheerful as she'd been downstairs.

Kaden shook his head and turned away. Whatever he'd been about to say, he wouldn't do so now.

I opened the door to find the woman standing outside, a tray of food in her hands. At the sight, my stomach growled, and I gratefully smiled at her. "Thank you so much."

She arranged the tray on a wooden desk with spindly legs in the corner, then headed for the door. "Eat up," she said, waggling her eyebrows with a nod to Kaden. "I think you'll need it."

I blushed, realizing she probably thought we'd spend the night making good use of the bed and all those pillows. I didn't have the heart to tell her we weren't together when she seemed to be our biggest supporter. "Have a good night," I said as I closed the door.

I sat at the desk, and Kaden joined me after a brief pause, pulling up the other chair. Together, we tucked into the meal—chicken with potatoes and Brussels sprouts. I normally hated Brussels sprouts, but tonight I loved every bite, I was that hungry. I didn't stop to think, just stuffed my face until my stomach was sated.

Once we were done, there was nothing stopping us from going to bed. We both stared at the thing, neither one of us ready to take the first step toward climbing into it. I swallowed hard, suddenly very aware of how close Kaden was, and how much I wanted him even closer.

Kaden's eyes raked over me with obvious hunger, but then he jerked his head away. "You can have the first shower." He stood and moved to the window, pulling aside the thick, flowery curtain. He peered out as if making sure no enemies waited outside. "Get yourself cleaned up."

"Good idea." I tore my gaze off of him. A shower. Yes. I did need to wash the blood and sweat off my body before I got in bed. My last real shower had been before I tried to escape the Leos, and since then I'd only had a dip in a lake and some quick bathroom cleanups.

I slipped into the bathroom and closed the door. Looking at myself in the mirror made me cringe. I had blood dried all along one side of my face, and my red hair was a tangled, stringy mess. Why the front desk woman hadn't turned us away on sight, I didn't know. I bet I smelled as good as I looked too. No wonder Kaden didn't want to fuck me.

I turned on the shower, which looked more modern than the rest of the house, thankfully. Of course, it still had that 1950's pink tile everywhere, but at this point, I'd take whatever I could get. At the first touch of hot water on my aching body, I couldn't help the moan that came out of my throat. I closed my eyes and tipped my head back, allowing the water to sluice through my hair and along my skin. I reached for the provided shampoo and lathered my hair up, rinsing out the blood and dirt that had accumulated over the last few days. Then I did a quick wash of the rest of me, already feeling a thousand times better. I couldn't wait 'til we rejoined the Ophiuchus pack wherever they were hiding and I could have regular showers again. Other wolves didn't care as much as I did about cleanliness, but—

The shower curtain jerked open, and I screamed like someone in a horror movie. The sound cut off when I saw Kaden standing there, staring at me with hunger in his eyes. He didn't have a shirt on. *Typical.*

"What are you doing?" I asked, my heart racing, and not just because he'd startled me.

His gaze lowered, devouring every inch of my naked body as the water ran over it. Then his eyes snapped back to mine and they smoldered with pure, carnal need. "I don't know. But I'm tired of fighting this."

My mouth fell open, but I was stunned speechless as his hands slid to the front of his jeans, popping open the top button. As they hit the floor, his cock jutted forward, rock hard and straining toward me. An answering flush of desire went through me, and I stepped back to give Kaden room to step into the shower with me.

He took a moment to rinse himself off under the shower, removing all traces of blood, and then turned back to me. His hands caught my face as the water slid over us, and I looked up at him, holding my breath. Expecting him to come to his senses and walk away again.

But he didn't.

"I'm done resisting."

Kaden's mouth crashed down on mine, and it was like a dam bursting free. He devoured me with his kiss, holding nothing back this time, claiming me with every stroke of his tongue. Our bodies collided, our wet skin slipping together, and I smoothed my hands against his hard chest. I was finally allowed to touch, and I wanted to sample every single inch of him.

His fingers tightened around my hips, and then he pressed me against the cool tile at my back. I broke the kiss with a gasp at the sudden change, but he immediately captured my mouth again, his kiss demanding. Hungry. Like he needed something only I could give him.

He slid his hands down to cup my ass, and then he was lifting me, wrapping my legs around his waist. No foreplay. Neither of us needed it. I grabbed onto his shoulders as his cock rubbed against my wet folds, lining up so easily, our bodies remembering how perfectly we fit together. Then with one hard thrust, he was inside.

It was so sudden and so good that I forgot how to breathe for a second. He bottomed out inside me, filling me up with his hard length, and it was like something clicked. Whereas kissing Jordan had felt all wrong, everything about this felt oh so very right.

I gripped onto his shoulders as he began to thrust up into me, fucking me hard and rough against the tile wall. Need for Kaden overwhelmed me, making me feel like a wild animal, and this time there was no heat driving it. I *wanted,* and Kaden *gave.*

He was just as hungry as I was, his cock demanding to go deeper, harder, faster. His fingers dug into my skin, holding me exactly where he wanted me. I cried out with each thrust, clutching Kaden's shoulders, and he nipped at my neck with his teeth. I threw my head back, legs clenching tighter around his waist.

He gripped my chin and dragged my head down, forcing me to meet his eyes. "You feel so fucking good," he said, each word punctured by the stroke of his cock. "I've wanted this ever since that full moon."

"Me too," I said, my nails digging into his shoulders. "I thought about it every single night."

Kaden growled in response, and his thrusts grew more frenzied, the beat becoming almost brutal. Each stroke in and out dragged his cock right along that sparking center of pleasure. I'd been on edge for so long, desperately wanting Kaden, and now I finally had him. He pounded me against the tile, and I swore I heard some of them crack, but neither one of us could stop. A frenzy of pure need had taken over, almost like when I'd been in heat, but there was no full moon to blame this time, just us.

It only took a few more thrusts before I was coming, my pussy tightening around him, wanting to bring his cock deeper inside of me. Kaden groaned, throwing his head back. His thrusts became erratic, and his hands tightened on my ass. He came inside of me and then stilled, his body caught in a beautiful arch of muscle as water droplets slid down his torso. I moaned, the pleasure still washing over me in waves, and I ground down on his cock to chase the last bit of my orgasm.

Kaden pressed his forehead to mine, and we came down off our high together, panting and shuddering. He set me down gently, and then pulled me under the spray with him. He kissed me again, hands roving over my body as he sluiced hot water over both of us. This kiss was gentler, calmer now that the edge had been taken off. I grasped the back of his neck, pulling him closer to me, unwilling to let go of him just yet. He seemed to be as boneless as I felt, but there was still an urgency simmering under the temporary feeling of being sated.

"That was..." I trailed off, running my fingers down Kaden's chest. He didn't flinch away, and I wrapped a hand around his arm, covering his snake tattoo. "Wow."

Kaden reached behind me to turn the water off. We stood, the silence suddenly loud and the drip of water punctuating my words. I was surprised to see that the hunger hadn't faded from his eyes. If anything, it only looked stronger.

Then he picked me up and hauled me over his shoulder, like he so loved to do, with one hand on my naked ass. I let out a little squeal in surprise, kicking my legs feebly.

"What are you doing?" I asked.

"Taking you to bed." He said as he carried me out of the bathroom. "I'm not done with you yet."

CHAPTER SEVENTEEN

KADEN TOSSED me onto the bed in the middle of the hundreds of pillows. I was still dripping wet from the shower, but I couldn't care less about that as all six foot whatever of the naked alpha stalked toward me.

His eyes raked over my naked skin. "The first night we did this we were both driven by need. The full moon made us wild. We fucked like animals, fast and desperate and insatiable. In the shower, I felt the same need. And trust me, I'm going to fuck you like that again. But not this time." He lightly traced a finger along the edge of my nipple, making me gasp. "This time I'm going to savor every single inch of you. I want to taste all the places I didn't have time to explore before. And then I want to fill you with my cock for hours."

Oh my *god*. My pussy clenched tight at the thought of everything he said he was going to do to me. Kaden was right. There would be no sleeping in this bed tonight.

"I've never been with anyone except you," I said, as I looked up at him with complete trust. "Show me everything."

He let out a low, possessive growl at my words, and then he descended on me. He started with a kiss, hovering over my body as his tongue slipped inside my mouth, but he didn't linger there. Instead he turned my head away so he could kiss along my neck. His other hand slid down my breast, cupping it, squeezing it, caressing it. Then he did the same on the other side.

Sex in the shower had been rough and fast, more like the mating frenzy than anything else. This was nothing like that. Kaden kissed his way along my naked skin, mapping out my body with his tongue and lips. It was like he wanted to claim every inch of me as his, and I let him. Gladly.

When his tongue circled my nipple, my back arched off the bed. I gasped as sparks of pleasure shot through me as he sucked the hard bud into his mouth, then moved to the other breast to repeat his actions. He worshiped my breasts with such lavish attention that I thought I might come from that alone, but just as the pleasure built up, his mouth moved back. Along my shoulders. Up my neck. Back to my lips.

He drew me into another kiss, nudging his thigh between mine and pushing my legs further apart. One of his hands slid down the front of my body, slipping between my legs to slide into the pounding heat of my pussy. He pushed two fingers inside, crooking them just so, and I moaned into his mouth, my hips rolling up to the pressure. After all his attention on the rest of my body, my pussy was glad to be back in the spotlight again.

Kaden broke away from my lips and began kissing his way down my body again, his eyes hot on mine as he watched the way I moaned for him. His fingers kept working inside of me, and then he pushed my legs apart wider. His gaze never left my face as he lowered his head, and then he licked one, long, delicious stripe up my slit.

I nearly leaped off the bed, so shocked and turned on by the way his tongue felt against my pussy. Kaden's hand pressed down on my hips, holding me in place as he repeated the action, then swirled his tongue around my clit. I threw my head back, arching my body up to meet him, overwhelmed with the sensation. I'd never felt anything like this before, and it was so good it was almost too much, but Kaden wasn't stopping. Not that I would let him if he tried.

He worked me expertly, drawing out every bit of pleasure he could with his tongue while his fingers moved inside of me, and it wasn't long before my legs were shaking. My hips lifted of their own accord, my body not even in control of itself anymore, and I found my fingers tangled in Kaden's hair, pushing his head down to my pussy, demanding more, more, more. And he gave it to me.

Searing pleasure ripped through me and my eyes rolled back in my head as Kaden masterfully tongued my clit in tandem with the thrusts of his fingers. Every coherent thought fled my mind and a long howl escaped my lips as a massive orgasm shook through me, unlike anything I'd experienced before. But he kept going, drawing the pleasure out, making one orgasm turn into another and another until it became almost too much, and I nearly begged him to stop.

Only then did Kaden sit back. He looked at me with obvious satisfaction and intense hunger. "You're beautiful when you come."

"I..." I shuddered, unable to move. I wasn't even sure what I'd been trying to say. I'd completely lost my mind, thanks to Kaden.

He slowly kissed his way up my body, taking his time to lavish attention on places he'd skipped before, like the curve of my hip, or the swell of my belly. Then he took my mouth again, and I could taste myself on his tongue, the feeling strangely intimate as he kissed me deeply. I felt his cock resting on my thighs, hard and ready to take me, though I had the sense Kaden would wait as long as I needed.

He rolled me over then, perhaps sensing I still needed a minute, and his hands and mouth moved across my back. It was somehow both sensual and relaxing, like a gentle, intimate massage. His hands worked lower though, and then he cupped my ass, kissing along the curve of it as he gave it a squeeze. Then he spread me wide and fingered my back entrance, tracing it like he was teasing me with the possibility. Would he fill that hole too? I gasped at the thought, both turned on and a little scared.

"Someday," he said, slipping his finger inside just a tiny bit, wrenching a moan out of me. His words sounded like a promise. Then he leaned close and licked my pussy from behind, just a short, quick one, and it was enough to have me jutting my hips toward him.

"Kaden, I need you," I begged.

I got up on my hands and knees, filled with a need for him to take me from behind. My inner wolf demanded it. She begged him to rut me like an animal, and somehow Kaden knew. He aligned himself behind me, gripping my hips, and the head of his cock nudged at my entrance, sliding along my slit before he seated himself inside of me. He thrust slowly, and I pushed my hips back, trying to pull him deeper, reveling in the feeling of finally having Kaden back there, right where I wanted him. He rocked into me until he'd bottomed out, and then drew back, making me feel every single intense thrust.

It was darker in the bedroom than it had been in the bathroom, but from this angle, I noticed a mirror behind the bed. In its reflection, all I could see was the glimmer of Kaden's eyes in the moonlight pouring in from the window. He ran his hands along my hips, up to my shoulders, and then he arched over me, slamming even deeper inside with his next thrust.

He pounded into me, and the position had heat gathering at the pit of my stomach once more with each thrust. Especially when he reached down my body to tease my almost oversensitive clit. I watched him as he fucked me from behind, still going slow to make sure I felt every inch of his hard cock as he claimed me. He looked desperate, yet somehow in full control at the same time. Like a man who was finally getting the thing he wanted most.

"You're mine," Kaden said, his voice a low growl.

I gasped at his words, which filled me with pleasure that wasn't physical. Did he really mean that?

"I don't care if we're not mates," he continued. "You're *mine*."

"I'm yours," I said with a moan. "Only yours."

The words seemed to spark something in him and his face turned feral. His teeth grew longer, turning to fangs, and then he bent over my back. Before I could react, he'd clamped his canines down on the juncture between my neck and shoulder.

I gasped, eyes going wide as his teeth sank into me. Kaden was *marking* me as his. It hurt, but in a good way, and the pain mixing with pleasure pushed me over the edge. Another climax swept through me, but it was different from anything I'd ever felt before. My body shuddered around the orgasm, Kaden's cock slamming hard as I felt his seed spill deep inside of me. His cock kept pulsing, his fangs sinking deeper into my skin like he wanted to imprint on me forever.

Finally, he released me. I watched in the mirror as he became fully human again, sweat gleaming on his skin as he hovered behind me. I couldn't believe it and touched my neck to confirm the bite mark was really there.

Kaden had just claimed me as his own in the most primal way.

As if I was his mate.

CHAPTER EIGHTEEN

I WOKE SLOWLY, a lazy sort of heat enveloping me. It took me an embarrassingly long time to realize why. My eyes popped open to the ceiling of the inn Kaden and I were staying at. Sunlight streamed into the room, letting me know that we'd slept well into the morning, possibly even into the afternoon.

I carefully cataloged the heat of Kaden's naked body alongside my own. His arm was still flung over my waist from where he'd pulled me close last night. When I glanced down, I saw the half-healed mark from where he'd bitten into me. A little thrill ran through me at the memory. Kaden had marked me as his own as if I were truly his mate. But would he regret it now that the night was over? Like the first time, when I'd been in heat?

I held still for a few moments, scared to move, trying to figure out what to do. Kaden had been notorious for leaving when things got too emotional for him. It was practically his signature move by now. I didn't want him to run away after everything that had happened last night. Or worse, tell me none of it meant anything, and that we couldn't do it again.

"What are you thinking about?" Kaden's low voice rumbled close to my ear, and I carefully controlled my reaction so I wouldn't jump.

"You," I said truthfully.

His eyes looked clouded with sleep, and I continued holding myself as still as I could, waiting for the moment he realized where he was, and who he was hugging close to him. But he just smiled at me, the look so open and un-Kaden-like that I frowned at him.

"What's that face?" He pushed himself onto one elbow and arched an eyebrow. His hand slid across my stomach, and I shivered at the sensation. We'd touched everywhere last night, but it still felt like the first time. I didn't think I'd ever get tired of it.

I turned over in his arms, chasing the last of whatever he was willing to give me. To my surprise, Kaden didn't immediately jump out of bed and run away. He trailed his knuckles along my side, seeming to enjoy the way my muscles flexed under the attention.

He must have seen some of the confusion on my face. "What is it? You look like you're waiting for me to bite you."

"You already did that," I said, waiting for him to tense up at the reminder of what we'd done last night. "I'm waiting for the other shoe to drop."

Kaden dipped his head and pulled me closer to him. He kissed me slowly, his mouth lazy as it claimed mine, and I melted against him, eyes dropping shut to revel in the sensation.

"I'm done," he said, looking me in the eyes, his gaze possessive. "I'm done pretending I don't want you. I meant it last night. You're *mine*. No one else can have you."

I shivered at that, my heart doing a funny extra beat, and Kaden's body moved over mine. His kiss deepened, his hard cock nudging between my thighs, seeking entrance. I opened up and he slid inside easily, my body already wet and ready for him from the moment I'd woken up. We both sighed as he filled me, and then he began fucking me slowly. Lazy morning sex, with the sun streaming down on us, while he held himself up on his strong arms and plunged in and out. I did nothing except let him pleasure me, and he gazed into my eyes the entire time. He never looked away, soaking up each moan from my lips, then watched me fall apart all around him before joining me with a groan.

When we were done, he pulled me back into the circle of his arms. I reveled in the feeling for a few moments before the real world began intruding along the edges. Doubts crept in, and I wished he would fuck me again to chase them away, but I knew we'd have to face them at some point.

"What about the mate bond?" I hated to ask, but I needed to know. If Kaden was only going to say he wanted me now to reject me later, I didn't think I could take it again. If this was going to work, I needed him to be okay with us being together, even with the mate bond intact.

"Fuck the mate bond," he said. "It's obviously bullshit."

Relief washed through me, and the last of the tension I'd

been holding in my body eased away. He was finally admitting what we had was real, and that the mate bond didn't matter. I knew that had to be difficult for him, after what he'd been through with his ex.

I took his face in my hands. "I choose you." I swallowed, my throat tight with emotion. "Even if Jordan wasn't my brother, I'd still choose you."

Kaden's next inhale was a bit ragged. He tried not to show it, but I could see in his eyes that the words meant a lot to him. He lowered his head and kissed me, the kind of long, deep kiss that you feel all the way in your soul.

When it was done, he sat up and played with my hair idly. "Come on. As much as I'd like to stay in bed with you all day, we should eat something and get on the road."

I groaned and rolled over, still limp from the orgasm he'd just given me. Kaden slipped out of bed and went over to the desk, flashing me his naked ass and his broad, smooth back. He'd left his phone there to charge overnight, and now he frowned down at the screen. I watched him for a few moments, reveling in the fact that he was *mine* just as much as I was his. I wanted to wake up to Kaden every morning for the rest of my life.

Finally, I shook myself and slid out of bed, making my way to the bathroom to take a quick shower. We did still have a mission to complete, and no amount of lazing around in bed would make the Leos stop coming after us.

I changed into a fresh set of clothes, the last ones I had, and ran a little travel brush through my hair. Kaden went for the shower next, and I pulled out my phone.

Thankfully, it had survived the crash, and I smiled as I read the messages from Mira. She'd made it to the Pisces pack safely, and the Ophiuchus warriors had taken down all the Leos hanging out there. Best of all, her mate was all right.

When Kaden joined me, we went downstairs for breakfast. The friendly woman, looking just as spry as she had in the middle of the night, eyed us knowingly, and I remembered how loud I'd been last night. Had she heard? I found myself blushing, even though it hadn't mattered to me in the moment, and yanked my shirt up to cover the bite mark on my neck.

I loaded up a plate with eggs, bacon, and pastries, and chowed down. My appetite was ravenous again after what we'd done last night, and Kaden ate even more than I did.

"It looks like we're only a few hours away from the Cancer village," Kaden said. "We'll need to cross the border into Canada as wolves to avoid having to deal with the human authorities."

I nodded and took a swig of coffee. That was how most shifters crossed the border without notice. The Cancer pack had done it all the time. "Hopefully we'll be able to find the survivors tonight."

Kaden made a noise of affirmation and then typed something out on his phone. I smiled at him as I finished eating. This would be sweet, if we weren't so focused on the fact that I was trying to find my ex-pack while being hunted by enemy shifters. I could imagine a future for us like this. Waking up with Kaden, eating at the kitchen island with him and Stella... All of that could be a reality if we managed to stop the Leos and the Sun Witches.

When we were done, we went back to our room and gathered our things. I was almost sad to say goodbye to the room of a thousand pink pillows. It had been a haven for us, a place where we finally let go of our inhibitions, but I knew we couldn't hide forever. We needed to get back on the road so we could reach the Cancer pack lands.

The woman was cleaning up the breakfast area when we came back down. "Did you sleep well?" she asked, a knowing twinkle in her eye.

"Yes, your bed was very soft, thank you," I said with a grin, my cheeks warming.

"We appreciate your hospitality," Kaden added.

"Of course, I'm glad I was able to provide you with a room to your liking. Good luck on your journey." She waved the broom she was holding at us. "I hope your marriage is a long and fruitful one."

I opened my mouth to tell her we weren't married, but what would be the point? We'd accepted her room with only one bed, and saying that nothing was going on between us would be a lie at this point. I just inclined my head and gave her one last smile.

We continued down the road for some time and then slipped into the dense conifer trees. The area smelled like Christmas, though the last bit of summer heat still warmed the air. Kaden breathed it in, completely in his element, and then he began to undress. I watched, mesmerized by the way he shed his clothes, so comfortable in his nakedness. Besides, seeing his nude, muscular body never got old.

Then it was my turn to get naked. As I shoved my clothes back in the bag, I felt Kaden's eyes on me too. His cock twitched as he took me in, and one side of his lips quirked up. I held my breath, waiting for him to cross the distance to me, eager for him to throw me down on the ground and have his way with me.

He shook his head as if snapping out of a trance. "If you distract me we'll never make it to your village."

I let out a long breath and nodded. It wasn't a 'no,' it was a 'later.' He was right, of course. We had to keep moving. I just lost control of myself a little whenever he was around me.

Kaden gave me one more heated look and then shifted. In the blink of an eye, a huge black wolf stood where Kaden had before. My shifting took a few seconds longer, but soon I stood beside him on four paws, my long white tail swishing behind me.

You're just as beautiful as a wolf, he told me. I ducked my head, enjoying his praise inside my head. Then he grabbed the bag in his huge jaws, and we sprinted off into the woods together.

It was a relief to be a wolf again. Last time I'd been so focused on getting away from the Leos that I hadn't had the proper time to revel in it, and I'd been in the desert, which would never be home to me. Out here, in the forests, I truly felt free for the first time in weeks. *And even better, I* thought, glancing over at Kaden, who loped at my side. *He's with me.*

We crossed over into Canada without a hitch, passing a stone marker that let us know we'd reached the border. Out in rural areas, there was no border patrol, and a sign simply told us to self-report to the authorities, which we obviously ignored. We continued on until we reached civilization, and then donned our clothes and took a bus through Vancouver. Once we reached the northern part of it, we got a quick bite to eat, then headed into the mountains to continue our journey as wolves.

The sun had set by the time we arrived at the outskirts of the Cancer pack lands on the coast. In the distance, I heard the crash of waves, and even though I'd never been at home here, it was where I'd spent the most time, and in some ways, it was good to be back in familiar territory. I knew these lands like the back of my hand, and I guided Kaden through the forest easily.

As we approached the edge of the village, Kaden stepped behind a tree and jerked his head at me to follow. We both shifted back and dressed as quietly as we could. There was no way to know how much danger waited for us inside of the village, and my anxiety crept back in.

Kaden pulled me close to him, and I was more than happy to press myself along his side, his warmth spreading out to me. "Are you all right?"

I nodded, taking a deep breath and squaring my shoulders. "I'm fine. I just never thought I'd come back here."

He took my hand. "Let's see if anyone's around."

The moon had barely risen in the sky, but it must have been enough for Kaden to tap into because he turned us invisible. He'd done it to me before during our battle with the Taurus, but I hadn't gotten to appreciate it then. Now I held out my hand, marveling at how I couldn't see it at all. As long as Kaden and I remained touching, the spell would continue.

We walked out of the woods, holding hands, and it would have been romantic if not for the knots in my stomach. We did a brief trek around the outer bounds of the village, noting that the houses there had no lights on and no movement inside.

Kaden squeezed my arm, and I used my power to teleport us into town. We could have walked, of course, but this was faster and would leave less of a scent trail. Also if any enemy shifters were hiding in town, we could catch them off guard completely.

Delphinus was a laid-back fishing village centered around the harbor, with one main street running down the center of it with quaint little shops, bakeries, restaurants, and more. It was late enough now that they should have been lit up from the inside, but the town remained dark. At this time of night, I would have expected people to be heading into the grocery store to pick up some food, or for a few older kids to ride past on bicycles, or at the very least an old truck heading down the road after leaving the harbor. But there was no one here at all.

As we looked around, we didn't even need my teleporting or Kaden's invisibility, because it was clear the town had been abandoned. The only flicker of movement came from a seagull walking along the edge of a fence, and the only sound was that of the waves crashing along the rocks nearby. Even the scent of the Cancer pack was faint as if they hadn't inhabited the village for at least a few weeks.

We did a thorough pass of the village anyway, making sure we wouldn't be ambushed, and that no sniper was waiting on top of the gas station to take us out, or something along those lines.

Kaden let go of my hand and came into focus again. "No one's here," he said. "No sign of a fight either."

"They must have left town."

Kaden shrugged. "It's your old pack. Where would they have gone?"

I gazed across the town I'd grown up in as I considered his question. With my entire family gone—and me presumed dead—the beta would have taken over. He'd hated me, as had his son, Brad. I had no idea where he would have taken the pack. We were at a dead end.

"I don't know." I let out a frustrated breath. "We could look through the town some more, see if there are any clues as to where they went."

"That could take days," Kaden said, his brow furrowed. "Is there somewhere we can stay while we're here?"

"Take your pick," I said, spreading my arms wide at the empty houses. Of course, breaking into someone's abandoned home and crashing there felt wrong. I shook my head. "I suppose we can go back to my childhood home. I might as well see if there are any clothes or shoes there I could use."

Kaden's eyebrows darted up at that idea. "I would very much like to see where you grew up, little wolf."

I sighed, as the sea air whipped at my hair. "Don't get too excited. I didn't exactly have a happy childhood there."

He took a wayward strand of hair and tucked it behind my ear. "I don't care. It's still a part of your past. I want to know about all of it—the good and the bad."

I swallowed hard, turning my gaze toward the direction of my old home. Even though I dreaded returning there, something in my gut tugged me forward, and I became certain that I had to do this. No matter how hard it would be.

CHAPTER NINETEEN

KADEN TOOK MY HAND AGAIN, giving me the courage to start walking down the road toward the largest house in the village, nestled atop a rocky cliff overlooking the waves. The alpha would never settle for anything less of course, but the house wasn't so grand that it felt out of place in the town either. The two-story house was painted white and gray, with lots of windows so the ocean could be seen from every room. A narrow path led down to the private beach, but we passed it by and headed straight for the front door. There were no lights on inside, not that I'd expected to see any, but each step still filled me with dread as I approached.

The door was locked, but I kicked aside the rock that we kept on the porch with the spare key, and pushed the door open. Once I flipped the lights on, I just stopped and stared. It looked exactly the same as it had the day we'd left for the Convergence. Dad's coffee cup sat next to the sink with the expectation that I'd wash it when we got back. One of Jackie's gossip magazines was splayed out on the counter next to the rest of the mail.

Kaden was completely silent, but I felt him hovering close to me as I walked through the living room. Jackie had redecorated the place recently, painting the walls stark white, then changing all the furniture to a modern gray, with black and white accents around the room. She loved to do this every few years to keep up with the trends, but to me, it felt staged. The room was spotless, with nothing out of place, like she wanted anyone who came into the house to think we had a picture-perfect life.

All sorts of emotions bounced around inside me, and I couldn't focus on any single one of them. In a way, it was nice to come back to this place where I'd spent most of my life. This home was all that I'd known, and I did have some happy memories inside it. Of course, they'd all been with Wesley, and at that thought, the heavy weight of my grief nearly crushed me. There were bad memories too, of course. All the times my parents had been cruel with their words or their hands. Or in other ways, the more subtle yet more painful ones, like when Wesley got Christmas presents and I didn't. Or how he was in every single family photo hanging on the walls here, but I was nowhere to be found.

Being back in this house made me so angry, and sad, and relieved that they were gone, and guilty for feeling that way, and so many other emotions I didn't even have a name for. I nearly bolted out, too overwhelmed by it all, until Kaden rested his hand on my lower back as if he knew I needed his support.

"Breathe," he said. "If it's too much, we can go."

I nodded, taking a long, slow breath, and pushed through the turmoil inside me. I wasn't sure I'd be able to sleep in this house tonight, but we should at least visit my room before we left. "I'm all right. Thanks."

I drew my shoulders back and set my jaw as we headed up the stairs. My parents' door was closed, which I was thankful for—I didn't need to see anything in there. Wesley's old room, which Dad had converted to a guest room, was open, but I kept going until I reached my door at the end.

My room was the smallest, barely larger than a closet. It was also bare except for the bed, nightstand, and dresser, with nothing on the walls. I glanced around, an odd sense of nostalgia washing over me. How many times had I walked in here after a long day, cradling my camera and thinking about how I wanted to escape all this at the Convergence? Well, I'd definitely escaped, though not at all how I'd expected.

I shook the memories away and got to work, rooting through my drawers for anything I'd left behind. I'd taken all my best shoes and clothes to the Convergence in the hopes of moving to a new pack, but I found a couple of things—a ratty pair of underwear, some socks with holes in the toes, and two t-shirts that were slightly too small for me. A pair of worn flip-flops peeked out from under my bed, along with an old My Little Pony backpack from when I was a kid. Better than nothing.

"This was your room?" Kaden asked. He sounded

almost shocked, as if he couldn't believe I'd been living in a place like this for the first twenty-two years of my life.

"Yeah, why?" I suddenly realized how small it was, and how worn-down the clothes I'd put in the backpack were. Compared to the wealth on display in the rest of the house, it was pretty shameful. Maybe he'd never realized just how different our upbringings were until now.

"It's so..." he paused. "Lifeless, compared to you. So bare. You really lived here for the first part of your life?"

"Yeah, although most of my possessions are missing," I said wryly. "I lost them at the Convergence. Not that I had much to begin with. My parents never let me be myself, not really. I was always more of an unwanted guest in their house, the half-breed that Dad liked to pretend didn't exist. A mistake that was better out of sight, out of mind."

Kaden let out a growl, and his hands were balled into tight fists, anger radiating off him like heatwaves. "You should never have been treated that way," he said, with such vindication that it shook me. "If he wasn't already dead, I'd challenge him as alpha right here, right now."

"Down, boy," I said as I punched Kaden lightly in the arm. But even as Kaden glowered at me, I couldn't help the smile that lifted my lips. I was secretly pleased that he'd be willing to do that for me.

Then I saw something out of the corner of my eye, something peeking out from under my pink pillow, now faded almost to white from too many washings. I lifted it up, surprised to see a photograph sitting there. I picked it up with shaking fingers as I took in Wesley's smiling face, drinking in the familiar features greedily. I had no pictures of him anymore, and even though there were other photos of him in the house, this was the only one I was in too.

In the photo we were on the beach of Nereus Island, which was an hour's boat ride away from here. We'd visited almost every year for vacation until Wesley went to college, and I guessed I was about fourteen here, which put Wesley at eighteen. He had his arm slung around my shoulders and grinned at the camera broadly. I looked a little subdued, but even I was smiling wide. He'd just told me a joke before Jackie snapped the picture, to be sure that my smile would be broader than usual.

Tears pricked at the back of my eyes as I remembered the moment. I could hear the scream of seagulls overhead and taste the salt in the air as if I were there now. It was the last vacation we'd taken together as a family, and one of my happiest memories of my brother.

"I miss him so much," I whispered. I'd thought about his death all the time, but admitting it out loud unlocked some part of me that I tried to keep under wraps. Tears poured down my cheeks, and Kaden's arms wrapped around me from behind. I turned and pressed my face against him, letting the grief wash over me. Kaden didn't say anything, but his presence was enough.

I pulled back and wiped at my eyes, opening my mouth to apologize to Kaden for using him as my personal tissue, but then I frowned down at the photograph. "I didn't leave this here."

"What do you mean?" Kaden asked.

"I haven't seen this photo in years. Wesley had it at his apartment." I flipped it over, and nearly dropped the photo in shock when I saw the writing scrawled on the back in blue ballpoint pen. Two simple words: *find us.*

I looked up at Kaden, as my heart began to pound even faster. "I know where they are."

THE CANCER PACK made most of their income by selling fish and crabs to restaurants and markets, so it was no surprise they had a lot of boats in the harbor. Big ones, small ones, with everything from sailboats to pontoons to jet skis. Dad personally owned a large sailboat that he could take a big group out on the water with, but it required at least two people to manage, and I had a feeling Kaden wouldn't be much help there. Dad had often used me as his crew because I would do the grunt work without complaint, while the rest of the shifters drank wine and ate cheese. But Dad also had a bowrider for when he wanted to speed across the waves, and that was the one I headed for now.

As we walked down the dock, I fidgeted with the ignition key I'd grabbed from the house. I hadn't been allowed to drive the speed boat when we'd gone out as a family, but Wesley had taught me whenever we got the chance to go alone. Of course, that was years ago now, but hopefully, it would all come back to me, like driving.

When we got to the boat, Kaden looked over the water with a grimace as I climbed inside and began checking things out. "I don't like this plan," he said. "Do you even know how to drive a boat?"

"First you question my driving, now you question my boating skills?" I patted the side in a *come on* motion. "I can get us to the island. I think."

"You think?" Kaden asked, eyebrows shooting up. He hadn't come any closer to the boat, and he was far enough away that I couldn't yank him into it either.

"Well, I haven't exactly had time to practice after being kidnapped *twice*. Being landlocked and held in a cell multiple times kind of puts a damper on that." I shoved the key in the ignition and was pleased when it started without a problem. "If there's one thing any Cancer knows, it's how to handle a boat. Even an outcast like me. I'm an excellent sailor too." *Although Wesley was better,* I thought with a pang.

I flipped a few switches and checked the gauges, wondering if I was forgetting something. It felt like forever since Wesley had shown this to me, but I closed my eyes and imagined he was beside me, guiding my hands to the right places, grinning at me when I got things right. I could do this.

Navigation. That was what I was missing. The boat had an onboard electronic navigation system with the location of the island already saved to it, so all I had to do was turn it on and the GPS would show me exactly where to go.

"Come on," I called to Kaden, who was still standing on the dock, looking entirely uncomfortable with the idea of being on a boat. "I thought snakes liked water."

"No, they like eating things that like water," Kaden mumbled. With a scowl on his lips, he stepped into the boat and sat down on one of the seats behind me.

"Finally," I said, rolling my eyes. I'd never expected the big bad alpha to be such a baby when it came to boats.

I slowly backed the boat up out of the slip and turned it around to point toward Nereus Island. Even though it was dark out, my wolf senses gave me an advantage, and everything Wesley had taught me was coming back now.

When I gunned the boat, Kaden's hands gripped the seat on either side of him, and he swallowed hard. I couldn't help but smile. He looked up at me, so undeniably grumpy that I had to cover my laugh with my hand.

"I've never been on a boat," he admitted finally, and still wouldn't look anywhere but at the horizon.

"Don't worry," I called to him as the boat started to pick up speed, slicing through the waves faster and faster until we were almost flying. "Even though I can't breathe underwater like a real Cancer, I'm a strong swimmer. If we do capsize, I can save you."

"I know how to swim," Kaden muttered. "I just don't want to have to do it in the middle of the ocean."

I rolled my eyes, but then I had a sudden thought. The Cancer pack, along with the Pisces and Scorpio packs, could breathe underwater because they were water signs. The other packs all aligned with the other elements, except for one. "What element is the Ophiuchus pack?"

"We don't have one. The packs got those powers after we

were exiled, probably from the Sun Witches. But our Moon Witch blood makes up for it."

"True, although I bet you'd feel a lot better if we could both breathe underwater right now."

Kaden clenched his jaw at that but didn't say anything else. I turned back toward the front, steering the boat a bit south to compensate for the wind. Even though I'd never felt like I belonged in my pack, I'd always loved this, with the wind blowing my hair back from my face and the smell of salt in my nose. I hadn't realized how much I'd missed the ocean until I'd set eyes on it again. Maybe there was a little bit of Cancer in me after all.

It took a little over an hour for us to reach the island. I saw the Nereus lighthouse peeking up from the waves long before anything else appeared. I pointed it out to Kaden and he finally came to stand beside me, more relaxed now that he realized I wasn't going to drown us.

I was surprised that the Cancer pack had come here, but I supposed there wouldn't be any way for an outsider to trace them except the picture I'd found. I hadn't even noticed all that many boats missing from our harbor. If Brad's dad really was alpha, at least he was doing a good job of keeping the rest of them alive.

Speaking of that asshole... As we pulled up, a group of shifters gathered at the edge of the dock, and I recognized Brad almost immediately in the illumination from the light- house above.

"Great," I muttered, as I maneuvered us into position and killed the engine. I knew logically he would be here, but

I'd hoped to at least talk to his dad before him. Last time I'd seen Brad and his mate, they'd broken my camera and beaten me up, and I couldn't imagine he'd be nicer to me now that his father was alpha.

Brad and a few other Cancer shifters who'd loved taking part in the fun of 'punch and kick the half-human' gathered around our boat, stopping Kaden and me from getting off unless we wanted to step into the water.

"What the fuck are you doing here?" Brad snarled.

"Visiting old friends," I shot back. "What, did you think I was dead?"

"We hoped you were," his mate, Lori, said from behind him. *Glad to see she's still a total bitch.*

Brad crossed his arms. "It would have been better if that Leo asshole had hunted you down and killed you. We heard that's what happened, anyway."

"You heard wrong," I snapped. "Step back, I need to speak with the alpha. You're in my way."

"I don't think so." He didn't budge. "You caused so many deaths already, why don't you just turn around and leave?"

I raised my eyes to the moon, wishing the goddess would give me the strength to deal with this piece of shit. "I said, I need to speak to the alpha. Or are you still as dumb as a bag of rocks?"

Brad snarled and launched himself at me, but then Kaden was there, stepping in front of me. He grabbed Brad by the throat, holding him mid-air with the kind of strength only an alpha would possess.

A deep growl radiated from Kaden's chest. "If you touch

her, I'll rip you apart with my bare hands. And I will enjoy every second of it."

Brad kicked his feet feebly, his eyes bulging out of their sockets, probably so shocked that someone was bigger and badder than him for once. He looked like he couldn't breathe, and I put my hand on Kaden's arm. As much as I hated Brad, I couldn't let Kaden kill him.

"Put him down," I said with a sigh.

Kaden stared Brad down for a few more moments and then dumped him on the dock. Brad clutched his throat, sucking in a breath, while his mate kneeled over him. The other shifters eyed Kaden warily but didn't move to defend their friend.

"This was obviously a waste of time," Kaden said, turning back to me.

I felt the old pit of anger flaring up in my stomach. I remembered every single time Brad and his gang had tormented me, and I wanted nothing more than to spit in their faces and turn the boat around. But I had to at least try. I had to be the better person, or I'd be just like them.

"Ayla?" a voice called out.

A voice so familiar it made my heart stop. The sound came from further up the dock, and I turned toward it, holding my breath as if it could keep the hope inside of me. I blinked a few times, trying to see if my eyes were tricking me. That line of shoulders, that carefree lope, that windswept hair—it was all too real.

"*Wesley?*"

CHAPTER TWENTY

I HOPPED onto the deck and ran up the wooden planks toward my brother, shoving aside a couple of Cancer shifters in my path. As I got closer, there was no mistaking it—Wesley was *alive*. My brother was here, in the flesh, and I launched myself at him.

Wesley caught me, and I saw the flash of his teeth in the moonlight as he grinned, just before I flung my arms around him. I buried my head into his shoulder, breathing in deep, and he hugged me tight. I never thought I would see him again, but he was here, and not dead.

My eyes were wet when I finally pulled back, and my throat constricted painfully. I drank in the sight of him for several moments, hardly believing my eyes. The fact that he was standing in front of me seemed so impossible, I wanted to stare at him for several more minutes to make sure he wasn't an illusion. "How are you alive?"

Wesley's eyes glimmered with tears of his own, and he

let out a strained laugh. "I could ask you the same thing. Last I heard, you disappeared from the forest without a trace after the Convergence. I thought the Leo assholes had gotten to you, and we searched all over for you. But we had to run before the Leos came back and looked for the rest of us." He looked me over as if seeing if I had any visible wounds. My mind flew to the bite mark that Kaden had given me, but if he saw it under the collar of my shirt, Wesley didn't say anything. He patted my shoulders with both hands, as if feeling the solid weight of me underneath him, and the grin on his face was the best thing I'd ever seen. Then he pulled me back into a hug. "Thank the moon you're alive. How did you get away?"

"It's a long story." That was an understatement. It would probably take me all night to tell him everything that had happened to me over the last few months.

When I pulled back again, Wesley was looking over my shoulder, his eyes fixed on Kaden, who had come down the deck to stand behind me. Wesley's grin disappeared, and I wondered if he remembered Kaden from the Convergence.

Remembering my manners, I gestured toward Kaden. "This is Kaden Shaw, alpha of the Ophiuchus pack. Kaden, this is my brother, Wesley."

Wesley tilted his head, studying Kaden. "I can see we have a lot to discuss." He motioned for us to follow him. "Come with me."

Wesley led us away from the dock and down the road into the main part of the island, where all the houses were located. The island wasn't very large and most of it was beach and forest, but there were a few small shops in one area, plus some vacation homes along the water and on the hills above it. It was the perfect hiding place for a pack looking to get away from other shifters—especially since very few people knew it existed outside of the Cancer pack.

Wesley began talking as we walked, and I kept up beside him, with Kaden lingering just a bit behind, still listening but doing his best to not intrude. "Many of the wealthier Cancer pack members have homes here," Wesley explained, mostly for Kaden's benefit. "Both for vacation, and for shelter in case of an attack. I never thought we'd need them, but here we are." He flashed me a grin. "Remember how we used to dare each other to sneak inside the other houses?"

I shook my head at the memory, a smile on my lips. "Yes, although I was never brave enough to do it. But you did, almost every time. I can't remember how many seashells I lost to you during bets."

"Turns out it was a good idea since I knew how to get into all of them." He went quiet for a moment. "After the Convergence, I moved the pack here in case the Leos decided to come finish the rest of us off. The pack members are all sharing the houses, making sure everyone has access to a kitchen and a bathroom. Some of the houses are pretty packed, but we're safe here at least."

It hit me then—my brother was the Cancer alpha now. He was the one making the decisions and shouldering the responsibility for the entire pack. I'd hoped and prayed for such a thing for most of my life, for a time when the pack would be free of my father and in my brother's capable hands. I'd just never expected it to happen this way. Or this soon.

"What do you do for supplies?" Kaden asked.

"We had years' worth of supplies stocked in the light-house," Wesley said. "My dad was prepared for an attack from the Leos at any moment, and he turned this place into the ultimate shelter. Plus we can fish for food, there are chickens and goats at a few of the houses, and we have weapons stockpiled too. If the Leos ever actually found us here, we would be able to defend it easily."

For once, I was glad for Dad's hatred and paranoia, though I wasn't surprised. The Cancers and Leos had been at war on and off for my entire life, and well before it too. Dad had always expected an attack, he'd just never foreseen it would happen at the Convergence.

"How many of you are left?" I asked as we walked along the path leading up to our house.

"Not enough," Wesley said, his face turning grim. "We lost so many at the Convergence."

I remembered all too well. The shock and fear when Dixon had murdered our father felt as fresh as if it had happened only yesterday, and I could still hear the screams and growls of the Cancer pack being slaughtered all around me. No matter how much time passed, I wasn't sure I would ever get over what I went through that night.

"Here we are," Wesley said, shaking me out of my thoughts.

I looked up at the familiar light blue two-story house with the white wrap-around porch and felt a smile tilting my lips up. So many memories were stored in this house, and most of them were happy. It felt strange being back without our parents, but I supposed this was Wesley's house now.

He opened the door and led us inside, and I heard the faint sounds of people in the other room. "Since it was just me, I gave most of the house up to other shifters who needed a place to stay, but we can move people around to get a room for you two."

"A room?" I asked, glancing back at Kaden. *Is it that obvious?*

"Your scents are intermingled, and..." Wesley's eyes caught on where my shirt had slid away from my neck, and he gestured awkwardly. "I just assumed you would be sharing."

I blushed hard. So he *had* seen the place where Kaden had marked me. I mean, that was the point of the mark, but I'd never thought my brother, of all people, would see it.

Kaden cleared his throat and stepped forward. "Yes, she's under my protection, and I'll be by her side."

Wesley nodded. "Why don't you head out onto the back porch? I'll get your room sorted, and meet you there so we can talk."

"If it's a problem, we can camp outside," I said.

"No, it'll be fine." Wesley grinned. "Besides, the Ophiuchus alpha is our guest of honor. I can't let him sleep in a tent."

Kaden shrugged, and I knew he'd be fine with it, but as the new alpha, Wesley probably felt he had to provide suitable accommodations. I was just grateful my brother was treating Kaden with the respect he deserved as an alpha, instead of the hostility other packs had shown at the Convergence.

Kaden and I passed through the living room, and I saw some other Cancer shifters sitting on the couches playing video games or reading a book. They were all young, somewhere between ten and eighteen, and I realized their family members must have died at the Convergence. *Orphans, like me. Like Wesley.*

As we passed by, one of the females looked up from her book, her eyes wide. Then the other four stared at us too, as if they didn't know what to say. I couldn't tell if they were shocked to see me alive, or wondering who Kaden was, or if they were just being typical teenagers.

I led Kaden out onto the back porch, which was set right on the beach, with the waves only a few feet away. I stopped and breathed it in, then we took our seats on the old wooden furniture that had somehow survived years of weathering. With the waves lapping at the shore and the moon overhead, it was peaceful, and for the first time in hours, I let my body relax.

Wesley came out and brought us some crackers, salami, and cheese, along with a couple of beers. "Your old room should be ready in a few minutes, and then you can go rest. I'm sure it was a long journey getting here. But first, let's catch up a bit."

I leaned forward, with one burning question I needed the answer to before we discussed anything else. "I saw the Scorpios take you down. How did you survive?"

Wesley popped open a beer and stared at the waves. "I barely did. The Scorpios attacked me with their poison claws, and I used my crab armor to block what I could, but eventually I passed out. I probably should have died, but I woke up and managed to crawl out from the pile of dead shifters around me. A woman from the Virgo pack found me and healed me. There were almost no survivors, but somehow I made it."

"You were too stubborn to die," I said with a wry grin.

Wesley took a swig of his beer. "I could say the same thing about you. What happened?"

I took a deep breath and cast my mind back to that night, as I recounted it for him. How I ran from Jordan and found the Pisces pack, only to be left for dead again. How Kaden had taken me in, trained me, and made me one of them.

"Look," I said, pushing the sleeve of my shirt up so Wesley could see the pack mark.

Wesley's eyebrows darted up. "Wow. I always expected you to join another pack, but I have to admit, I never thought it'd be that one." To my surprise, he leaned forward and offered his hand to Kaden. "Thank you for helping my sister when I couldn't. I owe you a debt."

Kaden shook my brother's hand and bowed his head slightly. "She's made a fine Ophiuchus."

"I don't doubt that." Wesley's eyes flicked to me. "I am sad you won't be in our pack anymore, but I guess it's better than having you be a Leo."

"If not for Kaden, I would be one now," I said with a slight shudder. "Jordan decided he wanted me back and he held me captive for a while, but the Ophiuchus got me out. Then we decided to come here to see if any of the Cancer pack was still alive. Thank you for the photo, by the way."

"I left it there in the hopes you might still be alive and would find your way to us. But if you didn't know I was alive, why come back at all?"

"We came to offer our help in getting revenge on the Leos," Kaden told Wesley. "And in return…"

I shot Kaden a sharp look, knowing he was going to say he wanted the Cancers to submit to him, but that was before we knew Wesley had become the alpha. Surely he wouldn't suggest such a thing now?

Kaden paused, meeting my eyes with a frown, and then continued. "In return, I want the Ophiuchus pack accepted back into the Zodiac Wolves."

A rush of relief went through me, and I was pleased he'd changed his mind because of me.

"The Cancer pack is small now." Wesley sighed and he suddenly looked tired, and much older than his twenty-six years. "Nearly powerless. I don't know how much help we'll be. We don't have the numbers to stand up to the Leos. Hell, right now I'm just trying to keep us alive."

"It must have been difficult when you became alpha," I said, my voice softening as I imagined what Wesley must have gone through. While grieving the loss of our parents and me at the Convergence, and recovering from his own near death, he'd had to become a leader to what remained of the Cancer pack and make sure they were safe. My respect for my brother grew ten-fold, and it was no wonder he looked a lot older now.

"It was no picnic, that's for damn sure," Wesley admitted. "I'd always wanted to be alpha, just not like this."

"I went through the same thing," Kaden said. "I had to become alpha and keep my pack safe when my parents were killed by the Leos. It was before I was ready, but I managed to make do as best I could. If you're anything like Ayla, you'll be fine."

Wesley nodded at him. "Thanks. I'm trying my best."

I made a little sandwich of cheese, crackers, and salami as I considered my next words. "The attack on the Cancers was only the beginning. Jordan plans to take over all of the Zodiac Wolf packs. They have the Sun Witches on their side, and they're nearly unstoppable already."

Kaden finished his beer and set it down. "If you join forces with the Ophiuchus, we can fight the Leos together. You know they'll come after you again at some point. You can hide on this island all you like, but someday they'll find you."

"What are the other packs doing?" Wesley asked. "We haven't reached out to any of them yet, in case they were working with the Leos."

I handed Kaden another beer as I spoke. "Most of them seem to be watching and waiting at the moment, but if you join us, the other packs might as well. No one wants to be ruled by the Leos, or have their pack nearly wiped out like the Cancers."

Wesley stared out at the waves as he considered our

words. "Even before I was alpha, I swore I'd do things differently than Dad. Better. Yet here I am, planning a war with the Leos, just like he did for decades."

"This is different," I said. "They struck the first blow, and this is much bigger than a feud between two packs. This is about the fate of all the Zodiac Wolves."

"That's true." Wesley tapped his fingers on the side of his beer. "I want to keep my pack safe, but I fear you may be right. We won't ever be truly safe until the Leos are stopped."

"Then you'll join us?" Kaden asked.

"Yes, I'll form an alliance with you," Wesley said, his face grim.

I let out a breath. "Good. Mira is talking to the Pisces alpha too, so hopefully, we get his support. But we'll need more packs to join us."

"I can try contacting some of them, but it would be better if we spoke in person to their alphas," Wesley said. "Especially since I'm a new alpha, and you two..." He spread his hands and shrugged.

I nodded slowly as I considered this. The different packs lived all over the US and Canada—it would take time to visit them all. A phone call would be a lot easier, but Wesley was probably right that they might not listen to us that way, if they even took the call.

"We need to call another Convergence," Kaden said.

"Good idea," I said. "And this time the Sun Witches are not invited."

"That could work." Wesley sat up a little straighter.

"We'll invite only the Cancer allies and the neutral packs, although I don't know if anyone will listen to me, or if anyone will come. None of them helped us during the Convergence, after all."

I looked over at Kaden, determination sliding through my veins. This was the most progress we'd made in a long time, and if this went according to plan, we might have a fighting chance against the Leos for once. "We have to try."

CHAPTER TWENTY-ONE

WE WENT to my old room not long after that, once it became clear I could barely keep my eyes open any longer. I had so much more to discuss with Wesley, like the fact that Jordan was my brother, but that would have to wait.

My room was all white and sea green, and one of my favorite parts about it was that this room looked just like Wesley's, unlike the one in our other house. It was the same size and had the same old white furniture, passed down from my grandparents' time. I fell asleep the second my head hit the pillow, not even waiting for Kaden to crawl into bed with me.

In the morning, I woke to the sound of waves and felt more at peace than I had in a long time. Kaden was beside me, Wesley was alive, and I was safe. I squeezed my eyes shut, savoring this moment, fearing it couldn't possibly last.

I showered and dressed first, then headed downstairs while Kaden got ready. When I got there, Wesley was already in alpha mode. He paced back and forth across the kitchen floor as he fried eggs and bacon for breakfast. Whereas last night he'd been hesitant about going after the Leos, now he seemed eager to take them on.

"You said that Mira was talking to the Pisces alpha?" he asked, pausing to lean against the counter. "I'm glad she's all right. Her parents weren't so lucky, unfortunately."

I nodded around a swig of coffee. I'd always suspected Mira had a crush on Wesley, and I'd wondered if Wesley felt the same. Then again, my brother had always had taken full advantage of his mate-less status with all sorts of women. That was before the Convergence though. We'd all changed a lot since that night.

"She'll get back to me as soon as she has any news." I grabbed some plates from the cabinet. "What about the Virgo pack? You said one of them healed you."

Wesley began serving the food. "I can ask, though they're usually pretty hesitant to get involved in any conflict."

We sat down to eat, just as Kaden joined us, his hair wet from his shower. Wesley caught me checking him out and made fake gagging sounds. I rolled my eyes. Maybe things hadn't changed that much.

"I've been thinking," Kaden said, as he accepted his plate of food. "There's going to be a solar eclipse in about a little over a month—when the new moon blocks the sun's rays from Earth. That would be the perfect time for all of us to meet. The Sun Witches will be weaker then, or at least that's what I'd assume. I don't know much about the power of Sun Witches, but those of us with Moon Witch blood always get stronger then, so it stands to reason they would be weaker."

Wesley paused with his fork raised in the air. "So your pack *does* have Moon Witch blood?"

"Yes, some of us do." Kaden glanced at me pointedly, and I realized this was the time to tell Wesley about my powers. I'd left that part out last night since I wasn't sure how he would react. Most of the Zodiac Wolves saw the Moon Witches as the enemy, after all.

"Do you know anything about my mother?" I asked after taking a deep breath.

Wesley shook his head. "No, I never met her. Why?"

"She was a Moon Witch, not a human like Dad always said."

Wesley dropped his fork, his eyes going wide. "She...what? How do you know?"

"When I was at the Convergence, the only way I got away from Jordan was because I unlocked some sort of... power inside of me. I can teleport from patches of moonlight. Kaden suspected I had Moon Witch blood, and the Sun Witches confirmed it while I was in captivity. They performed some sort of spell on me."

Wesley stared at me like I'd grown a second head and I tensed, but then he cracked a grin. "That sounds pretty sweet. You'll have to show me later."

I relaxed immediately and mentally scolded myself for ever doubting my brother. He always loved and accepted me no matter what. "I will."

Wesley grabbed some more bacon and sat back down

again. "I'll go through Dad's files and see if there's anything on your mom. I've already started looking through them, trying to find anything to help me as alpha. I already found something in his email about you."

"How did you pull that off?" I asked, blinking in surprise.

"His password was really easy." Wesley snorted. "King Crab."

"How very like him," I said, rolling my eyes. "Really, it was almost like he *wanted* you to crack it. What did you find?"

"Correspondence between the Sun Witches and Dad. They were working together."

"What?" My brain ground to a halt at those words. No, that didn't make any sense. Why would the Sun Witches betray the Cancer pack at the Convergence if they were working with Dad?

Wesley's face turned grim. "There's no easy way to say this, but it looks like Dad paid the Sun Witches to use their magic to create a mate bond between you and Jordan."

I fell back against my chair, all the air escaping my lungs from the force of those words. Dad was responsible for all of this mess—and it confirmed that the Sun Witches could create fake mate bonds. Kaden took my hand, subtly letting me know *I'm here with you,* and I squeezed it tight. "Why would he do that?"

"I think he was trying to end the war with the Leos," Wesley said. "He wanted to create a connection with the

Leos, to bridge the gap between our two packs so we could stop fighting."

Another thought struck me, and I swallowed. "That, or he hated me so much he wanted to send me to live with our mortal enemies."

Wesley's uncomfortable silence let me know he'd thought of the possibility as well.

I stared at my food, this new revelation changing everything. Had Dad really wanted to end the conflict with the Leos? That alone surprised me, but he might have thought he'd kill two birds with one stone by sending me to them. Shit. No wonder the Sun Witches had acted so strange with me at the Convergence. I'd kept thinking they were giving me odd looks or staring at me more than anyone else and now it made sense. Then I suddenly remembered Evanora's words just before I'd been mated to Jordan. *The gods? Not even they can save you from what's coming.*

"That explains a lot," Kaden said. "About why you were mated to Jordan."

"What do you mean?" Wesley asked, frowning.

"Jordan is my half-brother," I said, gritting my teeth around the words. I hated speaking them out loud, but Wesley had a right to know, as well.

"You must be joking," Wesley said, looking between the two of us. His eyebrows shot up as we didn't answer. "You're not joking?"

"Trust me, it's the last thing I'd want to joke about." I took a long sip of coffee, but couldn't suppress the shudder that went through me.

"How?" Wesley asked, his voice incredulous.

"Our Dad is also his father," I said. "Jordan has the Cancer alpha's blood in him. That makes him *your* half-brother, as well."

Disgust and horror flickered over Wesley's face in quick succession. "I can't believe it. You're telling me that the Sun Witches mated you to your own brother?"

"Yes, although I don't think they knew he was my brother at the time." I cocked my head as I considered. They'd seemed pretty surprised when Debra had announced it at the altar, I realized. She must have kept the secret close to her chest all these years. Then a horrible thought struck me. "Oh god. Do you think Dad knew we were related?"

"I don't think so," Wesley said, shaking his head. "Dad was a monster in many ways, but he wouldn't have done that to you."

I nodded. Even that seemed a bit too cruel for our father. I didn't think he'd take it quite that far, just to torment me. "I wouldn't be surprised if the Leo alpha female never told him. And since they weren't mates, it never would have occurred to him that he could get her pregnant."

Wesley slid a hand over his face. "Damn, he really slept around a lot. What an asshole. I hope we don't have any other half-siblings running around out there."

A startled laugh burst out of me at the thought. "Oh god, let's hope not. Damn, I never thought I'd feel sorry for Jackie, but I do. Sort of."

Now it was Wesley's turn to laugh. "And I never

thought I'd hear you say anything positive about her." He bumped his shoulder against mine. "Hey, when all these brothers and sisters show up, just remember we were the original pair, all right?"

I bumped him back, grinning. "Don't worry, Jordan is not going to replace you as my favorite brother anytime soon."

We finished eating, and even though this new revelation was horrible in so many ways, it felt like a weight had been lifted off my chest. Now I knew for sure that the mate bond was a complete lie, an elaborate scheme created by my dear old Dad. *Even beyond the grave, he's fucking my life up,* I thought. Of course, he'd paid the price for it. Whatever he'd been trying to do obviously hadn't worked, since the Leos had rejected me and then used it as an excuse to kill everyone.

Once we were done eating, I went to wash the dishes, while Wesley began asking Kaden more questions about the Ophiuchus pack. I half-listened as they talked, and then Wesley went to make a few phone calls to the other packs' alphas.

When he was gone, Kaden grabbed me and dragged me into his lap. "Your brother is a good man. He will be a great alpha."

"He's the only thing that made living here bearable. Finding out he's alive is...everything." I leaned against Kaden and then had a new thought. "If the mate bond was a spell cast by the Sun Witches, do you think it can be broken with magic too?"

Kaden played with my hair, his eyes thoughtful. "I'm not sure. The only spells my parents taught me were basic things to protect the pack, like setting up wards. For complex magic, we'd probably need a real witch."

Damn. There was no way one of the Sun Witches would be willing to help us. That only left one option: the Moon Witches. But no shifter had seen them in decades, not even the Ophiuchus pack. I wanted to find them, but I didn't even know where to begin looking.

THE WAVES LAPPED against the shore, a strange sort of music to my ears. For so long, I hadn't thought of myself as part of the Cancer pack, and I'd tried to pretend that I didn't love the sound of the sea as much as the next shifter. But there was something about it, something that eased the constant tension in my shoulders and made everything seem a little less daunting.

It was late, and I'd crept out of the house to walk along the beach. There were too many things to think about, and I didn't want to keep Kaden awake with my pacing. I dug my bare toes into the sand as I continued walking, and tilted my head up to look at the stars. The moon had risen higher, and I found my gaze drawn to it, as usual. This time, I didn't feel the serenity and strength it usually gave me.

Where were the Moon Witches? I didn't have the faintest clue as to where I'd find them. Hell, I didn't even know where to begin looking. Had they gone into hiding?

Or had every bit of their existence been systematically wiped out by the Sun Witches, except for the small traces of their blood in the Ophiuchus pack? Was my mom still alive, or had she perished with the rest of the Moon Witches?

If Kaden hadn't appeared at the Convergence, I would have never believed that he—and the Ophiuchus pack—existed at all. Were the Moon Witches biding their time to make their comeback as well? Now seemed like the perfect time to do so—and we could certainly use their help. If they were keeping up with what was going on with the packs, hopefully they'd realize now would be the time to stand up to the Sun Witches. But so far, they hadn't made an appearance.

I shook my head and sighed. I was beginning to get frustrated with these insurmountable tasks we were having shoved onto our plates. *Oh, just locate the Moon Witches, and find a way to make all of the other packs ally with you, while trying not to get captured again by the Leos and Sun Witches. Easy peasy.*

A scuff of feet on the sand behind me sent me into an immediate defensive position. I half expected Brad to find me and try to beat me up again, just out of spite, but it wasn't him who stood behind me. I blinked, fists still clenched. "You scared me."

"You shouldn't wander off like that," Kaden said. "It isn't safe, especially when we have the Taurus pack hot on our tails."

I rolled my eyes. I liked that he wanted to keep me safe, but sometimes he could be a bit overbearing. "Ooh, the big bad alpha, looking out for me to make sure I don't get eaten up by the Cancer pack. Hold on, let me find a patch of sand soft enough to swoon onto."

Kaden's lips didn't so much as twitch. "You *do* need to be more careful. So many people want you hurt—or dead."

"Sorry," I said with a sigh. "I just had to clear my head. This is all so overwhelming."

"I get it. It's a lot to take in. Being lied to your entire life can't be an easy thing to swallow." He tilted his head back to stare up at the sky, and I remembered when we'd first kissed, on the roof of his house as he showed me the stars through his telescope. He'd pushed me away after that, believing we could never be together, but now we knew the mate bond was a lie.

"It is a lot, but it's easier with you here." I turned toward him and he opened his arms wide, drawing me into his embrace. I rested my head on his shoulder, breathing in his scent, feeling safe and content. I just had to ignore the niggling feeling in my gut that said this happiness could never last.

CHAPTER TWENTY-TWO

WE SPENT the next week living with Wesley and the orphan shifters. I got the sense Kaden was impatient to return to the Ophiuchus pack, but I hadn't seen my brother in months. The thought of leaving Wesley so soon after finding out he was still alive physically hurt. But we couldn't stay on this island forever, even if it was the perfect hideaway. We had our own path, and Wesley had to take care of the Cancer pack.

The days passed like something out of a dream. During the day, Kaden often played video games with the young shifters, while Wesley and I chatted on the porch. Wesley caught me up on all the pack news, including who had survived and who hadn't, and the improvements he planned to make to the pack already. He wanted to find a new beta but decided it was too much change all at once for the pack.

In return, I told him more about my time with the Ophiuchus pack and all the things I'd learned, and then told him about everything that happened when I was being held captive by the Leos. We discussed the Sun Witches, and how it seemed as though they were controlling much more of our lives than we'd believed.

Wesley also spent time reaching out to the other pack alphas, without much success. There weren't any immediate responses, but I had no doubt that Wesley would keep us updated if he found anything out. Mira was also silent, and I hoped that everything was going well with the Pisces pack.

A month didn't give us much time to try and convince multiple packs that going against the Leos was a good idea, but I hoped that it would be enough to at least get them to come and hear us out. I just wanted this to be done, impatient for the confrontation to happen already. I was sick of running and hiding and being scared. I wanted the Leos to be taken care of, so I could enjoy my time with Kaden and the Ophiuchus.

On our last night on the island, I was so mentally tired that I fell asleep the moment my head touched the pillow, one of Kaden's arms curled protectively around my side. When I opened my eyes the next morning, I was in the exact same position we'd fallen asleep in. I took a moment to look over Kaden's handsome face, my chest bursting with affection. He looked less broody when he was asleep, closer to his actual age, and I wished I had my camera to capture the moment forever.

Breakfast was silent, and when I went to pack up our stuff afterward, I found that tears were prickling at the back of my eyes. I managed to hold them back all the way back to our boat, but when Wesley enveloped me in a hug, I couldn't stop the tears from flowing. This felt too much like a true goodbye for me to think of it being anything else. At the Convergence, there hadn't been time for goodbyes, just the heart-pounding need to get away from the danger. I didn't want to leave Wesley, but I tried to reassure myself that we *would* see each other again this time.

"I'll see you at the solar eclipse," I said, with a sniff. "Stay safe and try not to almost die again."

"You too," Wesley said, giving me a sad grin. "I don't know why you're always such a magnet for danger, but I'm sure you can take care of yourself. And you have someone on your side who will help you now."

Kaden nodded as he shook hands with Wesley. "She'll be safe with me, I swear it."

"Good," Wesley said and stepped back. "I love you, Ayla."

My throat closed around the swell of emotion. I deposited my bag into the boat before going and giving Wesley one more hug. "I love you too," I managed to get out.

Then I swiped my hand across my cheeks and got in the boat. I needed to focus so we could get going. I pushed the emotions associated with Wesley into the little box I kept in the back of my mind. It had previously held my grief over his death, but now I didn't have time to deal with the fear of losing him again either. We had so much to do before I could even allow myself the luxury of worrying.

Once Kaden manned up enough to get in too, I started the boat. Wesley watched in silence from a little bit up the dock, and then we were off. I made sure everything was running smoothly before I turned around to face the island. Wesley raised a hand in farewell, and I echoed him. He became smaller and smaller until he was just a speck on the island, but I was sure he watched us until we were gone from view as well. I turned ahead and focused on steering us back to the mainland.

The boat ride was silent for the most part. I noticed that Kaden was less leery of the boat this time, and I couldn't help the small, wry smile at that. *I'll make a seafarer of you yet,* I thought. We docked, and Kaden went ahead to make sure the village was still empty while I turned the boat off and loaded our bags onto the dock.

"Anything?" I asked as Kaden slipped back onto the deck. He shook his head. Good. We seemed to have lost our Taurus tail, and I was more than happy about it. I didn't know how far Jordan was able to trace the mating bond, but I hoped I'd be able to escape it for a little longer.

"Ready?" Kaden asked as I hoisted myself onto the dock and picked my bag up. "I figure we can make it to another town by nightfall if we get started now."

"We are not walking all the way to the Ophiuchus pack." I started heading into the town, and Kaden followed me. "We can take one of my Dad's cars."

We trekked back up to my childhood home, but this time I only had to enter the garage, much to my relief. The SUV we'd taken to the Convergence was gone. Wesley had told me he'd left it at the Convergence partly because he was too injured to drive, and partly so the Leos would think he was dead. The only downside was that all of our stuff had been left behind there too.

Luckily, Dad owned a couple of other cars, including a dark red SUV that Jackie always drove, a beat-up white truck he used when he went fishing, and his newest purchase, the one that Jackie had yelled at him about repeatedly—a silver Aston Martin. Totally impractical for a rural area like this, but he'd always been a big fan of James Bond, and during his latest midlife crisis, he'd gotten it anyway. That was the car I headed for now.

I was surprised by the lack of guilt I felt at the thought of stealing one of his cars. He was dead, and besides, he owed me. A car was the least he could do in the wake of the personal hell he'd set up for me with the Leos. Not to mention all the years of abuse at his hands.

I grabbed the keys off the hook and tossed them to Kaden with a grin of triumph. "A present."

Kaden raised an eyebrow at me. "I hope Wesley won't miss this."

I shrugged. "I doubt he'll care, but we can make sure to get it back to him at the solar eclipse."

Kaden tossed our meager possessions in the trunk and climbed into the driver's seat. He turned the car on and waited for me to buckle my seat belt before pulling out of the driveway and out of the town. As we left, I stared out the window. The last time I'd seen this view was before the Convergence. I'd hoped then, as I did now, that I'd never have to see this place again unless it was to visit Wesley. It wasn't my home, even though it had been where I'd grown up, and relief flooded me as we got farther away. I'd been worried about being torn, but while I still loved Wesley, the Ophiuchus pack was my home now. *Kaden* was my home. Not that empty village filled with a thousand bad memories.

Once we left the pack lands and pulled onto the highway, Kaden floored it, showing us what the car could do. He'd said it would take three days of almost non-stop driving to reach where the Ophiuchus pack was hiding, but maybe it would be sooner if we kept up these speeds.

"Hey, so you know how this is technically my car?" I asked with a grin. "That means you should let me have a turn behind the wheel."

Kaden slanted a glance over at me that said, *bullshit.* "Hmm."

I raised my eyebrows at that non-answer. "Come on, what do you think I'm going to do? Drive us off a cliff? You've seen me drive. I'm not *that* bad."

He tapped on the steering wheel for a moment. "Fine. Once I start getting tired, you can drive."

I leaned over and kissed his cheek. "Wow, what a charmer. He's even going to let me *drive.* I'm honored."

"Let's just hope we don't run into any of your Leo friends along the way," he muttered.

"LEFT," Kaden said with a scowl. "I said, *left.*"

I gritted my teeth and backed up the car, then turned down the half-hidden road I'd just passed. We'd entered a densely packed forest a few hours back, and Kaden had directed me down all sorts of winding, dirt roads that looked like driveways, if that. This was certainly off the map, and I couldn't imagine a cluster of buildings big enough to house the Ophiuchus pack out this far.

We'd left the Cancer pack three days ago and driven to Manitoba, where the Ophiuchus pack lands were located. But instead of heading to Coronis, we'd continued farther north, the area getting more and more rural and remote with each hour. Now we were getting close, and I was pretty sure I'd never be able to find my way out of here on my own. Shit, it would be a miracle if our Aston Martin made it without getting stuck in the mud. We really should have taken the SUV.

"Happy?" I asked as we continued down the sad excuse for a road, the trees forming a tunnel over us. "I had no idea you'd be such an annoying backseat driver, though I guess I should have known."

Kaden shrugged. "You insisted on driving, even though I told you it would be tricky."

"Only because you looked like you were falling asleep at the wheel!"

"I was not." He sat up straighter. "Get ready to turn left again. Here!"

I quickly rounded the corner, determined not to miss it this time. When I did, the tunnel of trees gave way to a group of small, brightly lit cabins with smoke coming from the fireplaces, with a shimmering lake behind them. A much larger lodge stood in the center of them, like something you'd see at a fancy vacation resort.

"Oh," I said, as I stopped the car, taking it all in. "This is beautiful. The Ophiuchus pack is here?"

"Yes. Just like the Cancer pack, we have a place we can escape to in case of danger." He hopped out of the car, obviously eager to be back with his pack.

When I opened the car door, I took a moment to stop and breathe in the air. The cozy smell of wood smoke and forest immediately soothed me. Even better was the sight of familiar Ophiuchus pack members chatting with each other, along with a group of pups playing in a grassy area by the lake. The sun had just set, and the last of summer's warmth still hung in the air, and everything about this moment felt perfect. This was where I belonged.

The pack members spotted us and waved, some of them calling for Kaden, and he waved back but walked toward one of the cabins right by the lake. This one was larger than all the other cabins, and though it was a far cry from his house in Coronis, I could still tell this was the alpha's home.

The door to the cabin opened, and Stella poked her head out. "Kaden!" She bounded down the steps and threw herself into her brother's arms. "I'm so glad you're back," she said, and then drew back to grab me in a hug next. "Ayla! Oh, thank the goddess!"

I stepped forward to hug her. "I'm so happy to see you again."

"I'm so relieved you're both home safe." She ran a critical eye over my body as if checking for injury. I shook away her concern. All the wounds from the Leo pack were long gone at this point. The only mark I still had on my body was from where Kaden had bitten me, and I didn't want to explain that to her yet.

"Come inside," Stella said. "I have pasta already cooking, and you can tell me everything that happened over the last few weeks. I'm dying to hear about it all."

"We'll tell you everything, but first I want to know how *you're* doing," I said as we entered the cabin. It was rustic inside and looked like it hadn't been updated in at least ten years, but it was comfortable too.

"Oh, you know, it's been a lot of work," she said as she went to stir the pasta. Under the kitchen lights, I saw dark circles under her eyes, and she looked older, as if she'd lived a year in the few weeks it had been since my capture. "People were not happy to leave Coronis, not one bit. We've gotten a lot of protests, which I get, but it's not like we had any other choice." She shrugged. "But other than that, we're managing."

"That has to be rough." I reached toward Kaden unconsciously, putting my hand on his shoulder as I turned to him. "But now Kaden's back, and he can boss everyone around. You're too nice to do that."

Stella's eyes were caught on my hand on Kaden's shoulder, and how he wasn't shaking it off. *Shit.* She narrowed her eyes, gaze flicking between us. "Are you...?"

"Stella," Kaden said, but it wasn't a true warning. He still made no move to widen the space between us, so I supposed it was fine that she knew.

She let out a laugh and went to punch her brother in the arm. "I knew it! Took you long enough." Then she spotted the mark on my neck and her jaw dropped. "Oh shit. Is that what I think it is?"

I self-consciously adjusted my shirt as my cheeks grew warm. Even though the wound had healed days ago, a tiny mark would always be there, showing everyone that Kaden had claimed me. She punched her brother again, squealing.

Kaden shoved her off with a grumble, and Stella went back to her side of the counter, practically bouncing on the balls of her feet. "Say it. I want to watch Kaden die with embarrassment on the inside."

"We're together," I said, the words feeling strange on my lips.

Stella's grin was wicked as she watched Kaden shake his head and run a hand through his hair. "You know you'll have to tell me everything. I mean, not the gory details, because yuck, but I want to know what finally changed his mind."

"That's enough," Kaden said.

"You know, I was about to start placing bets on how long it would take you two to finally get together." She cackled as Kaden glared at her, but she ignored all his protests. "So who made the first move?"

I shook my head and opened my mouth to humor her, but another sound came from outside. It sounded like someone was walking up to the door, and before I could look back over at Kaden and Stella to see their reactions, the person hammered on the door so hard that it groaned.

Someone shouted, and it sounded a little further away, and then there was the sound of someone else on the porch. "Shit," Stella said. "I was hoping that this wouldn't happen."

Kaden stood up and put himself in front of me. I could see he was preparing himself for a fight, metaphorical hackles raised as he faced the door. I looked over at Stella, who looked grim. Kaden's free hand was clenched into a fist as he opened the door.

Tanner stood outside, and I let my guard down a little until I saw his face. He was angry and looked as ready for a fight as Kaden did. I blanched. What was going on?

"Tanner," Kaden said, cool as a cucumber. "I don't suppose you're here to welcome me home."

Tanner was big and muscular, and I'd always thought he looked like a surfer, with long blond hair—but now he'd cut it short, almost military-style, and it gave him a much harder edge. He filled the doorway, blocking the outside light fading into dusk, and I watched him take in the room. His eyes settled on me, and the anger in them flared.

"She needs to leave," Tanner said, raising a hand and pointing to me. "She doesn't belong here."

Shit, I thought. *Not this again.*

CHAPTER TWENTY-THREE

I STOOD UP, my fight or flight systems engaged, and I wasn't about to flee. This was my pack, and I wasn't about to be kicked out of it. I'd spent my whole life being an outcast, and I was sick of it.

"What the fuck, Tanner?" I asked. "I thought we were friends."

"That was before you brought the Leos." Tanner's lip curled, but he stepped back.

At first, I thought he was backing down, but as I looked over his shoulder, I realized he was letting us see the crowd gathering outside. Faces I'd grown to know and trust stared back at me. Some looked angry, others nervous, and a few looked confused.

"The pack doesn't want her here," Tanner said. "She's not one of us."

Suddenly, the presence of the crowd made startlingly clear sense. They were here for a confrontation with their alpha. With *me*. Flashbacks of being in the Cancer pack ran down my spine, and my throat tightened. I thought I'd escaped the shame of being the unwanted member of the pack, yet here we were again.

A deep growl issued from Kaden's throat. "She's a member of the Ophiuchus pack, just like you and me. Pack mark and everything. I assume your memory is good enough to remember that she passed the tests and accepted the mark." Tanner opened his mouth to speak, but Kaden raised his hand to stop him. "And beyond that, Ayla is my mate, and the pack's new alpha female."

A flurry of whispers went through the crowd as people looked amongst themselves as if trying to figure out what to do, or how to react to this news. I was just as shocked as everyone else hearing Kaden speak those words. I knew we were together and that he'd claimed me, but for him to announce it to the entire pack was beyond anything I'd ever expected. And calling me his alpha female? Oh shit. I was so not prepared for that.

"There's no mate bond between the two of you," another man said with a scowl. I recognized him as one of the men who rescued me. The one who'd thrown me in the back of the van. "She's still mated to the Leo alpha."

That brought up another flurry of whispers among the crowd. I spotted Harper and Jack out there, both of them looking worried, yet neither of them could do anything to stop this.

Kaden tilted his chin up as he addressed the crowd. "I've

marked Ayla as my female, and anyone who has a problem with her has a problem with me."

This time the unrest was a bit louder, and I saw some of the expressions change to horror. A few people shook their heads. I'd never seen so much blatant disrespect shown toward Kaden.

"Fine." Tanner drew himself up taller and glared at Kaden. "I didn't want to have to do this, but I see no other choice. I challenge you for alpha."

Many people gasped, and I watched another ripple of unease go through the entire crowd. Even the other pack members weren't expecting that. I wondered how long it had been since anyone had challenged Kaden for alpha. Dad had been challenged every few years, including by Mira's father, but he'd always won. And the loser? Always ended up dead, or their entire family shunned, as in Mira's case.

"You can't do that!" Stella cried out and stepped forward as if she was going to get between Kaden and Tanner.

Kaden held up a hand, and she stopped in her tracks. "No, it's all right," he said to her, his voice softening ever-so-slightly. When he turned back to Tanner, it hardened again. "Anyone can challenge the alpha. But I want to make sure you really want to do this. I've been challenged before, and I'm sure you remember. I. Don't. Lose."

Tanner paused, and I almost expected him to back down, but after a moment he jutted his chin forward. "A lot of us blame you for starting the war with the Leos. We were perfectly fine before this, living in hiding. We didn't need to get involved in Zodiac Wolves bullshit." He looked behind him, where some of the shifters were nodding in agreement. "Now, some of us are dead, including my brother. After we fought the Leos, we had to leave our homes and come here to live in fear." His eyes fell back on me. "Ayla is the reason why. She brought the Leos straight to us because she's mate bonded to one of them."

Guilt twisted my gut. He was right—about all of it. "I'm sorry. I never wanted to bring any harm to the pack. You're like my family."

Kaden raised his hand once more, and I lapsed into silence, but he kept his eyes on Tanner. "You seem to have forgotten that we were planning to go to war with all of the packs anyway. That's why we went to the Convergence, which I distinctly remember you being at. That's what we've been training for all these years."

Another ripple of unrest went through the pack, and I saw a few of the confused faces turn to shame. He was right, but it didn't stop the guilt from weighing down my stomach. They wouldn't have been found if not for me.

Kaden continued speaking. "We finally have a chance to make that happen. Ayla and I have been putting a plan into motion that could turn the tide for us. We can defeat our enemies and stop living as outcasts. We won't have to hide anymore."

Tanner didn't look swayed. A few of the others were wavering, but I could still feel the tension in the air. Some of them were looking for violence, and I didn't think Kaden's words would be enough.

"That doesn't matter," Tanner said. "We've been training for *your* personal vendetta against the Leos, that's all. You've become so blinded by your rage and hurt that you can't see that you're taking it out on the pack, and now we're suffering because of it. Now you're taking the Leo alpha's woman, and things will only get worse. Your parents would have never wanted this." He shook his head, his eyes full of scorn. "I'm going to be the new alpha and protect the pack. You can't, that much is clear."

Rage turned every angle in Kaden's body extra sharp as he stood still enough for me to wonder if he was even breathing. For several long moments, no one dared to move. Then Kaden gave a terse nod. "Fine, we'll fight tomorrow. Just after nightfall."

Tanner stared Kaden down for a few moments longer, neither of them backing down. Then, he turned away and melted into the crowd. Kaden looked out at his pack members, but none of them seemed to want to stand up and speak against the alpha. Soon enough, they were slipping away as well, and we were left, just the three of us on the porch.

"I can't believe you agreed to that," I said to Kaden, my stomach twisting with fear.

"Agreed," Stella said.

"What choice did I have?" Kaden asked, crossing his arms. "If he wants to challenge the alpha, that is his right."

"I'm going to go try to talk some sense into the pack members," Stella said, and the anger left her all at once, leaving that tired, drawn look that I'd seen earlier. "I knew some people were upset about the direction we were taking as a pack, but I didn't think it had gotten so bad. Most people understand that we couldn't live in hiding forever, and we just need to remind them that we are dying off too quickly to not rejoin the other packs. I just don't think they realized that doing so comes with defeating the Leos too."

"And the Sun Witches," I muttered. We still needed to catch Stella up on everything that we'd learned over the past few weeks.

"Eat some pasta and try to relax," Stella said. "I'll be back soon."

Then we were left alone. My earlier good mood from the thought of returning to my true family had dissipated in the wake of this new information. I had no idea that there were Ophiuchus pack members who opposed Kaden going to war with the Leos. I'd never gathered that before I'd left with Jordan. Everyone seemed to look up to Kaden, and every time he'd come up in conversation, they'd been singing his praises as an alpha. But maybe I just hadn't spent much time with that side of the pack.

"I'm worried," I said, before I turned around to face Kaden.

"I'm not," Kaden said, all cocky alpha energy.

I closed my eyes and wished that I had just an ounce of that surety. Before I could open them again, I felt Kaden shift closer. He wrapped me up in his arms, pressing the length of his body against my back.

"I won't lose," he said. "I never have before, and I don't

plan to when I fight tomorrow night either. Tanner might be big, but I've helped train him. I know his weak spots."

"Then he knows yours too." The worry didn't leave the pit of my stomach, mixing up with the guilt. I swallowed, trying to tamp it all down.

"I don't have any weak spots," Kaden said, and that made me roll my eyes. *Sure, other than an alpha's pride.*

Another thought was twisting my stomach in knots. "Did you mean it?"

"Hmm?" Kaden's arms tightened around me, and I tilted my head back so I could see his face.

"That I'm the new alpha female."

"Of course." He touched my neck, in the spot where the mark branded me. "What did you think this meant?"

"I didn't think it through, I guess." I bit my lip. "I'm not exactly alpha female material, after all."

Kaden kissed my forehead. "You are. I wouldn't have chosen you otherwise."

I shook my head. I was grateful for Kaden's belief in me, but all my life I'd been an outcast. Even once I joined the Ophiuchus pack I was the newbie, and now it seemed half the people in the pack hated me. Maybe more than half. How could I possibly lead them as their alpha?

Then again, if Tanner had his way, *he* would be alpha tomorrow, and I wouldn't have to worry about any of this. Unfortunately, for that to happen Kaden would have to lose. I'd likely be cast out, since it was clear they didn't want me here. Which meant in twenty-four hours, I could be pack-less again. Worse, Kaden could be dead.

He had better not lose.

———————

WHEN I WOKE the next morning, Kaden was already gone. In fact, the cabin was completely empty. He and Stella must be out there talking to pack members. As I poured myself some coffee, I wondered if I should go out there to do the same, or if my presence would only make things worse. If I was a true alpha female, I'd be out there among my people, or beside my alpha...but I wasn't. No one would respect me if I tried to act that way either. I was still too new, and I hadn't even been born into this pack. Why would they ever accept me as their alpha female?

They wouldn't. Especially right now, when they blamed me for what happened with the Leos. I understood their feelings because I felt the same way. Even now, I was putting them at risk by being here. Shit, maybe I should leave. Maybe that would make Kaden's life easier, along with everyone else in the pack. All I wanted was for them to be safe.

I was halfway ready to pack my bags when someone knocked on the door. I tensed, but then I made myself get up and open it. Clayton stood on the other side, and he wrapped me in a big bear hug when he saw me.

"Glad you're back." He let me go with a grim look on his face. "I heard what happened last night. I would have put a stop to it before this went so far, but I was hunting in the woods when it all went down."

I gestured for him to come inside, and then went to pour him some coffee. "It was definitely not the welcome we hoped for when we arrived."

Clayton accepted the coffee with a nod. "It's bullshit. Tanner has gone too far this time."

"I thought he and I were friends. Or at least, I didn't realize he hated me so much."

"He doesn't hate you. Or Kaden, for that matter. But he's always been skeptical of the plan to go up against the Leos. He thought we would be safer if we stayed hidden as a pack and didn't get involved with the other Zodiac Wolves. Then his older brother was killed when the Leos attacked Coronis, and he needed to find someone to blame. I'm sorry to say that with you gone, it was easy for him to point to you as the enemy. Especially since you left with the Leos. That didn't look good."

"I only did that to protect the pack," I said with a sigh.

"I know that, but Tanner didn't believe it, and many others felt the same. There has always been a small group of people who opposed Kaden's plan to try to rejoin the Zodiac Wolves, but after the Leo attack, that group has grown larger and more vocal. Especially with Tanner as their spokesman."

I sipped my coffee as I considered. "Would it be better if I left?"

"No," Clayton said, his voice adamant. "I know it seems like the entire pack is against you, but I promise, there are lots of us who support Kaden—and you. People are just scared right now. They lost their homes, and some of them lost family members too, and they're not sure what's going to happen next."

I slumped down on the couch. "Kaden and I have been trying to form alliances with some of the other packs. At this point, I fear there's no way we can stay out of the fight with the Leos and the Sun Witches. They want to take over all the other packs—including ours. If Tanner becomes alpha..." I swallowed hard at the implications.

"He won't," Clayton said.

Another knock sounded on my door, and when I got up to answer it, I found Harper outside, along with Jack and Dane. They had a box of donuts with them.

"We came here to show our support," Harper said, pushing her way inside without an invite. "We brought food too, cause we figured you were probably starving."

"Thank you," I said as I took the box, my eyes filling with grateful tears. I knew they'd been friends with Tanner, so it meant a lot that they'd chosen to come here and publicly show they were on our side.

Dane followed Harper inside, though he stopped to rest his hands on my shoulders and give me a firm nod. I wondered why he never spoke, but it didn't really matter—I accepted him as he was, just as he accepted me. I owed him a debt too since he'd shown the truth to Kaden about why I'd left with the Leos.

Jack rested a hand on my shoulder next and gave me one of his charming smiles. "Don't worry. This will all blow over soon. And even though Tanner is one of the pack's best warriors, no one is better than Kaden."

I blew out a long breath. "I hope you're right."

Everyone settled around the couch, and we all ate donuts and drank coffee, catching up on things that had happened over the last few weeks. Harper told me all about how they'd taken down the Leos stationed with the Pisces pack, and I told them about how we'd found the Cancer pack, along with my brother. Grant, Clayton's mate, showed up at some point and joined us too, eating the last of the donuts.

I glanced around the table at my friends, my heart warming despite my fear over what would happen tonight. Maybe I wasn't a total outcast in this pack after all—and my place here was worth fighting for.

CHAPTER TWENTY-FOUR

THE SUN FELL behind the mountains far too quickly. I knew we had to get this over with, but I wished I would have gotten a bit more time with Kaden before he had to go fight Tanner. When he'd come back from speaking with some of the pack members he seemed frustrated, and he'd asked for some time alone to gather his thoughts. To give him some space, I'd gone out to the lake and smiled at a few shifters there, but they all avoided me. No one wanted to even talk to me until they saw what happened tonight.

Now it was time, and together Kaden and I walked out of the cabin. Most of the pack was already gathered in a circle in front of the lodge, leaving room for Tanner and Kaden. I felt every single eye in the crowd on us as we walked over, and my heart raced faster. Tanner stood on one end of the crowd with a group of shifters gathered around him, while Clayton stood across from him with many other pack members at his side, including our friends. A pack divided—all because of me.

Nerves sparked along my skin as I watched Tanner's face, which was dead serious, like he was willing to take this to the bitter end. I'd seen my share of alpha challenges before, and I knew how brutal and bloody they could get. Kaden was an exceptional fighter, but I couldn't help but worry. All of the worst-case scenarios began playing in my head, an endless loop of Kaden's throat getting ripped out in new and horrifying ways. Each one was worse than the last, and it made me realize something.

Even without the mate bond, I loved Kaden. Everything that had brought my life meaning, the feeling of having a family, of being home, most of that came from him. More than that, Kaden believed in me when no one else had, and he gave me a chance to become a better person. I couldn't stand it if I lost him.

I looked at Kaden, finding it suddenly hard to swallow. He stared back at me, and heavy emotions flickered across his eyes too. The rest of the crowd seemed to fade away until it was just the two of us.

"Come here, little wolf," Kaden murmured, as he pulled me into his arms. He leaned down and kissed me, not as long or deep as I would have liked, but I closed my eyes and savored the press of his lips against mine.

"A kiss for luck," I said, as he drew back. "Maybe you'd better have one more, just to be sure."

"Good idea." He pulled me tighter and kissed me longer, making my cheeks flush.

I took his face in my hands. "Stay alive, or I'll kill you myself."

Kaden's smile turned cocky. "No need to worry. I have no plans of dying tonight."

He turned away to face Tanner, and stripped off his shirt in one smooth motion, making the tan muscles of his body ripple and flex. Tanner did the same and tossed his own shirt to the ground.

Clayton reached up and clasped Kaden on the shoulder, and the two of them shared a few words between beta to alpha. They spoke for several moments, heads bent toward each other to keep their conversation private among the crowd. With the hum of voices all around us, I couldn't make out what they were saying.

As they spoke, Stella walked up to me. She hadn't been back to the cabin all day, and she looked just as exhausted as she had last night. "I think I managed to talk some sense into them," she said wearily, running her fingers through her long, dark hair.

"I'm sure you did great. People listen to you." I took her hand and gave it a squeeze. For years, Stella had been playing the role of alpha female, even though she'd never asked for such a role.

"He'll be fine," Stella said as she watched Kaden, almost like she was convincing herself instead of me. "He's the best fighter we have."

"I've never seen him lose a fight," I added. "Back when we were looking for the Cancer pack, we took down several Taurus wolves. Most of them were his kills."

Stella nodded and clenched her jaw while Clayton, who was officiating the challenge, stepped forward and called for silence. It fell immediately, and it was startling how quickly things went from lively to quiet.

"State your intentions," Clayton said and stepped back.

Tanner moved to the center of the circle. "I challenge Kaden for the right to be the alpha of the Ophiuchus pack."

"I accept your challenge," Kaden said as he stepped into position, facing Tanner down. He sounded unbothered, and he stood with his hands loose at his sides.

Tanner, however, looked like he was on edge. His eyes darted around the clearing. The feeling of unease crept back up and my fingers tightened around Stella's.

"Do you both agree to fight without weapons until the death, or until one concedes?" Clayton asked, and both Tanner and Kaden gave their verbal consent.

"And none of your moon magic either," Tanner said.

Kaden bowed his head. "Fair enough."

Clayton nodded. "Begin."

At first, the two male shifters just circled each other, not daring to look away. Tanner was the one to throw the first punch, with a loud roar of defiance. Kaden sidestepped it calmly, and I realized Tanner was angry as hell. That alone would give Kaden an edge.

Kaden threw the next punch, but Tanner managed to side-step it as well, and I watched Kaden correct for the momentum. The next punch from Tanner connected with Kaden's side, and I sucked in a breath as Kaden turned away. His teeth were bared, and I knew that it had hurt. Kaden followed up with a series of brutal, quick punches.

He wasn't playing around any longer. I saw the shift go from wary to deadly serious. Tanner huffed out a breath as one of Kaden's hits connected, and then he followed up with another one, not letting Tanner recover.

Tanner stepped back, lips drawn back in a snarl of his own, and then he shifted into a large gray wolf. He lunged at Kaden and I flinched, but I'd forgotten Kaden could shift in the blink of an eye. His large black wolf appeared instantly, and he met Tanner, blow for blow.

They rolled around in the dirt, a flurry of teeth and claws and fur. The crowd was completely silent as they watched, as if all of us were holding our breaths, waiting to see what would happen next.

There was a yelp, and when the two males parted, Kaden's muzzle was bloody, and it was Tanner who was limping backward. The tang of blood hit the air, and I scrunched up my nose. It was almost too much, grating on my already over-exposed nerves.

The two shifters attacked each other again, and it was clear as time went on that Kaden had the upper hand. He was a better fighter, and their wolves were equal in size, but Kaden was faster. Kaden had Tanner pinned, and another yelp emanated from the two fighting shifters.

A sudden movement caught my attention out of the corner of my eye. A pretty brunette female broke free of the crowd, looking at the fight with obvious malice in her gaze.

She paced back and forth a few times along the edge of the circle, obviously agitated.

"That's Lindsey," Stella said quietly. "Tanner's mate."

Lindsey ripped off her dress and shifted into a brown wolf. She was smaller than the two wolves tussling on the ground, but it didn't matter. Kaden's back was to her, and she looked like she was getting ready to attack him. Her muscles bunched as she readied herself to leap, and I made a split-second decision.

Fuck no, I thought, and let go of Stella's hand. I wasn't going to let Tanner's mate mess this up, not when Kaden was fighting fair and square. As she lunged forward, fangs bared, I began shifting without even stripping out of my clothes. My white wolf body slammed into Lindsey's before I even had time to fully comprehend that I was completely shifted. I'd never done it so fast before, but then again, I'd never been fighting to protect my alpha before. My *mate.*

I pinned her down, but Lindsey twisted out of my hold before I could get a solid grip on her to keep her away from Kaden. She tried to continue on her way to attack Kaden, but I bit down on her tail and dragged her back. Lindsey snarled and turned her attention to me finally.

What the fuck are you doing? Kaden's voice in my head made me jump.

Protecting you, I sent back. The only thing I got in return was an impression of Kaden's complete distaste with that idea. He thought he was the one who was supposed to be protecting me, but he had his own hands full with Tanner. Lindsey had been the one to break the rules and try to join in, and I wasn't going to let her throw the match. And as she faced me with her ears raised and her fangs bared, a new sense settled over me.

I wasn't just fighting for Kaden. I was fighting to be the alpha female of this pack.

Just stay out of my way and don't get yourself killed, Kaden said.

No shit, I thought, and then threw myself back into fighting with Lindsey. I was larger than her, but she was slippery, like an eel. I could pin her down, but not long enough to get her to submit. She would always manage to find a way to break free of the holds I'd put her in.

Finally, I just flopped down on top of her. She couldn't escape me this way, and though it wasn't the most elegant way of pinning her, I had her in a vulnerable position. I didn't know what to do next, but Lindsey continued struggling.

Submit, Kaden told Tanner. He had Tanner pinned, his jaws around the other shifter's throat. Even though Tanner was moments away from death, he snarled at Kaden and snapped his jaws, back paws trying to catch purchase on his belly.

You'll have to kill me, Tanner growled back, and his voice sounded defiant, even though I heard the fear underneath it. He believed Kaden really would end it all, right here, right now. It was within Kaden's right, especially since Tanner wasn't conceding.

I'll kill you, and Ayla will kill your mate. Do you really want that? Kaden asked. He snapped his jaws at Tanner's throat in warning.

I looked down at Lindsey, who didn't look ready to die. She looked scared, eyes wide. She wasn't even fighting against me anymore. I didn't want to kill her. This was supposed to be my pack sister, someone I could rely on to have my back when things got tough. But she was challenging Kaden as alpha, and as such, she was challenging me. If it came down to it, I would sink my teeth into her neck and watch the light fade from her eyes.

Lindsey must have seen that reflected in my face because she began struggling again. Not to fight, this time, but to free herself. *Please,* she sent out, but it was directed at Tanner, not at me.

Tanner's eyes flicked over to Lindsey, and then he dropped his head. *I concede.*

Kaden immediately let go of Tanner, who leaped up out of biting distance. I let Lindsey wriggle out from under me a final time. Tanner waited for her to join him, and then the circle of Ophiuchus pack members parted to let them through. They ran into the woods without shifting back to human form.

"Kaden remains alpha," Clayton said, sounding relieved.

Kaden raised his dark head and let out a long howl that seeped right through my skin, into my bones, down all the way to my soul. On instinct, I lifted my snout and released my own howl, which joined in harmony with his, a song of both triumph and relief, along with a dash of sorrow. A few seconds later, other members of the pack, both human and wolf, began to howl with us too.

When the howls died down, Kaden shifted back to human form, and I did the same. We were both naked and covered in blood, but it didn't matter. A roar went up around the circle of Ophiuchus pack members. Most of them cheered, looking happy to see their alpha triumph. Stella was one of the loudest, jumping up and down.

Not everyone looked overjoyed to see Kaden win though. Some of them turned away and followed after Tanner and Lindsey. Clearly, Tanner hadn't been the only one who thought that Kaden was taking the Ophiuchus pack in the wrong direction.

Kaden looked around, surveying the remaining members of his pack. His eyes burned with fire, the kind that came from the victory he'd just won, and that same feeling poured into me. "Is there anyone else who wants to challenge me?"

The Ophiuchus pack grew silent, and I saw a few of the shifters look down, as if ashamed. No one stepped forward to challenge Kaden. I wouldn't have wanted to either. Every line of his body sang with the power he held, and just from standing next to him, I knew he was a force to be reckoned with.

Kaden spread his arms wide. "Everything I do is for you, for this pack, and I will always lead us as I see best. If you have an issue with what I'm doing, you're welcome to speak with me about your concerns. And as for Ayla..." He grabbed my hand, and a shock went through me at the contact. "She is my alpha female. She proved herself worthy of that tonight. Together, we will take down the Leos, rejoin the Zodiac Wolves, and lead our pack into the future."

I gazed across the gathered shifters, trying to steady my racing heart and trembling hands. One by one, they lowered their heads in a sign of submission. I was being accepted as alpha female. I could hardly believe it. I hadn't wanted the job and had never imagined I would ever have a shot at it, yet when the time came to fight for my place, I'd taken it. And I'd have done it a thousand times over, to keep Kaden safe.

I looked up at Kaden, the victory resounding in my blood. *This* was right. *This* was what I'd been looking for my entire life. I was Kaden's mate, and I was the alpha female of the Ophiuchus pack.

CHAPTER TWENTY-FIVE

KADEN and I left the crowd behind, our hearts still pounding, the battle still fresh in the air. Adrenaline raced through my veins, making me borderline jittery. I looked over at Kaden and opened my mouth to ask him *what do I do with this feeling?*

The resounding lust I saw echoed in his eyes made me realize what I was feeling wasn't entirely the aftermath of the fight. We'd battled together, won together, and we both felt the need to experience that victory together, to reaffirm to each other that we were still truly alive.

As I looked at Kaden's naked body, covered with sweat and blood, rippling with pure masculine alpha power, desire poured over me. It was so strong I very nearly staggered on the spot. I needed Kaden close to me now. I wanted as much of our skin touching as was humanly possible. My wolf had tasted blood, and now she demanded sex too.

I surged toward Kaden, and he let me come, reaching for

me as well. Our lips crashed together and Kaden gripped my
naked ass tight enough that it was almost painful. He kissed
me thoroughly, tongue demanding entrance. I gave it to him,
throwing myself into the kiss with just as much vigor. Our
wolves were still close to the surface, and we were barely
human as we came together like animals in heat, except
there was no full moon urging us on now.

Kaden kissed me like he wanted to devour me. I melded
my body against his and felt the hot throb of his cock against
my thigh, already primed and ready. I wanted to take him
inside of me, right here, right now. I didn't care who saw.
The overwhelming energy boiling inside of me now had an
outlet, and I'd be damned if anyone got in the way of that.

Kaden made a noise, half growl, half groan, and then
pushed me back. I blinked at the sudden distance between
us, trying to get my brain to move on from the pounding
need.

"Cabin," Kaden said, and he sounded just as reluctant as
I felt to follow his own order. When I opened my mouth, he
held up a hand. "There are pups around. We don't want to
traumatize them for life."

Right. That got me moving. It was only a few steps to the
cabin, and I felt Kaden's presence behind me with each one.
I wanted to say *fuck it,* and let him take me right there, but
before I knew it, we were inside.

Kaden slammed the door, and then pinned me against it
just as quickly, as if he couldn't even wait for us to be inside.
I let out a gasp as my back hit the rough wood. I wasn't going
to complain about it, not at all. Desire zinged through me as

Kaden crowded into my space, kissing me all over like he couldn't control himself.

"You were fucking brilliant," he said, and then licked a stripe up my neck.

"You were too." I arched my body against his, hands smoothing over his shoulders. I wanted to touch him everywhere I could manage. I wanted to *taste* him too.

I grabbed his arms and used my shifter strength to spin us around, so his back was to the door. Before he could take control again, I slid down his body to my knees, like I'd done back at the car when I'd healed him. Only this time, I was pretty sure he wouldn't stop me.

I took his cock in my hands, feeling the hard strength pulsing there. His eyes burned with possessive fire as he looked down at me. As his hands slid into my hair, I stroked my tongue along the underside of his cock, eliciting a loud groan from his lips. He tasted of salt and sin, and it only made me want more of him. I'd never done this before, but my primal instincts told me what to do, and I slid the head of his cock between my lips.

"Oh god," he said, throwing his head back against the door. "You have no idea how long I've wanted to fuck that sexy mouth of yours. Every time you talked back to me, I'd think of shutting you up with my cock."

Was that so? My eyes narrowed and I gave his balls a squeeze, hoping to make him yelp. It backfired though when he liked it, his cock thrusting into my mouth, and another moan escaping his lips.

"Keep that up and I'm going to be cumming into your throat soon," Kaden growled.

That's the point, I thought. I wanted to take him over the edge, to make him lose control, to see his face when he exploded for me. He'd never let me touch him like this before, in a way that seemed submissive at first, until I realized I had all the power. His alpha female, truly.

I sucked and licked his cock, and his hips began to move as if of their own accord. I loved the feel of them nudging against me as if he couldn't stop himself from plunging deeper, and I grabbed his very firm ass to encourage him. His hands tightened in my hair, and my name kept tumbling from his lips as he got his wish to fuck my mouth. And then in one glorious instant, he lost all control, yelling my name as his seed surged onto my tongue. I swallowed it up, greedy for everything he could give me, knowing I would always want more of him.

"Little wolf, you will be my undoing," Kaden said, as he yanked me to my feet. Then he grabbed my ass and picked me up, wrapping my legs around my waist, slamming me back against the door. "Now it's my turn to make you scream."

"So soon?" I teased. "Don't you need a minute to recover?"

"Don't insult me." He lined his cock up with my entrance, showing me how hard he was. "I'm an alpha and you're my woman. I could fuck you all night without stopping for a break. As you well know."

"Promises, promises..." I rutted against him, finding his cock and letting it slide along the folds of my pussy.

"Do you need another demonstration?"

His cock plunged into me fast and hard, making me cry out. His grip on my thighs was ironclad, and the slight edge of pain made the pleasure pooling in my core even sharper. Kaden paused as he bottomed out, breathing as hard as if he'd just stepped away from the fight. I wound my legs tighter around his hips, and my eyes rolled back in my head at the pressure of his cock deep inside of me.

"Are you just going to stand here all day or are you going to fuck me?" I asked.

Kaden growled in response, and one of his hands moved to my hair. He wound it around his fingers and yanked my head back. Stars danced in my vision, blackening the edges, and I ground my hips against him, wishing he would fuck me in earnest already. For a few heartbeats, he let me slide myself along his cock, and the friction was enough that it had me begging for more. Then Kaden bit into the curve of my neck, hard enough that I knew that it would bruise. Another mark to let everyone know that I was *his*.

Kaden laved his tongue along my neck, sucking and soothing the area. He drew himself out so that only the tip of his cock remained inside of me, and I nearly whimpered at the loss. Before I could complain more, Kaden drilled his cock back inside of me. The wooden door shuddered behind my back as he pounded into me, and my nails dug into his skin.

He slid me up and down on his cock, and the wooden

door behind us continued to bow and shudder. No doubt anyone who passed by would be able to figure out what was happening without any problem. Not that I cared at this point.

My orgasm crashed over me, hard and fast. I tightened my legs around Kaden, burying him deep inside of me as I shuddered and clenched. He grazed his teeth against my neck as I came, and waves of pleasure washed over me.

Kaden held himself completely still as I came, letting me bounce up and down on his cock to get myself off, but I could tell he wasn't done yet. He set me down, and the moment my feet touched the floor, Kaden spun me around.

Still trembling from my climax, I splayed my hands on the wooden door as Kaden kicked my feet apart. I pressed my cheek against the rough wood, while Kaden trailed one hand down my back and settled it just above my ass, where he pressed, hard. I moaned as he pushed his cock back inside of me, and set the pace once more. It was brutal and unforgiving, and when Kaden slid his other hand between my thighs, I nearly screamed in earnest. His fingers slid to my clit, parting my folds so he could swirl one finger around the tiny nub. Each brush of his fingers against my clit sent pleasure sparking through me. I closed my eyes, focusing on the rising pleasure that nipped at the heels of my last orgasm. It was almost too much, too good.

Then Kaden pulled us both to the floor, so I was sitting on his lap, facing away from him. He kept thrusting up into me with one hand on my clit, the other one pinching my nipple until I cried out from the mix of pleasure and pain.

Kaden's rhythm didn't stop, and the pleasure continued zinging through me as he picked up his tempo, drilling into me from behind.

He brought to me a second, knee-shaking orgasm, the pleasure crashing into me from the combined pleasure of his fingers working my clit and the drag of his cock on that spot inside of me that made my vision white out at the edges. I cried out Kaden's name as he brought me to that edge and sent me spiraling over it.

I clenched around Kaden hard, and his breathing turned ragged. He bucked like a wild animal as he came inside me, and I rode his cock, unable to stop myself from demanding more, more, more. I threw my head back and impaled myself on him, and it felt so good that I wasn't sure if I was still coming from the last orgasm, or if my body was giving a valiant effort to eke out one more.

When the pleasure faded, we were both breathing heavily, hearts pounding in tandem. I turned to face Kaden, and he wrapped his arms around me, staring at me in the darkness. At some point during our ravenous fucking, true night had fallen, and there were no lights on in the cabin. Not that it mattered to us.

Kaden cupped my chin in his hand. "You fought for me."

"Of course I did." The startlingly tender motion caught me off guard. "Good thing I was trained by the best."

He rumbled his approval, deep in his chest. Then his thumb slid down to touch the mark on my neck. "How does it feel to be the new alpha female?"

"Terrifying," I admitted.

He chuckled at that, his voice low. "I felt that way too at first. But you'll get through it, just like I did."

"Are you sure it should be me?" I asked, finally voicing the biggest fear inside me.

"I'm sure." He pressed a soft kiss to my lips. "There is no one else I would rather have at my side, ruling my pack with me."

I kissed him back, clinging to his strength, his surety. I had no idea how to be alpha female, and with tensions so high in the pack, I could tell it was going to be an uphill battle to get everyone to accept me—but I had to try. For Kaden. For my pack.

CHAPTER TWENTY-SIX

THE NEXT MORNING we called a meeting at the lodge and invited every pack member to attend. It was obvious that far too many people had doubts, concerns, or questions about what was going on, and things had only gotten worse while Kaden had been gone for a few weeks. That was partly my fault, and I told Kaden we should tell the pack everything. Yes, *everything*. Kaden was hesitant, mainly out of a need to protect my privacy since it involved airing out a lot of my family's dirty laundry. But I strongly felt that we had to be open and honest with our people, and also felt it should be me who did a lot of the talking. The pack needed to hear why I'd left with Jordan from my own mouth, along with everything I'd learned while in captivity, and afterward with my brother.

When I got to the part about Jordan being my half-brother, the pack's outrage and horror told me I'd made the right decision. The Ophiuchus were already skeptical of the

Sun Witches and how they used magic on the Zodiac
Wolves to control things like shifting and mate bonds, and
this sent them over the edge. By the time we got to the end
of our recap and explained our plans going forward, many
more of them were on our side than before.

There were still some pack members who didn't trust
me, or saw me as an outsider, or simply thought I was still
too new or too young, but that was to be expected. Kaden
said many had felt he was too young when he became alpha
too, and change wouldn't come overnight. I'd have to keep
working to build their trust and loyalty like he'd done. I'd
fought for my title and won, but the battle wasn't over yet.
That didn't bother me though. This was my pack, and I
wasn't going anywhere.

We spent the rest of the day and long into the night
meeting with people individually, listening to complaints
and concerns and trying to alleviate them. Though Kaden
had only been gone for a few weeks, it seemed like everyone
needed to talk to him about something urgently. I took the
time to try to memorize everything I could about each
person, committing their names to memory. Tanner and
Lindsey never showed up though, and I wondered how
many others had stayed back with them too.

By the time we returned to the cabin that night, my
brain was fried. Stella fed us something, and I passed out on
the couch not long after, in the middle of her telling us about
her day. I vaguely remembered Kaden carrying me to bed,
and that was it.

When I went down to breakfast the next morning, I

found Kaden already up and making me pancakes, with no shirt on. Yum. I got a nice view of his corded back muscles as he flipped them, and when I got close, he pulled me in for a scorchingly hot kiss that left my knees weak. He fed me a bite of pancake, and it was delicious and fluffy. The guy was hot, smart, powerful, *and* he could cook? I'd really hit the jackpot.

After breakfast, we headed outside to spend another day meeting with pack members. The morning was misty, the days growing cooler now that fall was approaching. A few of the leaves had even started to turn already. We passed Stella sitting with a group of pups by the lake, doing her best to continue her kindergarten class without an actual school. We spoke to others who were fishing, or chopping wood, or hanging out in front of the lodge. We knocked on the doors of people's cabins, seeing if there was anything we could help with. I had never realized that so much of being an alpha was just checking on your pack and seeing how they were doing or if there was anything we could fix, whether it was an argument between neighbors, or a broken toilet, or a kid who'd lost their toy in the woods. Then again, this was Kaden's way of being an alpha, and it was vastly different from how my father had led the Cancer pack.

When night fell, I thought we would head back to the alpha's cabin and relax, but instead, Kaden led me out into the woods. The moon was a perfect crescent overhead and millions of stars twinkled down at us. I shivered a little, wishing I'd brought a jacket.

"Tonight I want to teach you how to cast wards," Kaden

said, as he took me deeper into the dark forest, using his wolf senses to guide him. "As the alpha female, you should know how to do it, especially since you have Moon Witch blood too."

"I'd love to learn how," I said, hurrying to keep up with his long strides. "I don't know anything about magic."

"Don't get too excited. All I know are a few protection spells that my parents taught me, which have been passed down through the generations. It's nothing compared to what a full witch could do, but it's served us well over the years."

"I wish we had some way of finding the Moon Witches," I said with a sigh. The mate bond with Jordan was always there, buzzing inside of me like an annoying fly, although I'd gotten pretty good at ignoring it. Being far away from Jordan helped, as did being around Kaden. But it would never truly be gone until we found a witch to break the spell.

Kaden took my hand and helped me over a log. "On the way back from the solar eclipse meeting, we could stop in Coronis. I'll check and see if my Dad had anything about the Moon Witches that I might have missed before."

"Good idea," I said.

We reached some invisible barrier that only Kaden saw, and he stopped and breathed in the cool night air. "I cast the wards when we first arrived here," he explained. "They keep our location hidden from outsiders, both human and shifter, and prevent them from entering without our permission. The magic should block your mate bond too, preventing

Jordan from finding you as long as you're within these borders."

I nodded. That made sense—Coronis had been warded like this too, and it was only when I'd left the pack lands that the Leos and their allies had been able to track me down. Then the Sun Witches had destroyed Kaden's wards, allowing the enemy shifters to attack Coronis. "How long do the wards last?"

"It's best if I refresh them every few weeks."

I reached a hand out and felt the magic pulsing against my palm. It felt cool and soft, a gentle brush against my skin, very different from the magic of the Sun Witches.

"Watch me do the first one, and then we'll move to the next location and you can try," Kaden said. He raised his hands and his face up to the moon as if catching its light, drawing it inside himself. Then he began chanting a few words I didn't recognize, though they sounded similar to what the Sun Witches said during their spells. He thrust his hands out and moonlight burst out of them, forming a wall in front of us that stretched wide, then faded from sight almost instantly. The magic was still there though, stronger now than it was before.

"What were you chanting?" I asked.

"It's Ancient Greek. Or so I was told." He shrugged. "I don't know what any of it means, but it works, so I don't question it."

We moved alongside the invisible barrier, walking around trees and over fallen branches, taking care not to twist our ankles in the darkness. When we reached a part where the magical barrier began to weaken again, Kaden stopped. He taught me the words he was chanting, making me repeat them over and over until I got the pronunciation correct. Then I spread my arms wide and looked up at the moon, drawing its power inside of me like I did when I needed to teleport. That part was easy enough by now. I began chanting the words hesitantly, and Kaden nodded at me, signaling I was doing it correctly. Then once I hoped enough magic had built up inside me, I tried to send it out into the existing wards, as he'd done. Nothing happened.

I tried again, pushing my palms out and willing the magic to be released, but it just stayed inside me, like I was hitting a wall. I let out a frustrated noise and tried a third time, wondering why I couldn't get this to work.

"I can't do it," I said. "I can feel the magic, but can't access it somehow."

"Hmm..." Kaden cocked his head as he considered. "Maybe you're too stressed, too tired..."

"I don't think so. I feel like I'm blocked somehow." I blew out a long breath. "I don't get it. I can teleport, and when the Sun Witches cast that spell on me, I released some kind of light that knocked them back...so why can't I do this?"

"Let's try again at the next location," Kaden suggested.

We continued on, but no matter how many times I tried, I couldn't create my own wards. Kaden worked hard to teach me, but I only felt like a bigger failure every time he could do it and I couldn't. So much for being a powerful Moon Witch. The Sun Witches had called me dangerous, but they'd be laughing now if they saw how I couldn't cast even the most basic of spells.

WEEKS PASSED, and leaves began to fall from the trees, the air growing colder and colder as fall settled in all around us. The moon grew full, and Kaden and I led the pack on a hunt through the forest, where I helped take down a white-tailed deer for the first time. I still couldn't access my magic no matter how hard I tried, but among my fellow shifters, I felt more connected to my wolf side than ever before.

The solar eclipse crept ever closer, and I'd never wanted to dig my heels in to stop the passage of time more than I did now. Yet at the same time, I was excited to see my brother again. Wesley and I kept in touch almost every day, and we'd settled on a location for the meeting—a cabin in Oregon that had belonged to our father. I'd never been there, but Dad had taken Wesley a few times on father-son expeditions, leaving me at home with Jackie. Though I had no interest in visiting anywhere that reminded me of my parents, Wesley said it was a perfect location because it was outside any of the packs' territories, but easily accessible to all of them. I wasn't totally convinced, but I didn't have any other suggestions either. Now the trick was getting some of the other pack members to actually show up.

"Ayla, are you listening?" Wesley asked.

"Yes, I'm here." I shook myself out of my thoughts and began pacing along the shore of the lake while clutching the phone to my ear. I realized I'd let Wesley talk for a few minutes without soaking in a single word he'd said.

"As I was saying, the Leos have everyone cowering in fear," he continued. "You know I've been reaching out, but the other alphas are hesitant to even *talk* to me, let alone agree to a meeting."

"I know you're doing the best you can," I said, rubbing at my temple with one hand. "At least the Pisces alpha agreed to come. That's a start. Now that he's said yes, others will follow." *I hope*, I mentally added.

Mira had texted me yesterday with the news that the Pisces alpha had finally been convinced to come hear us out. I suspected she and her mate had been relentless in badgering him until he'd finally caved in, and I'd never been so thankful for such a persistent friend.

"I think the Libra alpha will come too," Wesley said. "He's definitely interested in hearing what we have to say."

"Good. Hopefully, more will show up too." I sighed as I gazed across the sparkling waters of the lake. "You'd think they'd all be more averse to being controlled by the Leos."

"Each pack believes it won't happen to them, or that if they keep out of the conflict, they'll be safe." Wesley sounded exhausted as he spoke. "We both know that's bullshit, but I can see how they might think that."

"I guess." I had a lot less faith in the other Zodiac Wolves after they'd abandoned our pack to die at the Convergence. We were supposed to be united, and yet at the first sign of blood, they'd all turn tail and fled. Now it was nearly impossible to get them to even speak with us. It almost made me want to say screw it and let them fall under the control of the Leos if they weren't willing to lift a hand to stop it. The only reason I didn't was that I knew that would come back around to hurt Wesley's pack, and Mira's, and eventually my pack as well. If the Leos and Sun Witches became too powerful, we were all doomed to fall.

We said our goodbyes and hung up, promising to speak again soon. I had the brief urge to throw the phone into the water, but I knew that it wouldn't accomplish anything. Instead, I gripped the phone tight and breathed through the feeling of hopelessness that ran through me.

A twig snapped behind me, and I spun, ready for a fight.

Kaden stepped out of the shadows. "Good form."

His words sent me back in time, to when he was more my enemy than my lover and had to teach me out of sheer necessity. So much had changed, and even with all the hardship, I wouldn't trade any of it for the world.

I launched myself at Kaden, who opened his arms to me. He'd been away on a trip to get supplies, and even though it had only been a few days, I'd found myself missing him terribly. I reached up and drew Kaden's face toward mine, tilting my head back so we could kiss.

I'd meant it to be something sweet, something brief, but the moment my lips touched his, I wanted *more*. Kaden seemed enthusiastic enough to deepen the kiss, hands sliding along my hips to bring me closer to him.

Then Kaden let out a grunt and drew back. "As much as I'd love to keep doing that, I have news."

I grimaced. "News?"

"Don't make that face, it's good news," he said. "I've located the Sagittarius pack. They were roaming close enough to our lands that I was able to catch the scent of them and follow them."

The Sagittarius pack were notorious nomads with no set pack lands and no place to truly call home. They liked it that way, and I'd heard that some shifters went to the Sagittarius pack if they felt like they wanted to live a truly free life. They were also the only pack that had been friendly with the Ophiuchus pack before the Convergence, though we hadn't been in contact with them since.

"That's great," I said. "What happened? Did you talk to them?" I looked over his body on impulse, trying to see if he'd been attacked. I didn't think the Sagittarius pack members would hurt him, but so many things had changed over the last few months. For all we knew, they'd gone and joined the Leos since then. Besides, I was just as protective of my man as he was of me.

"I talked to a few of them, yes," Kaden said, brushing away my concern. "They've agreed to a meeting tomorrow with their alphas. I'd like you to come with me."

"Of course. I'll do whatever I can to help." Hope filled the hole that frustration had hollowed in my stomach from my conversation with Wesley. This felt like the biggest break we'd had yet.

"I'm confident they'll be willing to listen. They aren't allied with the Leos, and we've always had a good relationship with them."

I nodded. "And if there was ever a pack that would fight to not be controlled by another one, it would be them."

"Exactly." Kaden reached for the bag on his shoulder. "I got you something while I was away."

My eyebrows darted up. "You did?"

"It's something I've wanted to get you for a long time, but I never had the opportunity until now." He handed me a box, messily wrapped as if he hadn't had time to properly do it. Or maybe he just sucked at wrapping gifts.

I didn't care though. I couldn't remember the last time I'd gotten a wrapped present at all. I tore the paper off with perhaps a little too much vigor, and then gasped when I opened the box. A new, professional camera was packed inside, its black edges gleaming proudly in the daylight. Happy tears immediately filled my eyes as I looked up at Kaden. "How...?"

"Jack and I managed to stop at an electronics store in Winnipeg during our trip." Kaden ran a hand through his hair. "Do you like it? I wasn't sure what to get, but the guy at the store said this was a good one. I know you lost yours at the Convergence, but I hope this one is a decent replacement."

"It's amazing." I traced the lens cover with one finger. This was the nicest camera I think I'd ever seen in person. I couldn't even imagine the possibilities of all the photos I could take with it. I wrapped my arms around Kaden's neck, careful not to crush the box between us. "Thank you. I love it so much, and it means the world that you got it for me."

Kaden brushed his knuckles down my cheek. "You've been working so hard these last few weeks. You deserve it."

We kissed again, and I squeezed him tight, amazed that he'd gone out of his way to get me a present like this. I remembered him listening in while Mira talked about how I'd lost my camera, but I'd never expected him to do something about it. My throat tightened with emotion as I realized it meant he trusted me too. I could take pictures of the entire camp, but he knew I would never do anything to betray the pack or our location to others.

"I'm so excited." I tore off all the packaging and pulled the camera out, inspecting every angle of it. "Now I can actually take photos again without relying on my shitty phone camera." I held the camera up and pretend to take a shot of Kaden. "Say 'cheese!'"

He scowled and held up a hand in protest. "I regret buying you this already."

I grinned and held the camera out of his reach. "Too late. It's mine now, and there's no taking it back."

"Just watch where you point that thing," Kaden grumbled. Back to his old grumpy self. Except I knew now that was all an act, designed to protect his big mushy heart.

I laughed and took his hand, then dragged him back to the cabin so I could show him just how grateful I was for his gift.

CHAPTER TWENTY-SEVEN

THE SAGITTARIUS PACK tended to roam the northern, more sparsely populated parts of Canada, and they were hard to track down sometimes. We were lucky they'd decided to stop only a few hours away from where we'd been living, and that Kaden had been able to find them and make contact.

We drove to their location the next day, but parked a short distance away and trekked the rest of the way, up a hill to where the pack had made camp in a large clearing. The first thing I saw were the many rows of tricked-out camper vans and RVs, followed by some tents that had been set up. Soft music filtered on the breeze, along with the smell of campfires and food cooking.

As we approached, two people suddenly appeared out of the bushes, their movements silent and graceful. Each one held a bow in their hands, cocked and ready to shoot. The Sagittarius were excellent archers, training in the skill from the time they were small children, and when they used their pack power—archer's sight—they never missed, no matter how far away their target was.

"State your purpose," the male said.

Kaden inclined his head slightly. "I am Kaden Shaw, alpha of the Ophiuchus pack, and this is my mate, Ayla Beros. We're here to speak with your alphas."

"You may pass," the female said before they both stepped aside.

We stepped into the camp, and I was impressed by how the Sagittarius had settled in with large tents set up in the center along with several fire pits burning. People sat on portable chairs just outside their RVs and drank beers, while kids danced and played around the tents. They looked so much at home, I understood why they never wanted to live any other way.

Two people walked toward us, both of them flashing warm smiles. They were both in their fifties or so, with dark hair and features that made me think they had some Inuit blood, as did many in their pack. A mixture of confidence and power radiated from them, marking them as the Sagittarius alphas.

The male reached out and shook Kaden's hand. "Welcome. It's good to see you again."

"Yes, it's been too long," Kaden said. "Thank you for meeting with us."

"Such a pleasure, Kaden." The female gave Kaden a friendly hug and then turned toward me. "So lovely to meet you. I was wondering if Kaden would ever find a mate."

I flushed at her words, but sensed a trace of humor in her voice and decided to go with it. "He just hadn't found a woman who could stand up to him until he met me."

Both alphas chuckled at that, and the female alpha clasped my hands in hers. "Oh, I like you already. My name is Mae, and this is Theo. Come, we have a meal waiting."

"Thank you," Kaden said, as we followed them through the maze of tents and campers. "We're pleased you happened to travel this way so we could meet with you."

"It wasn't an accident," Theo said. "There is change in the air and rumors on the wind of an upcoming meeting among alphas who have no interest in becoming subjects of the Leos. We decided to take a trip close to your pack lands, hoping you would venture out this way and shed some light on the matter."

"We'd be happy to do so," Kaden said.

This was already going better than I'd hoped. Warmth bubbled up inside of me as we made our way through the camp, and I enjoyed peering into some of the open campers, surprised at how nice they were, like mini luxury homes on wheels. A lot of the tents were pretty fabulous too, and I realized I'd been expecting something totally different when we arrived here. But it was clear the Sagittarius traveled in style.

The alphas led us to one of the large tents, which had twinkling lights at the entrance, and a long picnic table outside. Inside, the place took glamping to a whole new level with a whole living room set up, including a big-screen TV. A younger couple sat on the couch, holding hands, and I assumed they must be the betas. As they turned around to greet us, Kaden stopped dead in his tracks.

Tension rose thick in the air as the betas rose to their feet, staring at Kaden. The male was very handsome, with short dark hair and a strong jaw, and he grimaced as he looked at us. The female beside him was gorgeous, with long black hair hanging down her back, so straight it looked like she could cut things with it. The female blinked, as if she couldn't quite believe what she was seeing, and then stepped forward almost as if she couldn't help herself. The male grabbed her arm as if to hold her back. I glanced between everyone, wondering what was going on.

"Oh..." Mae said, looking between the female beta and Kaden, a frown pulling her eyebrows down. "I'm so sorry, I forgot."

"Is there a problem?" I asked.

"No, no problem," Kaden responded, but there was still a thread of tension in his voice as he stared at the betas.

The female smiled at Kaden, and there was *something* in that smile, something I was still missing, along with a hint of sadness in her eyes. "How have you been, Kaden? It's been so long."

The male growled, low enough that it was just a rumble. He put his arm around the female beta possessively, and she looked back at him as if she'd just surfaced from a dream.

Kaden stared levelly at the male, not breaking eye contact. A muscle twitched in his jaw from where he clenched it. "I'm fine," he said, in polite, clipped tones. "How are you, Eileen?"

Eileen. The name sparked something in my memory, and everything slotted into place. The tension between Kaden and this female, the way the beta was acting possessive for no particular reason—Eileen was Kaden's ex. His childhood love, the one that Kaden had thought would become his alpha female when he took over for his parents. Then they'd gone to the Sagittarius pack to trade, probably during a meeting a lot like this one, and the mate bond had been activated between her and the beta. She'd left the Ophiuchus pack for good after that.

"I'm well, thank you." Eileen looked over at her mate. "I think you remember Devin."

"Of course," Kaden said.

Everyone was being overly polite, but each word was strained. The moment was so awkward and uncomfortable, I wanted to walk away from it. Except as I watched Kaden stare at Eileen, another emotion, dark and new, sprang up. I'd never felt it so deeply before, it took me a minute to figure out what it was.

Jealousy. And a huge side dish of possessiveness too. I wanted to bite Kaden, to show Eileen that he was *mine,* but would Kaden accept that? Did he still have feelings for Eileen? This was the woman who had broken his heart, and if she hadn't found a new mate, they would probably still be together right now.

Kaden rested his hand on my arm, calming my beast slightly. "This is my alpha female, Ayla."

Eileen's eyes widened as she took me in. "Maybe we should leave."

"Yes, maybe you should," I snapped. *Down girl*, I told my wolf, who was ready to come out, fangs blazing, and fight for her man.

Eileen tugged at Devin's arm, and then they walked away from the tent. Kaden watched them go for far too long, and I clenched my jaw and looked away from him.

"I'm sorry about that," Theo said. "I forgot about your...situation. I wouldn't have invited them otherwise."

"It's fine," Kaden said.

"Please sit." Mae gestured at the couch, obviously eager to move on quickly from the awkward moment. "Would you like some wine?"

"That would be nice, thank you," I replied, with a forced smile.

As we sat, the tension faded out from Kaden's body, and he looked like he always did. My Kaden, who was trying to win over the packs so that we could stop the Leos. If not for the anxiety fluttering in my gut, I would have thought that what I'd seen was just a trick of the light.

The alphas were eager to please after that, and we sat and drank wine, making small talk for a few minutes. They were surprisingly funny and launched into story after story that had even Kaden chuckling, and soon we forgot about the uncomfortable moment.

Then we moved to the picnic table, where a young woman, who I thought might be their daughter, served us some kind of deer stew with some thick, flaky bread. It tasted much better than I expected, based on how it looked, and the warmth seeped into my bones. While we ate, we got down to business, telling the Sagittarius alphas our long tale about the Leos and the Sun Witches.

The two alphas looked shocked, but somehow not surprised by everything we told them. "Dixon came to bully us after the Convergence," Theo admitted. "We sent him packing, along with the rest of the Leos, telling him we had no interest in an alliance. We've managed to remain neutral, even amongst all of the fighting over the years. We're sympathetic to your cause, but we have no intention of taking sides in this battle now."

"You won't be able to be neutral forever," Kaden said. "The Leos don't want alliances anymore—they want subjects. I can't imagine a pack that values freedom so much would ever be okay with that."

"Should it come to that, we would fight to the death to maintain our way of life," Mae said. "But I find it hard to believe such a thing would come about."

"Believe it," I said. "The Cancers never thought the Leos would almost wipe out their entire pack in one night either, yet here we are. Which pack will be next?"

"It is a shame about your former pack," Mae said, then glanced at her husband. They shared a look, communicating in the way that only long-time married couples could.

"Please, just come to the meeting," I said. "That's all we ask."

Theo met Mae's eyes again and then nodded. "All right, we will come to this meeting. I can't promise anything, but we will listen at least."

"Thank you," Kaden said and bowed his head.

I let out a long breath, my shoulders relaxing as relief rushed through me. It was a small step, but at least it was in the right direction. With Wesley working on some of the other packs, we might have a decent showing at our meeting after all.

"You must be weary," the female alpha said, as she stood. "I'll show you to your tent."

It was a clear dismissal. They probably wanted to talk more about the matter, which was reasonable. Besides, it had grown late with all the wine and storytelling. Mae led us across the camp to an empty tent, which was small and cozy, perfect for two people. A bed had been made on the ground inside, with plenty of blankets to combat the chill in the air.

"That went well, I think," I said once we were alone.

Kaden grunted. "As well as can be expected, I guess. The Sagittarius value independence above all, and I think once they see that the Leos want to take that away from them, they'll come on board."

We undressed and got in the bed, but we didn't curl up together, and some of the unease from earlier crept back in. *Maybe he's just tired,* I told myself. *Or maybe he's thinking about his ex,* that annoying voice inside my head said back.

"Are you okay after seeing Eileen?" I asked.

"I'm fine." He shifted around so he was propped up on his elbow, looking at me in the dark. "We were over years ago. I don't feel anything for her anymore. It just..." He paused. "It surprised me to see her, that's all."

"You and me both," I said with a stilted laugh.

Kaden slid his fingers into my hair, pulling me against

him. "Oh, little wolf, are you jealous?" He pressed his lips to my neck. "I promise you, the only female I want to share my bed with is you. Or my heart, for that matter."

"Good," I said, wrapping my arms around his neck. "It would probably strain our relations with the Sagittarius pack if I tore out their beta female's throat."

He chuckled at that and settled me against his chest. "So fierce. No wonder you're my alpha female."

As he held me close and kissed me, I found myself believing that he didn't have feelings for Eileen anymore. Not in that sense anyway. He didn't want to be with her, that was clear, but it was also obvious that she'd wounded Kaden greatly, and that wound hadn't entirely healed. She'd been the entire reason Kaden hadn't wanted to be with me, after all. He'd worried I would go with my mate, unable to resist the bond, like Eileen had. It was only once Kaden learned that my mate was my brother that he was willing to fully give in to being with me.

Kaden fell asleep quickly, but I was too restless. I slipped out of the tent to find somewhere to pee, unsure if I should go in the bushes or what. I didn't see any portable toilets nearby, so I slipped into the bushes to do my business, moving away from the rest of the camp as much as I could.

When I returned, I spotted someone sitting on a log in the forest by herself and paused. Eileen.

"I won't bite," she called out to me.

"Yeah, but I might," I said, as I approached.

She took me in, and I did the same to her. With the men gone, she was more relaxed now, although I also smelled wine on her breath too, which probably helped. Not that we could get drunk as shifters, but sometimes the idea of alcohol was enough to calm the nerves.

"I noticed the mark on your neck." She sounded sad as she spoke, not hostile. "And I heard Kaden made you his alpha female."

"Yes, he did," I said, feeling defensive despite her calm tone. "What of it?"

"He tried to do the same to me, you know." She stared down at her hands in her lap. "We were in love like you are now, and we didn't care that we didn't have a mate bond tying us together. We thought we would be together forever. I spent my entire life believing I would lead my pack with him." She sucked in a ragged breath. "And then the mate bond appeared with Devin, and everything changed."

I stood still, listening to her side of the story, unable to tear myself away. "You couldn't fight it."

"No. I tried at first, but it was no use. I didn't want to leave Kaden or my pack, but I had to. Trust me that it broke my heart to leave, just as much as it broke Kaden's." She sighed. "And now Kaden is in the same position I was in."

My hackles rose. "What are you talking about?"

She looked at me with dark, haunted eyes. "What happens when Kaden finds his true mate?"

I opened and closed my mouth, her words sucking all the air from my lungs. I'd been so focused on breaking the mate bond with Jordan that I'd just assumed that when it happened, Kaden and I would be mates. But what if we weren't? What if we met with other packs, and Kaden found his true alpha female among one of them? What if this was all a temporary fling, a dream that we'd one day wake up from?

Eileen stood up and moved close, resting her hand on my shoulder. Her eyes were kind, sympathetic, but also wary. "I just don't want Kaden to get hurt again."

"That's the last thing I want too," I said, my voice trembling slightly.

She nodded and released me. "There's no easy solution to this problem, and no answer clearly written in the stars, so all I will say is...be careful with your heart. And Kaden's."

She slipped off through the trees like some kind of midnight sprite before I could form a good reply. I looked up at the waning moon, begging the goddess Selene for a sign that Kaden and I were meant to be together, but she was silent. Eventually, I gave up and went back to my tent, where I wrapped my arms around Kaden, terrified to ever let him go.

CHAPTER TWENTY-EIGHT

WE RETURNED to the Ophiuchus camp and counted down the days until the solar eclipse. More packs had finally responded to Wesley and said they might attend, giving us a small glimmer of hope, and I couldn't wait to see my brother again.

We spent the first official day of fall preparing to leave the next morning for Oregon, another long drive that would take days. Jack had already yelled that he was going to drive the Aston Martin the entire way until Harper reminded him he'd have to trade off and graciously volunteered herself for a turn. After a hard look from her brother, she grudgingly added Dane to the list of drivers too.

Flying would be faster, but it carried a higher risk of the Leos finding out what we were doing, especially since we had to cross the border into the US. Kaden had a plan though—he and a few others had passports for the border crossing, and the rest of us would pretend to be dogs. Who would believe someone would drive around with wolves in their backseat?

As the sun set and dusk crept across the sky, I set out looking for Kaden, since I hadn't seen him in a few hours. I had no mate bond to guide me to him, but I raised my nose and followed my senses until I found him in the forest, chopping wood. With nothing on but a ripped pair of jeans. *Yes, please.*

I leaned against a tree and pulled my camera out to capture the way the muscles in Kaden's chest moved as he brought the axe down on the piece of wood. Not to mention those strong arms, which were almost as thick as the wood he was cutting, and his big hands, which handled the axe like it weighed nothing. His masculine power made me all hot and bothered, and I wanted to tear off those jeans and climb him like a tree. Who knew I was so into sexy lumberjacks?

"Are you going to stare at me all day or did you have something to say, little wolf?" Kaden asked, before bringing down the axe again on another piece of wood.

I snapped another photo. "You need to come pack for tomorrow. Someone else can do this."

"I want to make sure the pack has enough wood while we're gone. It's getting colder and I think it might rain soon."

I sighed, but it was just like Kaden to decide he had to do this right now, and no one else. Other alphas would have delegated the task, but not Kaden, no. At least it gave me a nice view.

He finished up the next piece of wood and then

stopped, turning toward me and spotting the camera. "What are you doing with that?"

"Documenting this moment." I clutched the camera to my chest. "I bet I could sell these for big money."

He rolled his eyes, set the axe down, and wiped the sweat off his forehead. "All right, I'm done."

"Too bad. I was enjoying the show."

"I can give you something better." He walked over and caught me around the waist and pulled me against him. I stiffened a little, unable to forget what Eileen had said the other day.

Kaden noticed and searched my eyes with a frown. "You've been distant ever since we returned from visiting the Sagittarius pack. Is something wrong?"

"I'm just stressed about the solar eclipse," I said, looking down.

"Hmm, I think there's more to it than that." He tilted my chin up so I had to look at him. "Spit it out, or I'll pin you down and drag it out of you."

I cracked a wry grin. "Is that supposed to be a threat?"

"Ayla..." His voice held a warning in it. "Tell me."

"Fine, it was something Eileen said the other night."

Kaden tensed, his next words a growl. "She spoke to you? What did she say?"

"Nothing bad. Not in the way you're thinking, anyway." I packed my camera in its bag, mostly to avoid looking at Kaden as I got the next words out. "She made me wonder what would happen if you ever found your real mate. Like she did when you were together."

"I see." He took my hand in his and began leading me forward. "Come. Walk with me."

As the sky darkened, he guided me through the forest, until we reached a part of the lake I hadn't visited before, nestled between thick trees. He moved to stand on the edge of the water and turned toward me.

"Do you remember when we first met at the waterfall?" Kaden asked.

"Of course. Your wolf almost tore my throat out."

"That's probably how it seemed to you, but the truth was my wolf lunged at you because he wanted to claim you right there. I didn't know what it meant at the time." His mouth twisted in a sardonic grin. "I thought I'd just gone too long without getting laid and my wolf was punishing me for it. But then I went to the Convergence and felt drawn to you there too. Enough so, that I stayed invisible to watch what happened after we left. That's when I realized what I felt had to be the mate bond—it just couldn't be completed because you didn't have your wolf yet."

My heart stuttered in my chest, and suddenly it became hard to breathe. "You knew back then?"

He rested his hands on my shoulders. "Yes and no. There was no doubt in my mind, at least until the mating ritual, when you were bound to Jordan. When I saw that, I assumed I must have been wrong, because how could you be mated to someone else when you were *mine?*"

"But now we know the mate bond is fake," I whispered, staring up at Kaden with wide, hopeful eyes.

"Exactly. Once I learned that I became certain that what

I'd felt back at the Convergence was real. I'm sure that after we remove the false bond with Jordan, our true mate bond will emerge."

"How can you be sure?" I wanted to believe Kaden was my true mate, but it was terrifying to put so much faith in something that might be setting me up for heartbreak.

"I've known it since the moment we first met. I tried to resist, tried to tell myself it couldn't be real, but eventually I had to face the truth. You are my mate." He took my hand and pressed it over his heart. "I think you know it too."

I nodded slowly, letting the certainty fill me. I'd felt something when we first met too, and every moment since, but for so long it had been a constant struggle between my feelings for Kaden and the mate bond's pull toward Jordan. I'd never been able to fully trust what I felt for Kaden because in the background Jordan was always there. Knowing he was my brother, and that the mate bond was all a lie, removed that barrier to some degree. I couldn't wait 'til I was completely free of the mate bond and could be with Kaden fully, without hesitation or fear of the future.

Kaden looked down at me, and in his eyes, I saw red hot possessive desire. I was helpless to resist as his hands slid up my waist. It had been days since he'd touched me like this, and I craved it like I craved food or water. As he lowered his head to claim my mouth, I softened against him instantly, melding my body to his. I'd never had something feel quite so right in my life. *Mate, mate, mate,* my soul hummed, growing louder than the mate bond for once, and I finally decided to listen to it.

Kaden's hand found my hair and wove the strands through his fingers. I moaned at the slight pressure and reached up to press my hands against his naked chest. His skin was hot beneath my fingertips despite the cool night air around us, and I pressed myself closer against him. He was already hard, the hot line of his cock nudging against my hip, and I ground against him a little. Tiny shocks of pleasure went through my body at the promise of what was going to happen next.

Kaden broke away with a growl and took the hem of my shirt in his hands. I lifted my arms obediently, letting him strip me, and then shucked my own jeans off. Once I was naked, Kaden's eyes skimmed over my body. I didn't think I'd ever get used to the way he looked at me, like he couldn't get enough, and never would.

"Off," I said, pushing at his jeans.

Kaden arched an eyebrow. "A little demanding tonight, aren't we?"

"It's your fault for doing that sexy lumberjack routine."

Kaden chuckled low in his throat and dropped his jeans, springing his cock free. I watched, each inch of bared skin taking my breath away. He was so beautiful, each line of his body perfectly sculpted as if by the moon goddess herself. The starlight reflected off his skin, and I wanted to reach out and trace the areas where light faded into shadow and map out every inch of his body to my touch.

"If you keep looking at me like that, I might not be able to hold myself back," he said.

He tilted my chin up and leaned down to kiss me once

more, and I wrapped my arms around his neck, needing to touch him to make sure he really was here, out on this lake with me. Kaden growled into my mouth as he wrapped his arms around my waist and tipped me over, lowering us both to the ground. The jolt of my back hitting the grass was enough to displace Kaden's lips from mine, but when I went to kiss him again, he pushed me back down with a firm hand.

I spread my legs, letting him settle in between them, pressing close enough that I felt the heat of his cock against my inner thighs. He looked down at me, the hunger in his eyes echoing the deep, pulsing thrum that had started up in my core.

The hand that had pushed me down traced along the front of my body, moving across my breasts, making my nipples hard. Each finger left a trail of fire in its wake, as he moved down, down, down.

"You're so responsive," he murmured, fingers just inches from where I actually wanted them.

I shifted my hips, trying to chase that feeling, to get him to touch me where I needed him.

Kaden's eyes flicked up to mine, a mischievous glint present even in the stark light. "Tell me what you need."

"Fuck me, Kaden." He was so close, so willing to give, and yet here he was, teasing me.

"I like it when you ask nicely," Kaden said. "You have such a mouth on you, it's hard to remember you can be reduced to this as well."

His fingers slipped inside of me, making me gasp. I was

so wet that there wasn't the slightest bit of resistance. My hips bucked, trying to get more friction, and he pushed me down with his other hand, holding me in place as he slowly pistoned his fingers in and out in a steady rhythm. I moaned as pleasure began flickering inside of me, but I wanted *more,* I wanted everything Kaden had to offer.

Kaden lowered his head between my thighs and slid his tongue along my clit, and the sudden burst of pleasure made my hips buck up to meet his mouth. He began fucking me with his fingers in earnest, while he sucked on my clit, and I shuddered at the feelings rushing through me. I wanted him inside of me, but I wasn't going to object to this. He was incredibly talented with his hands and tongue, that much I knew already. The pleasure built steadily, an ache that bloomed out in a wave of heat throughout my whole body. Kaden hummed against my clit in approval as he continued fucking me with his fingers. He *enjoyed* pleasuring me, and that made it so much hotter.

The pressure built, and the closer I got, the more he upped the pace. I was almost screaming by the time my release came, my fingers digging so hard in Kaden's biceps I had no doubt I was breaking the skin. He didn't stop, fingers working me through my orgasm, tongue stroking my clit, bringing wave upon wave of pleasure.

Then Kaden lifted himself up, while my body still trembled from what he'd just done to me. "Now I think you're ready for me to fuck you."

"Yes, please." Even though I'd just come, my pussy clenched from the anticipation.

Kaden kneeled above me like a dark god, stroking his cock slowly, while he looked down at me like I belonged to him, and no one else. "I'm going to claim you right here, under the stars and the moon for all the gods to see," he said, his voice edging into a growl. "You're mine, now and forever."

Mine. I shivered at the word as it wrapped around my heart.

Kaden lowered himself to me, and with one smooth stroke, he filled me completely. His hands grabbed my wrists and yanked them up, holding me down as he began to thrust into me. I couldn't move at all, completely at his mercy as he pinned me down and claimed me, over and over.

"I'm yours," I whispered. "Any way you want me."

Kaden growled, and on the next downstroke, his mouth found mine and he plunged his tongue between my lips. I could *feel* Kaden's possessiveness with his kiss and with the way his cock pulsed inside me.

He pulled back suddenly and lifted my legs up over his shoulders, changing the angle so he hit me even deeper. I gasped as he entered me again, feeling impossibly stretched and full.

"Mine," he growled as he pounded into me, pushing me into the dirt. "Say it. Say it again."

"I'm yours," I cried out. I tried to say more, to give voice to the feeling that was swelling up inside of me alongside the pleasure, but all I could do was repeat the word over and over again, the pressure growing at an almost dizzying rate. Kaden's fingers pinched my clit, and then all I could do was scream out my release. Kaden's perfectly timed thrusts lost their rhythm as I clenched around him, coming harder than I had the first time, dragging him along with me over the edge.

When his cock stopped pulsing, he lowered my legs and draped himself over me, pressing his nose into my neck and inhaling deeply. "Mate," Kaden said, his voice feral.

"Mate," I whispered back.

He cupped my cheek, the gentle touch a sharp contrast to the pleasure he'd just given me. I pushed my head into his hand and closed my eyes. We were really here, together, and nothing else mattered in the moment.

Tomorrow we'd have more work to do, and I knew that the path ahead of us didn't have an easy route. For now, I was content to doze, nestled against Kaden's side and breathing in his scent, knowing we were going to do it all together.

As mates.

CHAPTER TWENTY-NINE

WE ARRIVED at my father's cabin in the early morning, a few hours before the solar eclipse was set to occur, and sent out Jack, Harper, and Dane to alert us when they caught wind of anyone approaching. Dad's cabin hadn't been used in some time, and Kaden and I quickly got to work clearing off cobwebs, shaking out the cushions, and lighting the fire. The cabin was pretty small, just two bedrooms, a cozy living room with a fireplace, and a tiny kitchen. We weren't expecting a ton of people though—unlike the Convergence, this was going to be a smaller gathering of only alphas and betas—and we planned to have the actual meeting outside, but we wanted people to be able to come inside to socialize, grab some food and drinks, and use the restroom as needed.

We'd stocked up on basics like toilet paper plus food and drinks on our way, and once the cabin was cleaned up a bit, it started to feel like we were hosting a party. I wished Stella had come with us, but Kaden thought it would be best if she and Clayton stayed with the pack while we were gone. At first, I thought it was because there were still some people in the pack that were unhappy with what we were doing, but then I realized it was because Kaden wanted someone able to lead and protect the pack if he and I were both killed. A sobering thought. While we were all trying to be optimistic about this, there was always the chance that one of the packs could betray us.

As I finished setting up the cheese tray, Jack bounded in as a wolf and quickly shifted to human. "Cancer pack members are approaching from the north."

Anticipation made my heart beat faster as I raced outside. I heard the Cancer pack members coming, and ran over to the edge of the clearing around the cabin. Wesley grinned as he ducked through the trees, and I waited for him to come closer before pulling him into a hug.

"I missed you," I said.

Wesley squeezed me tighter. "I missed you too."

I closed my eyes and breathed in his scent, a mix of saltwater, cedar, and hope. It was so familiar to me and I'd spent a good amount of time thinking I'd never have the chance to smell it again. I pushed back tears as I pulled away from my brother. I couldn't fall apart right now. We had a lot to do still.

"We've gotten most everything set up already," I said. "Now we just have to wait."

"Perfect. I brought beer and dozens of cheap eclipse glasses for everyone." He waved his other pack members forward, and they headed into the cabin with their bags of supplies. "Can't have people hurting their eyes, after all."

"Good thinking. We brought your car back." I nodded to the Aston Martin parked beside the cabin, which was covered in mud and looked very out of place here.

Wesley let out a sharp laugh. "I forgot about that car. Such a typical Dad thing to buy. Hey, maybe I can sell it. I bet I could use the proceeds to feed the pack for a month."

I grinned, thinking how very different Wesley was from my father—and how Dad would probably roll over in his grave knowing Wesley was going to sell the car.

"Any news?" I asked. We hadn't talked for a few days, since we were both getting ready and then on the road.

Wesley's face fell. "We heard back from the Aquarius pack finally. They've sworn to serve the Leos."

"Oh shit." They'd been one of Cancer's oldest allies. Damn, that was a huge blow to our cause. If they weren't willing to come forward, would anyone be? Not many packs would have the courage to stand up to the Leos, not now when so many other major players were taking their side.

"It'll be all right," Wesley said. "I'm confident others will come."

Wesley and I walked over to where Kaden was setting up a long picnic table. They shook hands, and I imagined a time when things were different, where the Ophiuchus pack might have not been exiled, and Wesley and Kaden might have known each other from childhood. Would they have been friends?

As the minutes ticked by, and the solar eclipse

approached, I began to worry that no one was going to show up, and all our hard work was for nothing. But an hour later, Jack returned to let us know that the Sagittarius Pack was coming. I breathed a huge sigh of relief and went to greet them.

To my surprise, it was Eileen and Devin, as well as a couple of tough-looking warriors who had clearly seen battles. I turned to see Kaden searching for the alphas, but neither of them had come.

"What does it mean?" I muttered to him, mindful of everyone's enhanced hearing. It almost seemed like an insult to send these two, when the alphas knew all too well the history between Kaden and Eileen. Then again, they were the betas, so maybe they were the only people the alphas trusted to send.

"I don't know," Kaden said. "But it doesn't bode well for us."

He looked on edge as Eileen and Devin walked up to meet us. The tension in the air was almost palpable as they stopped before us.

"Welcome," I said, hoping to break the ice a bit.

"Mae and Theo couldn't make it," Eileen said, her voice formal. "An emergency with their daughter pulled them away. They send their apologies and regrets, and have entrusted us to make decisions for the Sagittarius pack on their behalf."

"We're pleased to have you," Kaden said. "Please relax and have some food and drink. I'm sure the others will be here soon."

"Thank you," Devin said stiffly and held up a bag. "We brought some dessert for everyone. Eileen baked brownies and a few pies."

"That's nice of you," I said, forcing a smile. A lingering awkwardness sat between the four of us, but we were all working through it as best we could. When they walked away to speak to Wesley next, I finally let out the breath I'd been holding.

The Pisces pack arrived next. When they emerged from the forest, my heart leaped in joy at the familiar face heading toward me.

"Mira!" I rushed toward her. I hadn't expected Mira to come, but she and her mate, Aiden, were there in the front of the small group, with the Pisces alpha only a step behind them.

She grinned at me and hugged me just as tightly as Wesley had done earlier. "I'm so happy to be here," she whispered to me. Whatever she'd said to finally convince her alpha to come, I was grateful for it. Even just getting him here was a good first step. They might not ally with us, but at least they were willing to listen.

Mira's gaze was caught on something over my shoulder, and when I turned to look, I realized she was staring at Wesley. I'd seen that look directed at Wesley before. Her lips parted a little, and then she shook herself and smiled at me again. I raised my eyebrows, surprised she still had her obvious crush on my brother even with her mate bond.

Wesley walked over to greet us, and Mira quickly looked down at the ground, as if she'd been caught doing something she wasn't supposed to be doing. He opened his arms to Mira, and she hesitated, before giving him a stiff hug. "I'm so glad you could make it," he said. "I'm sorry about your parents. They were fine people and will be missed."

Mira glanced up and gave him a sad smile. "Thank you."

"We miss you in the Cancer pack as well," he continued. "I hope you're adjusting well to your new life as a Pisces?"

"Yes, they've been very kind to me." Mira rubbed at her chest absentmindedly, and I followed the motion with sharp eyes. *That* was where what I felt for Kaden popped up. Not in my gut, like with Jordan and the mate bond, but in my heart. Could her mate bond be fake too?

I opened my mouth to say something, but then Aiden joined us, and Mira quickly looked at him with obvious affection. He was broad-shouldered and muscular, handsome in sort of a dopey way, with sand-colored hair and green eyes. Mira introduced everyone, and he gave us warm smiles, but I couldn't forget that the last time we'd met he'd dragged Mira away from me, leaving me for dead. I couldn't muster a smile for him, so I settled with a simple nod. Mira's face changed as she looked at Aiden, obviously enamored with him, and I began to doubt my earlier assumptions about her and Wesley. She probably just felt awkward around him now that he was alpha. That would be understandable. I'd just wished they were mates, since I wanted two of my favorite people together, and had probably been seeing what I wanted to see.

Wesley moved to speak with the Pisces alpha next, whose name I remembered was Amos. They shook hands, and my brother said, "Thank you for coming. We appreciate your support."

"I'm sorry about your family, and for not assisting the Cancer pack before," Amos said, looking Wesley square in the face. He was probably in his sixties, with gray hair and a weathered face, wearing a flannel shirt and jeans, but somehow looking more dignified than anyone else here. "We don't have many fighters, but we should have stood by your side during all of this. If there is anything we can do to help your pack recover, please let me know."

Wesley bowed his head and offered his thanks for the offer, and to my surprise, Amos turned to me next.

"I also must apologize to you for not helping when you came to us at the Convergence," he said to me. "We should have taken you in, and I have regretted my actions ever since."

"Thank you," I said, a lump forming in my throat. "I know you were only trying to protect your pack."

His face was grim. "Yes, but I should have known there was no staying out of this conflict, and done what was right. I won't ask for your forgiveness, but I swear the Pisces pack is done swimming away from the fight. We will stand with you however we can."

His words gave me hope, and I felt even better when he went to speak to Kaden next, and the two shared polite formalities. It was so very different from how Kaden had been treated at the Convergence, and it made me think change was actually possible.

It was almost midday, and the solar eclipse was starting

to go into effect. Everything dimmed slightly, and I watched as the shadows of the trees changed, the leaves becoming slivers instead of the full shapes cast onto the ground. Wesley and the Cancer pack handed out eclipse glasses, and we all put them on. The tension ramped up in my chest again. The meeting was scheduled to start soon, but no one else was here. Would the Pisces and Sagittarius be the only packs to attend?

The solar eclipse was nearing its totality when the Libra pack arrived, the alpha and a few other shifters stepping out from the trees. The Libra alpha was young and unmated, probably around the same age as Kaden, and freaking hot too. He was dressed like he was attending a business meeting, with his shirtsleeves rolled back to reveal tattoos running along his muscular arms. I remembered Wesley telling me he was a fairly new alpha, and that, unlike my brother or Kaden, he hadn't inherited the role—he'd challenged the previous Libra alpha and won. To my surprise, he greeted Kaden politely and formally, much like he would any other pack alpha.

Before I could speak with him, three men and one woman emerged from the trees with the Capricorn symbol on their arms, surprising us all. Wesley had been hopeful they would arrive, since they'd been allies of the Cancer pack, but they hadn't committed either way. I didn't recognize any of them, even though I'd met the alphas a few times before, and I guessed Capricorn hadn't sent its alphas, just the betas and a couple of warriors. I tried not to let it bother me too much—at least they'd sent someone at all.

Kaden stepped forward to greet them, but they ignored him and walked past, marching straight up to Wesley. The man at the front gave my brother a firm nod. "I am Pierce, beta of the Capricorn pack. We are here to honor our alliance with the Cancer pack." He shot Kaden a sharp glance, then turned back to Wesley. "Though we find your new company...problematic."

My hackles rose at his tone. How dare he talk about *my* alpha that way.

"It's nice to meet you," Wesley said, diplomatically ignoring the beta's last words. "Grab some eclipse glasses and a beer and settle in. We'll start soon."

I glared at the betas as they walked to the picnic table with the food and glasses on it. Kaden, sensing my anger, walked over to me and put a hand on my shoulder.

"It's fine. We knew not everyone would accept the Ophiuchus immediately. It's a relief they're here at all."

Since when had he become the level-headed one? I crossed my arms, still annoyed by the way they'd acted. "I guess."

We waited a bit longer, but time was running out. The sun slowly faded away behind the moon, becoming smaller and smaller as totality approached. That meant we only had another hour or so before it was all over.

As we waited for other packs to arrive, I watched the other alphas and betas interact with each other, along with the other shifters they'd brought. This wasn't the same joyful interactions that I'd seen at the Convergence, but it was good to see so many shifters in one place, getting along despite being from different packs.

After another fifteen minutes passed, and the sun was the smallest sliver of light, Kaden said, "No one else is coming. Totality is about to begin, and we need to get this meeting started too."

I sighed but knew he was right. If the other packs weren't here already, they weren't coming. Besides, we knew the Aries, Taurus, and Scorpio packs were already allied with the Leos, so they hadn't been invited, and we'd just learned that the Aquarius pack had fallen to them too.

"Damn, I'd hoped that Virgo and Gemini would make it too," Wesley said, and I heard the disappointment in his voice.

"Four of the packs are here," I said, trying to find the bright side. "That's a good start."

Wesley squared his shoulders and nodded. "You're right. It's more than we had before, and if they agree to ally with us, we stand a chance."

"It'll be enough," Kaden said, his eyes gleaming with determination. "Let's get started."

CHAPTER THIRTY

THE TOTALITY BEGAN, leaving only a small corona of light above us, casting the area in murky darkness. We walked toward the area we'd set up earlier, a circle of picnic chairs where all the alphas and betas would be able to see and hear everything. Wesley invited everyone to join us, and anticipation raced through me as the shifters gathered around for the start of our own mini Convergence. The alphas and betas sat in the chairs, while their other pack members gathered behind them. I took my own seat in the Ophiuchus section, my stomach clenched tight with nervous energy.

"Thank you all for coming," Kaden said, after calling for silence. "We've recently learned that the Leos are planning to take over all of the packs and make them submit to their rule, with the help of the Sun Witches. We're here to discuss how we can stop them."

A ripple of unease went through the gathered shifters.

Wesley moved to stand beside Kaden, an obvious show of support. "You all saw what happened to the Cancer pack at the Convergence," Wesley said. "The Sun Witches stood by and did nothing while my entire pack was slaughtered, including my parents. It was only by sheer luck that I survived to be able to make it back to my pack and take us into hiding." He looked around the gathered shifters, pausing for a moment as a few of them whispered. "We recently got news that the Aquarius pack have bowed to the Leos' rule. The Aries, Taurus, and Scorpio packs are already lost, and we don't know about the Gemini and Virgo packs. They might also be under the control of the Leos for all we know."

"Of everyone here, who will be next?" Kaden asked as he looked in turn between all the various packs. "You've seen how the Leos operate. They want absolute subjugation, and I don't know about you, but I'm not willing to take that lying down. We have to stand up to the Leos and the Sun Witches if we want to retain our autonomy and freedom."

"How do you know all this for sure?" asked the Libra alpha, who had called himself Ethan earlier.

"The Leos captured me, and their alpha told me his plans," I said, rising to my feet.

"Aren't you Jordan's mate?" the Capricorn beta, Pierce, sneered. "Oh, wait, no. He rejected you. What are you even doing here, half-breed?"

The word twisted something in my gut. It had been ages since I'd heard it, and I'd forgotten how much it hurt.

Kaden stepped in front of me and growled, low in his

throat. "Ayla is the Ophiuchus alpha female, and you will treat her with respect, *beta*."

I cleared my throat, shoving my shame and anger down so I could keep my voice level. "Yes, Jordan is my mate, which is how I know all of this is true. The Leos are working with the Sun Witches, and together they want to unite the Zodiac Wolves—under their rule."

"The Sun Witches have always been neutral allies," Pierce said, sitting back and crossing his arms. "Why would they help the Leos do this?"

"The Sun Witches have been lying to you for years," Kaden snapped. "They lock up your wolves until adulthood, spew you lies about a bullshit Moon Curse, and create fake mate bonds when it suits them."

"Why would they do all that?" Ethan asked.

"To control you," Kaden said. "It's just one part in their plan to take over all of the Zodiac Wolves."

"For what purpose though?" Ethan tilted his head, his face thoughtful. "I'm willing to believe that the Leos want to rule us and that the Sun Witches are helping them, but how do we know anything else you say is true? Like about the mate bonds?"

Wesley spoke up at that. "I found evidence that my father paid the Sun Witches to create a mate bond between Ayla and Jordan. If they created that bond, they could have faked other ones too over the years."

The other alphas and betas looked surprised at that, but I was even more surprised to see Eileen stand up and speak. "Though I am the Sagittarius beta now, I grew up as an

Ophiuchus. I can confirm that we gain our wolves as children, and we do not suffer from any full moon curse, nor do we need a spell to find our mates."

The other alphas and betas argued back and forth about the Sun Witches for some time, and I tuned them out and looked up at the eclipse through my glasses. The totality had ended, and the sun was growing larger behind the shadow of the moon. Our time was running out.

Eventually, Kaden held up a hand to silence everyone. "The Ophiuchus pack is prepared to fight, and we have allied with the Cancer pack. We will both do whatever it takes to retain our freedom from the Leos and the Sun Witches. Will anyone join us?"

The silence was crushing. My nerves became a jumbled mess as the alphas and betas considered their next move. Then Amos, the Pisces alpha, stood up, and my heartbeat picked up faster. He could make or break this. "The Pisces pack will join you."

Thank the moon goddess, I thought.

"I was full of doubts, like many of you are," Amos said to the others. "I regretted not doing more to help the Cancer pack at the Convergence, but I thought I could keep my pack neutral and safe. Then Jordan sent a group of Leos to my village and demanded we submit to them. They took my nephew hostage, and kidnapped his mate, holding their lives over my head." His eyes landed on Aiden and Mira when he said those words, his face solemn. "Thanks to the Ophiuchus pack, Mira was returned to us, Aiden was freed, and the Leos harassing my pack were taken down. That was when I realized there is no hiding from this conflict. Our only option is to stand together and fight, or we might as well give up and submit to the Leos' rule."

"Are we sure we can't negotiate with the Leos?" Ethan asked, rubbing his chin. "I've heard that the new alpha is much more level-headed than Dixon was."

"No, there is no negotiating with them," I said. "There was a time when I thought Jordan might have an ounce of goodness in his heart, but I was wrong."

Pierce narrowed his eyes at me. "And what do the Ophiuchus get out of this alliance you're proposing?"

"We only ask for our exile to be over, and to be allowed back into the Zodiac Wolves," Kaden replied.

I gave him a supportive smile. He'd come so far from when I'd first met him, when his only goal had been to wipe out the other Zodiac Wolves or make them bow to his rule—not very different from what Jordan wanted. The difference was that Kaden had changed and come to see there was another way. A better way. Because of *me*, I realized.

Pierce snorted. "I can speak for all the Capricorns when I say we don't want the Leos to take over our pack, but we'd rather that happen than to ally ourselves with *snakes*. We've been the twelve Zodiac Packs for years, and we have no interest in changing that. You were cast out for a reason."

Eileen's dark eyes glimmered with fury. "You stubborn goats never want anything to change."

The Capricorn beta gave her a cold smirk. "And you never stick around long enough to know what real change looks like. Your pack runs away whenever things get hard."

Devin jumped up at that with a growl, but Wesley stepped between the two betas, effectively cutting off their line of sight to each other.

"Now isn't the time to be fighting amongst ourselves," Wesley said. "We're here to make a decision about our future, not drag up old petty disputes. Will any of you ally yourselves with the Cancer, Pisces, and Ophiuchus packs against the Leos and help us plan an attack?"

The Libra alpha looked thoughtful but didn't say anything. The Capricorn beta still looked pissed. That left the Sagittarius.

Kaden turned toward Devin and Eileen. "What do you say?" he asked them. "Your pack has long been allied with ours."

Devin shared a look with Eileen before turning back to Kaden. "Though our pack values freedom and independence above all else, we're hesitant to commit to something this big."

Damn. If we couldn't even get the Sagittarius on our side, we were totally fucked. The others would back down too, and all of this would have been for nothing. I wanted to tear my hair out.

"I know it's a tough decision," Wesley said, though he shared a look with Kaden that said he knew we were in trouble.

Eileen rested a hand on Devin's shoulder, then leaned over and whispered something in his ear. He looked down at her, considering, and then nodded to Kaden, looking grim. "Sagittarius will stand with you," he said.

I nearly let out a loud whoop but held it inside, trying to remain calm and collected. The Sagittarius joining us was a huge victory—they had amazing warriors, and like the Leos, they were a fire sign, which would give them some resistance to the Sun Witches' attacks.

"And you?" Wesley asked Pierce. "We've been allied with your pack for so long. Are you willing to put aside your differences to help us go against the Leos? Or are you going to let your hesitation lead to your downfall?"

The Capricorn beta grimaced. "You're right, son of Harrison. Though we have some...reservations, we will never bow to the Leos. We are still your allies."

Wesley inclined his head. "Thank you."

I could hardly believe it. After everything Pierce had said, I'd expected the Capricorns to walk away from this meeting without pledging their support. That only left the Libra alpha undecided.

"Where does the Libra pack stand?" Kaden asked.

Ethan tapped his fingers against his lip as he considered. "I'm not sure yet. I think we're being too hasty in making this decision. There's still a chance for diplomacy. If we could only sit down and talk with the Leos—"

The Pisces alpha shook his head. "That's not going to work. I know your pack likes to mediate, but now isn't the time for that."

The debate continued in the background, but suddenly I couldn't focus on it. The mate bond tugged at my gut hard, making my mouth fall open in a silent gasp. It had been dormant for weeks while I'd been with the Ophiuchus and

I'd almost forgotten what it felt like, or how persistent it could be. Especially when my mate was close.

Jordan was here, and the goddamned mate bond was still pulling me toward him.

No—pulling *him* toward me.

CHAPTER THIRTY-ONE

I JUMPED up and grabbed Kaden's arm. "The Leos. They're here."

"What?" Kaden asked, gaze sharpening. "How do you know?"

"The damn mating bond," I grumbled. "Which means that Jordan knows where I am too. I'm like a fucking homing beacon for him."

"Shit," Wesley said, his eyes going wide. "I guess we'll be putting those alliances to test now."

"The Leos are on their way," Kaden announced to the others. "We must prepare for an attack."

The other shifters scurried to their feet, springing into action. Kaden ordered those who weren't fighters inside the cabin, while everyone else would fight outside of it. I saw Eileen hand Devin a long bow and some arrows, then give him a long kiss before heading into the cabin. I shooed Mira and Aiden after her, along with the Pisces alpha.

Jack rushed over and confirmed that the scent of the Leos was in the woods, along with the smell of others—Sun Witches.

Kaden glanced up at the sky, where the sun had completely emerged from the eclipse, and then swore under his breath. We'd spent too long deliberating, and now the Sun Witches would be back at full strength.

He turned to me and pulled me against him. "I don't suppose I can convince you to get inside too."

"No way. This is my fight too. And don't even try to use an alpha command on me again. We both know that didn't work last time."

"Of course it didn't." Kaden's fingers tightened around my chin. "Because you're my alpha female. The only one who is my equal in this world." His mouth crashed down on me and he kissed me hard. I gripped his face and kissed him back with the same vigor, in case this was the last time.

He pressed his forehead against mine. "I know you'll fight, and there's nothing I can do to stop you. Just know that I'll be fighting alongside you the entire time, and I'll be damned if I let them take you again."

"I'm not getting captured this time," I said and ran my thumb across his lips. "Just don't die on me, all right?"

He gave me a wry grin. "I'm not going anywhere."

Snarls came from outside the clearing, the crack of twigs and the scuff of feet against the forest floor coming from all sides. We were surrounded, so suddenly and completely. A rush of fear went through me, along with anticipation for the thrill of the battle to come. I was ready to face the Leos again, and get my revenge on them for everything they'd done to me and my family. *Bring it on*, I thought.

We just had enough time to settle into a makeshift battle formation before shifters emerged from the trees. Leo, Aries, and Taurus all melted from the forest, followed by orange-cloaked Sun Witches. They surrounded us instantly, pressing us into a circle. Kaden stood to my right, with Wesley on the left—the two men I cared about most and would fight to defend. Pierce and Devin stood behind me, with some of their shifters surrounding them, and to my surprise, the Libra alpha Ethan was there too. He'd ripped his button-down shirt off, revealing more tattoos, and I wondered what he thought of his precious diplomacy now.

"Attack!" Kaden yelled.

We raced out to meet the approaching attackers, many of us shifting as we ran. I settled into my wolf form with surprising ease as I loped toward the fight. The clash of fur against fur was punctuated with brilliant blasts of light from the Sun Witches as our two forces collided. The Leos let out their lion roar, causing the shifters near them to either flee or freeze in terror, but then the Libras raised their arms and used their own power to neutralize it. The affected shifters stopped and shook off their fear, then got back into the fight. Sagittarius warriors shot arrows into the enemy lines, using their archer's sight power so they hit every target. The Capricorns used their pack power, goat leap, to launch themselves across the clearing, soaring as if they were flying, until they landed on top of some of the other wolves and tore them apart.

Beside me, Wesley activated his crab armor, making him almost impervious to damage, just before an Aries hit him with a ram charge, knocking him back almost to the cabin. Kaden sank his poison fangs into a Leo who dared attack him, and I felt the mental presence of Harper, Dane, and Jack nearby too, each of them fighting together in sync.

I darted under a stray bolt of sunlight and lunged toward a nearby shifter, gripping him around the leg and trying to throw him across the clearing. He stood his ground, using his immovable powers so that it ended up being me who fell. Fucking bull stance. I couldn't take the Taurus down with my poison bite, and without any moonlight, I couldn't use my other powers. Luckily Devin shot an arrow that hit the Taurus wolf in the eye, and I let out a short yip of thanks before scampering off.

At my side, Kaden ripped his way through enemy shifters like a machine. Wesley brushed up against me, a brief press of fur against fur to give me strength in the battle, and I was relieved he had survived the ram charge.

The enemy wolves reached the cabin, breaking down the door, and I saw Eileen just inside. She shifted into a small black wolf and snarled. Mira wasn't anywhere in sight, and I hoped she had escaped to safety with Amos somehow. The Pisces pack could swim incredibly fast underwater, but Amos was right—they weren't warriors. At least on land.

Help protect the cabin, I sent out to the other Ophiuchus warriors, and felt Harper, Dane, and Jack acknowledge my order and move into position. Through the pack bond, I felt Kaden's approval.

Devin and the Sagittarius archers had the same idea, and they moved to fight against the wolves trying to get into the cabin. Devin suddenly went down under a Leo's jaw, and Eileen let out a ragged howl before clawing at the shifter on top of her mate.

I wanted to help them, but I couldn't pause to focus on their fight. All I could do was tear through flesh with my paws and teeth, to bowl shifters over and hope they wouldn't stand up again.

Then I caught a glimpse of Evanora in her red robes, standing at the back of the battle with her daughter, Roxandra. I snarled, but before I could lunge toward her, Jordan stepped into my line of view. He was still in human form, and he held his hands out as if saying *don't attack.*

The instant he stood before me, in all his shirtless glory, the mate bond flared to life, nearly knocking me over. It was *madness.* He was my brother, for fuck's sake, and I didn't want him, but the mate bond drew me toward him anyway. Rage turned my vision red. The Sun Witches had done this to me, to *us.* How *dare* they meddle with my life, trying to force me to want my own brother?

"Ayla!" he called out, but before I could decide whether to lunge at him with my fangs or turn and flee, a bolt of bright white power slammed into my side.

I hit the ground hard, my vision temporarily going dark, and heard a female voice say, "Capture her, I want her alive."

I swung my head around to see Evanora closing in on me with a few of the other Sun Witches. I stood up on four paws and shook myself, but before I could do much of anything else, I felt someone grab onto me, holding me in place. I instantly knew it was Jordan by the way the mate bond purred.

"It'll be easier for everyone if you go along with this," Jordan whispered into my ear. Nausea roiled in my gut alongside the ever-present desire of the mate bond. "I'll protect you."

I shifted back into human form just to tell him to *fuck off*. Of course, that meant I was now naked and squirming in his arms. "Get off me," I screamed. But he was too damn strong, and no matter how hard I struggled, he didn't let me go.

A huge black wolf snarled and charged toward us—Kaden! He looked terrifying in his rage, and in another few seconds he would tear Jordan apart, and at this moment, I would let him. But then the Sun Witches all turned to face him and fired beams of burning light directly into his side.

I watched it happen in slow motion, unable to move. The first few beams didn't take him down. He shook them off, and I thought *he's stronger than they are*. Then one knocked him over, and though he got up, it looked like it was a struggle. He shifted back to human and grit his teeth, then chanted some sort of spell of his own, but with the sun out now, I wasn't sure how much it did to protect him.

"Attack again, he's getting weaker," Evanora said, and they shot more beams of light at him. The sounds of fighting faded into the background as I zeroed in on what they were doing to Kaden. Light licked across his skin like fire, and he let out a roar full of pain and rage as his body was burned by the power of the sun.

I managed to tear away from Jordan, just as Kaden went down and didn't get back up again. "Kaden!" I yelled, but he didn't move.

Something built up in me, an emotion so intense and sudden I didn't even have time to process it before it was pouring out of me. I let out a feral scream, and with it came a huge wave of silvery light. It blinded me as it erupted out of me, such a large amount of power that for a moment I felt like I was on fire, except somehow it was icy cold. I let it all out, my grief and fury rushing out of me, somehow releasing all of the pent-up moon energy inside me.

When it cleared, everyone near me was down, and they weren't moving. Jordan. Evanora. Roxandra. Dozens of other shifters and witches too, both friend and foe. I didn't know what had just happened, and I didn't care. All I wanted was to get to Kaden.

Get back up, I pleaded with him as I rushed forward. *Come on, you promised me you wouldn't die.*

Kaden didn't twitch.

He can't be. He can't.

But the evidence was right there. Kaden had been struck with so many beams of the Sun Witches' power, and I'd seen much less take down other shifters. There was no way Kaden could have survived that many.

I stumbled toward him and crouched down. *Please be alive,* I thought, but Kaden didn't move. The hot slide of tears down my face didn't even phase me as I touched his blackened face. The smell of burning hair and singed flesh was almost overwhelming.

I pulled him into my lap as well as I could. "Come on," I said, not knowing what I was hoping for, but trying to pour the energy into him. I had no idea what I was doing, but surely, *surely*, I could do this to save him. Why have all this power if it meant that he died? Then I remembered. I could lick his wounds closed. I looked over his body, trying to decide where to start. There was *so much*.

Another wave of light washed over the clearing, but this one was softer than the harsh beams of the Sun Witches. I looked up, but wrapped my arms harder around Kaden and held him against me. I didn't care if I lived or died, whatever came next, just as long as I could do it holding Kaden.

Women in purple and midnight blue hooded robes appeared beside me as if stepping out of the light, and I blinked at them. Then another woman appeared, and her robe was black with silver thread. She had long white hair and a crown made of glittering stars with a crescent moon in the center. She stopped in front of me, and I stared up at her, not quite believing that she was real.

"You must come with us," she said. "But you must do it now, before the Sun Witches wake and try to stop us."

"I'm not going anywhere," I said, gripping onto Kaden tighter. "My mate—he's dying. Or dead, I don't know." A sob wracked through my body at the words, at the realization that I couldn't save him. What if it was too late for Kaden? What would I do then?

The woman's eyes were kind but steely. She rested her

hand on my shoulder. "You cannot help him. Not yet, at least. Come, now."

The light around us became bright, blinding me. I held my hands up to shield my eyes, and then suddenly, I was elsewhere.

CHAPTER THIRTY-TWO

I SWEAR, *if I open my eyes and find I'm in another damn cell, I will scream,* I thought as I squeezed my eyes shut. It was a ridiculous thought, but I wasn't exactly mentally stable at the moment. In fact, I was pretty sure I was one small step away from a complete meltdown. Kaden was *dead*, and I was...who the fuck knew where I was.

I finally made myself open my eyes, and it was a small relief to find I wasn't in a cell. Unfortunately, I was on a beach, surrounded by the purple-robed women. They all looked down at me with varying levels of concern, while the soft waves of the ocean lapped at the shore behind them. It was night now, and the full moon hung over us, which made no sense because it had been both daytime and a new moon just a minute ago.

Worst of all, there was no Kaden in my lap, only sand.

"No," I said, scrabbling uselessly at the sand as if I'd find him underneath it. "No, you can't do this!" My voice raised in pitch and volume with each word, the desperation causing me to almost scream. "Take me back to Kaden! He's my mate! I can't leave him!"

The women just stared at me, though a couple of them looked uncomfortable now. They clearly weren't going to do anything, so I decided I'd have to do it myself. I didn't know who they were or what they wanted, but it didn't matter. All that mattered was getting back to Kaden, helping him, saving him. Maybe there was still time. If I could lick his wounds closed, maybe...

I shoved myself to my feet, trembling with anger and fatigue, and tried to teleport away. It was no use. I stayed right where I was, even with the moon giving me power. They must be blocking me somehow, and it was enough to loose a scream of frustration from my throat, primal in its intensity.

"I don't think you understand," I sobbed and screamed, the words hardly making sense. "I have to get back to Kaden. He's *dying*. Why did you take me and not him?" I turned to the woman in the front, the one in the black robes and crown who had spoken to me back in the clearing. "Why?"

The woman dipped her head, her crown glittering on her brow. "I'm sorry, but there's nothing we can do for him now."

The confirmation that he was dead hit me like a dagger to the heart. I couldn't breathe around it for a few seconds, the pain was so sharp. *No, no, no.* I refused to believe he was gone.

"It was more important than anything else that we got

you out of there, Ayla," the woman in the crown said. "The Sun Witches wanted you, and we couldn't let them have you."

When she met my eyes, I knew that this woman had made many hard decisions in her life. She was used to cutting her losses, even when they hurt. I wanted to turn away from that. I didn't want to look at her. I wanted *Kaden*.

"We've been looking for you for a long time," she continued. "When you tapped into your power fully for the first time back in that clearing, we finally got a clear read on your location. We could feel it from here."

"You're Moon Witches," I said, flatly. Of course now was when I'd find them, when I'd lost the most important thing to me, when I didn't care at all about breaking the mate bond anymore, because what was the point? Fate was cruel. So very, very cruel.

"Yes. I am Celeste, the high priestess of the Moon Witches."

I didn't give a shit who she was at that moment. I was just...numb. Tears slid down my cheeks, a relentless stream, but there was nothing I could do to stop them. "Why would you take *me*?" I asked. "Kaden is more of a Moon Witch than I am. Why not save him?"

She lifted a hand and sent the other witches away. They faded away, leaving just the two of us in the sand on this strange beach. "Once you're calm, I promise to answer all your questions."

Calm? Fuck calm. I shook my head, wanting to scream again. Everything was happening too fast, and I couldn't breathe. Grief over Kaden's death was still roaring through me, sharp enough to be a wound, but one that I couldn't locate the source of. It hurt all over. Guilt wormed its way into my heart too over the way I'd just left Kaden's body there. It hadn't been my choice, but I couldn't help but feel it. And what about everyone else back at the cabin? My brother, Mira, everyone that had just allied themselves with the Ophiuchus and Cancer packs, all left for dead. Who knew what would happen to them now?

"I need to go back," I said, but it came out as more of a whimper. "Take me back and let me fight."

"I cannot," Celeste said.

I launched myself at her, suddenly furious at this woman for taking me away from my mate and my people. She raised a hand and an invisible barrier of moonlight stopped me, knocking me back onto the sand.

"Come with me and we'll talk," she said, extending her hand.

I snarled up at her, ready to shift into my wolf form to take her down. "I don't want to talk. I need to return to my mate and my pack. Take me back. *Now*."

Her voice softened as she looked down at me with far too much kindness. "Ayla, I can help you save them. I might even be able to help you save him."

Save him. Her words finally got through to me and I slumped down in the sand, losing all my fight in an instant. "How?"

"Come with me and I'll show you everything." She gave me a sad smile, and then turned away and walked along the beach toward a house in the distance. All the lights in it were on, as if inviting me inside.

The thought entered my mind to run, but I quickly tossed it aside. I didn't even know where I was. What if I was on another continent entirely? I had no idea where to go, or what to do next.

I wrapped my arms around my knees and sobbed into them. I'd never felt so alone in my entire life as I did in that moment. Not when I'd been the outcast in the Cancer pack, or when I'd become packless, or when I'd first been taken by the Ophiuchus pack. Not even when I'd been trapped in Jordan's cell with no way of escape. Now, with my mate dead, my friends fighting for their lives and possibly dead themselves, and me stuck who-knew-where, I was completely, utterly *alone*.

As if in accordance with my thoughts, fat raindrops began pattering down onto the beach. Each one that hit me stung, chilling me to the bone. I glared up at the moon, wondering why Selene hated me so much. Was my pain not enough that she had to send rain too?

My hand found my Ophiuchus mark. I was one with them, even if they were far away. Even if Kaden was dead. When all hope had been lost in the past, I'd promised myself I'd always try to make my way back to my pack. I just had to get up and take that first step.

You can do this, little wolf.

Kaden's voice in my head gave me the strength I needed to drag myself up off the sand and square my shoulders. He would want me to keep going, to keep fighting, to not give up on him, no matter what.

I stumbled toward the house at the end of the beach, each step becoming stronger until I was striding forward as if I hadn't just suffered the worst loss of my life yet. That Moon Witch had said something about saving Kaden and the rest of my pack. She had the answers I needed. I wasn't sure why she'd brought me here, but now that I'd found the Moon Witches, I would make them help me defeat the Leos and the Sun Witches.

And maybe, just maybe, I'd find a way to save Kaden too.

ABOUT THE AUTHOR

Elizabeth Briggs is the *New York Times* bestselling author of paranormal and fantasy romance. She graduated from UCLA with a degree in Sociology and has worked for an international law firm, mentored teens in writing, and volunteered with dog rescue groups. Now she's a full-time geek who lives in Los Angeles with her family and a pack of fluffy dogs.

Visit Elizabeth's website: www.elizabethbriggs.com

Join Elizabeth's Facebook group for fun book chat and early sneak peeks!